THE CENTAUR'S DAUGHTER

BY ELLEN JENSEN ABBOTT

MARSHALL CAVENDISH

Website: www.marshallcavendish.us/kids

This book is a work of fiction. Names, characters, places, and incidents are products of the author's imagination and are used fictitiously. Any resemblance to actual events or locales or persons, living or dead, is entirely coincidental.

Other Marshall Cavendish Offices:
Marshall Cavendish International (Asia) Private Limited, 1 New Industrial Road, Singapore 536196 • Marshall Cavendish International (Thailand) Co Ltd. 253 Asoke, 12th Flr, Sukhumvit 21 Road, Klongtoey Nua, Wattana, Bangkok 10110, Thailand • Marshall Cavendish (Malaysia) Sdn Bhd, Times Subang, Lot 46, Subang Hi-Tech Industrial Park, Batu Tiga, 40000 Shah Alam, Selangor Darul Ehsan, Malaysia
Marshall Cavendish is a trademark of Times Publishing Limited

Library of Congress Cataloging-in-Publication Data

Abbott, Ellen Jensen.
The centaur's daughter / by Ellen Jensen Abbott.
    p. cm.
Sequel to: Watersmeet.
Summary: Two years after arriving in Watersmeet, Abisina, now seventeen, questions her decision not to take a leadership role as the struggle to provide for refugees, some of whom hate others, threatens the folks' very survival.
ISBN 978-0-7614-5978-1 (hardcover)   ISBN 978-0-7614-6087-9 (ebook)
[1. Fantasy.] I. Title.
PZ7.A1473Ce 2011
[Fic]—dc22
2011000034

Book design by Alex Ferrari
Maps by Megan McNinch
Editor: Robin Benjamin
Printed in China (E)
First edition
10 9 8 7 6 5 4 3 2 1

mc Marshall Cavendish

For Dicky Jensen, my mom,
who is not terribly fond of fantasy,
but is terribly fond of me

ACKNOWLEDGMENTS

Thank you to my editor, Robin Benjamin, who has the wonderful ability to see the story beneath my flood of words. Thank you to my agent, Ginger Knowlton, for her advice, support, and grace. Thank you to the circle of women who support me in my life, both writing and otherwise: Elizabeth Cook, Charlotte Feierman, Margaret Haviland, Jane Jaffin, Deanna Mayer, Beverly Patt (my Journey Sister), Judy Schachner, and Barbara Shirvis. Thank you to my students and colleagues at the Westtown School, who put up with bouts of hysteria and late papers as deadlines loom. Thank you to the members of the KidLit Authors' Club, who make book events a million times more fun.

Thank you especially to Ferg, William, and Janie, without whom none of this would matter.

Communities in the Northern Kingdom

WATERSMEET

Keepers
Glynholly: faun, current Keeper
Rueshlan: shape-shifter (human/centaur), killed in the battle with the White Worm, Abisina's father
Vigar: human, original founder and Keeper

Humans
Abisina: daughter of Rueshlan and **Sina**, born in Vranille
Elodie: Abisina's patrol partner and close friend
Findlay: Abisina's close friend and, perhaps, more
Frayda: Rueshlan's companion, disappeared from Watersmeet
Neiall: Council member, supporter of Abisina

Centaurs
Kyron: supporter and protector of Abisina
Moyla: supporter of Abisina

Dwarves
Alden: Council member, father of **Breide**
Haret: Abisina's best friend, grandson of **Hoysta**, from south of the Obrun Mountains

Fauns
Anwyn: supporter of Abisina
Erna: friend of Elodie, from south of the Obrun Mountains
Ulian: Abisina's patrol partner, cousin of Glynholly

FAIRY MOTHERLAND
Lohring: the new Fairy Mother
Neriah: daughter and heir to the Fairy Mother
Reava: younger daughter of the Fairy Mother

Communities in the Southern Kingdom

Dwarves of Stonedun
Dolan and **Werlif**: brothers
Prane: cousin to Dolan and Werlif

Centaurs of Giant's Cairn
Icksyon: herd leader
Madra: Icksyon's tracker

Fauns
Darvus: Erna's mate

Humans of Vrania
Charach: shape-shifter who became the White Worm, slain by Rueshlan
Sten: Abisina's uncle, once married to Sina's sister, **Nonna**
Theckis: from Vranille, leader of Vranham
Vran: founder of Vrania

Humans of Vranlyn
Brack: a former outcast from Vranille
Corlin: leader of Vranlyn
Dehan: from Vranille, married to Ivice
Heben: reluctant supporter of changes in Vranlyn
Ivice: mother of **Landry**, married to Dehan
Jorno: a former outcast from Vranille
Thaula: daughter of a healer
Trima: mother of **Espen**

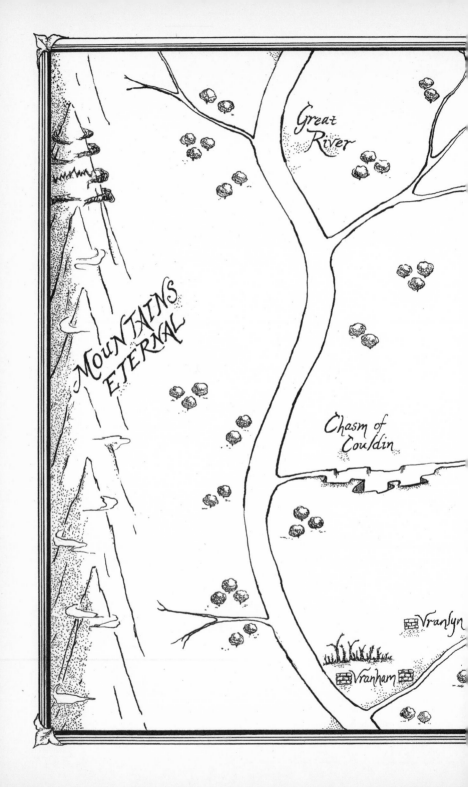

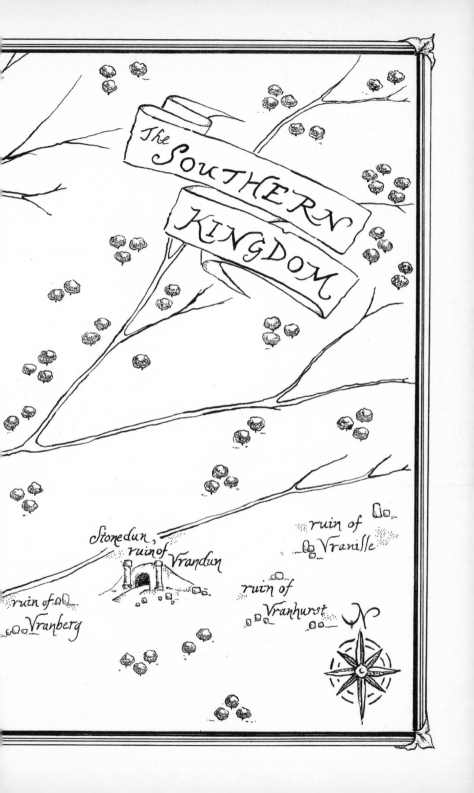

PROLOGUE

As the girl climbed higher into the Mountains Eternal, she kept looking back. She wasn't hoping for a last glimpse of home. The land behind her had ceased to be home long ago. It was fear that made her look. Even when she and the other refugees had climbed far above the clouds, she was sure the creatures were chasing them. Every scrape of sword against rock, every rattle of arrows in quivers became claws or pincers or worse in her mind.

Finally, she couldn't spare the energy to look back. Her breath came in short gasps and brought so little air, her chest felt crushed. The people in front of her spread into a longer line as the weaker ones slowed. She could hardly make out the boy far at the front, let alone the Green Man beyond him. She was glad she had offered to bring up the rear; she was better than the boy at encouraging the weak.

They neared the jagged ridge that would give them their first glimpse of the land they sought. She spotted the Green Man, twice as tall as a normal man, climbing steadily. But his green pallor had faded, and the leaves that covered his body had wilted. At the base of the mountains, ferns, saplings, and flowering bushes had sprung abundantly from his footsteps, but here, the gray outlines of lichens were the only evidence that he had passed. His strength—the force that made this journey possible—was waning. Could he get them down the other side?

The boy waited for her as she crested the final ridge. "I can't see it," he grumbled. "The clouds have already closed in. We'll have to wait until morning." She squeezed his hand, but he continued to frown.

Before dawn, the Green Man led the two of them away from the others, all asleep. Standing close to their guide, the girl breathed easier. He was still powerful. At a wave of his hand, the clouds tore apart. The valley lay below them, pearly gray in the dim light.

Dawn broke and illuminated a vast system of rivers, silver veins beginning in the east, threading closer and closer to the mountains and drawing the girl's gaze to a shining ribbon of water wending its way south. She gasped at the beauty. The boy, too, drank in the sight. Their eyes met, and they smiled.

"What do you see?" the Green Man asked.

The boy didn't hesitate. "Power."

"This river here,"—the boy pointed to the band of silver far below their feet—"it harnesses the strength of the rivulets and streams that serve it. It is a force pushing through the land, bringing down rocks and trees, even these mountains we stand on!"

The Green Man turned to the girl. "And you?"

Her words came more slowly. "The great river gathers the smaller threads of water, weaving them into itself, gaining strength."

"Yes," the Green Man said quietly, and for a moment, it felt as if her lungs filled with air.

The boy scowled.

"This is your new home," the Green Man continued. "To the north, along this great river, you will find one of my best creations: a stand of trees that will be your refuge. Use it well." He drew a brilliant box from the pouch he carried. "For you," he said, putting the box in the girl's hands. "Open it when you have arrived."

The Green Man turned to include the boy again, but the boy looked away. "Today and through the night," the Green Man instructed, "prepare for your new life. Empty your minds. Your breath will last, but you must eat and drink nothing. You will make your descent clean, with nothing of the old world about you."

The girl nodded. The boy gave no sign that he had heard.

The Green Man strode away then, leaving them on the barren ridge.

The next morning, the girl woke to find the boy—and half their followers—gone.

She would never see him again.

CHAPTER I

THE MUSKY ODOR OF THE ÜBERWOLVES HUNG IN THE AIR. Abisina scanned the trees, her shoulders tense. Überwolves could steal through the forest silently, despite their height and bulk, gliding on hind feet, claws bared, nostrils wide to catch a scent. They were smart, far smarter than their wolf cousins. So it was strange that she could hear rasping snarls. Didn't they know two humans and a faun trailed them? Or was this a trap—the growling to mask the sound of another überwolf circling back?

Next to Abisina, Elodie glided forward. She was a slight girl with ebony skin and long, tightly curled black hair. On Abisina's other side, Ulian slipped among the shadows. Like Abisina, both had arrows on their bowstrings. For years the überwolves had hardly bothered Watersmeet, but last summer after the death of Rueshlan—Abisina's father and the

Keeper of Watersmeet—refugees from the south began to arrive, followed by wave upon wave of überwolves.

Ulian paused. Like most fauns, he was thin with pronounced muscles in his shoulders, arms, and chest. The red hair on his head matched his goat-legs. He signaled that he was going to the right. Elodie moved left, leaving Abisina to continue in the middle. They would attack from three sides when Ulian gave the sign.

This better not be a trap, Abisina thought as the others slipped away. The snarling intensified, a high-pitched whine mixing with guttural growls. There was more space between the trees ahead; the überwolves had stopped in a clearing. Abisina almost smiled. The wolves would be in the open while she and her patrol could shoot from the trees.

Abisina crouched next to an oak and leaned around it for a better view. *Three überwolves. Two females and a male.*

The silver-haired beasts hunched over something that Abisina couldn't see. Their rear legs ended in paws with deadly claws. Their front paws were more like hands, clawed but with long separated fingers and thumbs. Abisina had seen them drop to all fours and run, though they preferred to be upright. Their faces were entirely wolf—long snouts and black lips, which pulled back to reveal cruel teeth. One of the females had a rough-hewn spear. The others carried no weapons. Their jaws and claws would be enough.

But what's on the ground that interests them so much? Abisina wondered. One of the wolves shifted, and then she saw what it was: a little girl huddled at their feet.

Alive—but for how long? She had to act now. *Where is Ulian's signal?*

Distraction. That was the key—to give Elodie and Ulian time to get in position.

With arrow nocked, Abisina stepped boldly into the clearing. At seventeen winters, she was tall, slender, and strong. Her green eyes stood out against her copper skin, and her black hair framed her face. She aimed at the male, let her arrow fly, and the wolf dropped. The female wolves turned their yellow eyes on Abisina.

"I'll take the child!" Abisina cried. The wolves couldn't understand her, but her friends would.

With a growl, the wolf on the right tensed to spring. The second one reached for its spear. Abisina had to choose.

She aimed at the second, the one with the spear, but it was the first wolf that leapt. Abisina switched her target. Her arrow went wide, grazing the überwolf in the side. She dodged the wolf hurtling at her but stumbled. Regaining her feet, Abisina pulled an arrow from her quiver and aimed at the second wolf again, but she hadn't recovered her balance. Her arrow embedded in the überwolf's thigh—not enough to stop it. *Ulian and Elodie, where are you?*

Abisina spun as the first überwolf lunged at her.

"Abisina!"

A whiz and a thud, and the überwolf fell back, its claws scratching Abisina's neck. The point of Elodie's arrow protruded from its chest. Ulian's arrow caught the other überwolf in the throat.

He had killed it—but the überwolf had thrown its spear before Ulian's arrow struck. That spear now pinned the faun to a tree.

In a few steps, Abisina was next to him. Blood ran down Ulian's chest. Dropping her bow, Abisina reached for the spear, but before she could grab hold, she heard the snarl of another wolf.

A male charged across the clearing toward Elodie, who held the little girl and couldn't shoot. With her bow useless on the ground, Abisina pulled the dagger from her waist-cord and threw, catching the wolf in the stomach. It stumbled, and Abisina snatched up her bow. The überwolf stayed on its feet, blood seeping through the silver fur. It ripped the dagger out and barreled toward Abisina. Her arrow flew, and she brought the wolf down.

Blood thudded in Abisina's ears. Across the clearing, Elodie looked sick. "I thought it had me," she gasped.

Abisina nodded. "A trap . . ." The girls stared at each other until a shuddering breath from Ulian forced Abisina into action. She grasped the rough spear shaft with both hands and pulled. It didn't budge. He would bleed to death if she couldn't get him off that tree! She threw herself at the shaft again. It shivered, but didn't come loose. If she broke it off at the point, she would never get him free.

"Elodie, quick!" Abisina called.

But the voice that answered wasn't Elodie's. "I will take him."

Abisina caught a glimpse of an enormous face—large eyes, twisty vines, and fur. *A hamadryad!* She had never seen one before. She'd hardly believed the fauns who told her that tree spirits could separate from their trees at will.

The spear splintered as the hamadryad removed it.

All the stories said tree spirits were shy creatures seen only by fauns, but Abisina risked a glance at him.

He towered over her, his twiggy hair spiking up from his head. His body was made not of vines but of twisted roots. The "fur" was root tendrils, white and delicate, moving constantly, feeling the air.

The hamadryad lifted Ulian with ease. The faun's shoulder bled profusely, and Abisina reached for the medicine pouch hanging from her belt. With shaking hands, she pulled out a small vial of green-tinged liquid and emptied it into the wound. Ripping off her tunic, she pressed the cloth against Ulian's shoulder. Something sticky dripped onto her fingers.

"You're injured, too," she said, noting a gash oozing sap in the hamadryad's chest. The root tendrils around the hole were turning gray and limp.

"It is nothing," the hamadryad rasped. "I will take him to his folk."

"But it's far," Abisina said. "Will you—can you leave your tree for that long?"

"For the faun, yes," he replied, and with Ulian in his arms, he strode away on gnarled feet.

"Was that a—" Elodie stood wide eyed at Abisina's elbow, the rescued child cradled to her.

"He's taking Ulian to Watersmeet."

"Will Ulian make it?" Elodie asked softly.

"He has a chance now." *But he's lost a lot of blood—and will lose more on the journey back.* Abisina's instincts as a healer told her what she couldn't bear to tell Elodie.

"How is she?" Abisina asked instead, taking the child.

The girl was three or four winters. Beneath her grimy tunic, Abisina felt her bones. This girl hadn't eaten a full meal in her life. The child's hair was light brown to her ears and then became blonde. Another Vranian refugee. The girl's mother had probably used a mix of chamomile, honey, and licorice root to lighten her hair. The Vranians punished those with dark hair—and other "disfigurements"—as Abisina knew too well. She had also grown up in a Vranian village—and been an outcast for her dark hair and skin. No amount of chamomile would lighten *her* black hair.

"Is she okay?" Elodie asked.

"I don't see any wounds," Abisina answered. Überwolves preferred live prey. "They must have been arguing about bringing her to the lair or sharing her among themselves."

The little girl stared at Abisina with empty blue eyes, a look Abisina had seen before. Frayda, the woman Abisina's father had been in love with, had the same vacant gaze in the months following his death. In the middle of winter, Frayda had simply disappeared from Watersmeet. Abisina had tried to search for her, but a blizzard hit. The snow and wind erased Frayda's tracks. The brutal battle, the death of so many folk, the loss of Rueshlan—it had been too much for Frayda. As Abisina held the little girl, she wondered: *What has this poor child been through?*

"Let me have your tunic, Elodie. She needs to stay warm. And we have to get her to Watersmeet."

They set off at a jog, Abisina carrying the girl, Elodie ready with an arrow. Überwolf tracks criss-crossed their path, but the chattering squirrels and singing birds told them that no predators hunted close by.

After a league, they stopped so Elodie could take the child. "Do you think the foragers have returned to Watersmeet already?" Elodie asked. "We should've reached them by now."

"They were terrified when we found the fresh wolf tracks. I'll bet another patrol brought them back," Abisina said.

"I wonder how much they gathered before—"

An enormous roan centaur broke through the trees, his wide chest hidden behind his full red beard.

"Kyron!" Abisina called.

"What happened?" he asked. "When the foraging party returned without you, I set out. Your neck is bleeding, Abisina. Where's Ulian?" Kyron caught sight of the girl in Elodie's arms. "Who've you got there?"

"I'm fine," Abisina assured him. "The überwolves had this little girl. And one of them got Ulian with a spear. A hama-dryad is taking him—"

"A dryad?" Kyron interrupted so loudly that the child winced. "Did you see him?" he continued, dropping his voice.

Abisina nodded. "He was magnificent—and our best chance for getting Ulian to Watersmeet . . . in time."

Kyron looked at Abisina sharply. "That bad? I don't know how many more losses our folk can take."

They started moving again.

"Last week two foragers, and this week Zayda was injured so badly, she won't be on patrol again," Elodie noted.

"Ulian is Glynholly's *cousin*," Kyron said.

"I'd forgotten that," Elodie replied.

Glynholly was Keeper, chosen to lead Watersmeet after Rueshlan died.

Kyron's face darkened. "Now she's got her excuse to close off Watersmeet."

"Glynholly knows we can't shut the refugees out," Abisina protested. "She was one of my father's closest advisors. She knows that the Keeper of Watersmeet is charged with providing a refuge for anyone in need."

"I was one of Rueshlan's closest advisors, too, Abisina, and I say that Glynholly is not thinking of the Keeper's charge right now," Kyron said. "She's thinking of protecting Watersmeet. The folk are scared. The Vranians coming from the south draw the überwolves to us. We can barely feed ourselves, much less them. The foraging teams are taking their lives in their hands every time they go out. Even with the patrols, some refuse to go."

It was true. The needs of the Vranian refugees had exhausted Watersmeet. Perhaps even worse was how difficult it was to work with them. For generations, the Vranians had been taught to hate nonhumans and anyone who didn't fit their Paragon of Beauty: blond, fair, and blue eyed. Women, too, were seen as unworthy. Anyone who deviated too much from the Paragon was labeled an outcast, forced to live on the edges of the society—if they were allowed to live at all. The folk of Watersmeet had to teach the refugees that outcasts and "demons"—the fauns, centaurs, dwarves, and darker humans—were actually responsible for saving their lives. They were having little success.

"I know there's talk about the 'refugee problem,'" Abisina began.

"I don't think you hear all of it," Kyron insisted. "Because of who your father was. And then there's your background."

"My background!" Abisina exclaimed.

"You grew up in Vranille. Your mother was Vranian. Folk assume that you would want Watersmeet to welcome 'your people.'"

"I should *hate* the Vranians for what they did to me and my mother. But if we shut them out, we'd be as bad as they are. Living in our own walled city, deciding who lives or dies. That's not Watersmeet."

"That's why I've always said that *you* should be Keeper," Kyron declared.

Other folk had asked Abisina to be Keeper—some had

begged—but she said no. She had lived in Watersmeet for only a few weeks before they'd gone to battle against the White Worm and the Vranians he held in his power. She had fought beside the folk from Watersmeet, but she could not *lead* them as her father had. Rueshlan was special. Powerful. He had been Keeper of Watersmeet for more than three hundred years and had the ability to shape-shift from human to centaur. When Watersmeet's governing body, the Council, was divided about going to battle, Rueshlan had stepped in and led them to unity.

"We can't turn the Vranians away now," Abisina continued. "My father died freeing them from Charach." She shuddered.

Charach. The White Worm. He was a shape-shifter who could be a man as beautiful as any Vranian could hope for, or a hideous worm with a ring of black eyes, poisonous breath, and a long, segmented body. It had been more than a year since her father had destroyed him, but his name could still make her tremble.

"Abisina!" Elodie interrupted. The child shook uncontrollably in her arms.

Abisina checked the girl's breathing. Fast and shallow. "I don't have the medicine she needs with me. Kyron, you'll have to take her."

"I can't leave you two out here alone."

"We're two of the best patrollers in Watersmeet," Elodie said. "We can get ourselves back safely."

Grumbling, the centaur took the child and galloped off. Abisina remained quiet as she and Elodie hurried on.

Was I wrong when I refused to be Keeper? Could I have stopped us from getting to this point? Kept my father's memory alive somehow?

There had been that one moment. Rueshlan and the Worm were both dead. Their armies stood on either side of the battlefield: Vranians, trolls, centaurs, minotaurs, and über-wolves on one side. The folk of Watersmeet and the fairies on the other. A new battle threatened, each side inflamed at the loss of their leader.

Abisina had stopped it.

But then, she had worn the necklace made of Obrium, the precious dwarf-metal. The necklace had once been Vigar's, the first Keeper. She had passed it to Rueshlan, who had given it to Abisina's mother when they had to part. Sina, in turn, had given it to Abisina. The necklace had a mysterious power. With the necklace held before her, Abisina had stepped between the two armies and persuaded them to stop the bloodshed.

Glynholly wears the necklace now, Abisina reminded herself. Placing it over the faun's head was one of the hardest things Abisina had ever done, and the necklace had haunted her dreams ever since. But it was the Keeper's necklace, and Glynholly needed whatever help it could give.

Abisina had also refused a seat on the Council. She had said that she didn't want to threaten Glynholly. But really, she couldn't imagine walking into the Council House if her father did not sit in the Keeper's chair.

Abisina sighed. Each choice had seemed right at the time, but now she wondered. Her father had warned her: "If we cannot come together—human, centaur, dwarf, faun, and fairy—some new Charach will rise."

If the folk of Watersmeet really were ready to turn on the refugees, war threatened again. And Glynholly did not seem willing to stop it.

The sun was setting when the girls came in view of Watersmeet. Abisina had called it home for almost two years, but she paused to gaze at the majestic Sylvyad trees growing in and around the three rivers that came together to form the mighty River Deliverance. The trees were giants, a unique species of pine that twenty or thirty men could not span with their arms stretched wide. The nest of Sylvyad roots made an island among the rivers, some roots rising to span the waters with natural bridges. The folk of Watersmeet built their community among the Sylvyads, carving out homes in the outer bark.

Glynholly fought beside my father to defend Watersmeet and what it stands for, thought Abisina. *She has to keep it open for those who need it, or my father will have died for nothing.*

CHAPTER II

ABISINA WENT STRAIGHT TO ULIAN'S WARD, THINKING guiltily of Haret and Hoysta. *Kyron will have sent someone to tell them I'm safe, but they'll wear out the floor pacing until I show up.* The dwarf Hoysta had saved Abisina when she fled her home. Haret, Hoysta's grandson, had come with Abisina across the mountains to Watersmeet. *And a more opinionated, stubborn, and loyal friend doesn't exist on either side of the Obrun Mountains. He'll understand that I had to go to Ulian's.*

After her father's death, Abisina invited Haret and Hoysta to live in her home. The move was meant to be temporary, but after a few months, the dwarves asked Abisina if they could carve out new rooms for themselves. The house was built for Rueshlan, who was tall both as a man and a centaur; dwarves needed tighter quarters—especially Hoysta, who had lived deep underground until she had come north to escape Charach. To Abisina's relief, once the dwarves built the new rooms, all talk of moving out stopped. Hoysta and Haret helped her ignore the gaping hole Rueshlan's death had left in her home and her heart.

In Ulian's ward, Abisina found a cluster of worried fauns gathered around the hamadryad. He looked shrunken and brittle, his root tendrils lying flat instead of standing on end.

"You must get back to your home tree," Bevan, an aging faun, was urging the dryad. "When we have news, we'll come to you."

Ulian's alive then! Abisina stepped away. In respect for the dryad, all folk but the fauns had left the ward.

"Please. Stay," a weak voice called.

The curly, horned heads turned to see who the dryad addressed.

"Thank you," Abisina said, politely avoiding the tree spirit's eyes. "How is Ulian?" she asked Bevan.

"Lennan's with him," he said.

If anyone can save Ulian, Lennan can, Abisina told herself. "May I go in?"

"The Keeper's there," another faun said. "You're not needed."

"Abisina is a healer and Ulian's friend," Bevan said. "She can help."

The crowd murmured, but Bevan took Abisina's elbow.

"The hamadryad looks awful," she whispered as Bevan walked her to Ulian's door. "Can't he be convinced to return to his tree?"

"We're trying." The faun sighed.

When Abisina entered Ulian's home, she could see almost nothing. The room was dusky and the windows were covered with cloth, a marked contrast from the early summer sunshine. The only light came from a few candles and a fire in the hearth. The air smelled of burning rosemary and juniper berries; Lennan was worried about infection. As her eyes adjusted, Abisina saw the dwarf healer leaning over a bed of branches. Glynholly stood nearby, watching anxiously.

Ulian lay on his bed, his face white, his breathing labored. His wound had been bandaged with poultices. Abisina smelled yarrow, garlic, and goosegrass. Lennan had built a frame around the faun's shattered shoulder with cords pulling in different directions, some bearing weights. She admired his skill. "How is he?" she whispered to the healer.

"Spear caught the lung; every breath costs him energy he needs for healing. The shave-weed extract you used helped staunch the bleeding, but the wound is deep. There's very little bone to work with—you can see the contraption I've had to build. If he slips into fever . . ."

"But can't you prevent that?" Glynholly broke in. Her desperation startled Abisina. Glynholly was not just Ulian's cousin; she had trained him as a youth and taken him with her on the campaign to defeat the Worm. He was more of a younger brother to her. But it had been months since Glynholly let her guard down like this—especially in front of Abisina.

"I will do what I can, Glynholly," Lennan replied.

Glynholly turned to Abisina. "Why did your patrol leave the foragers?"

"The wolves had a refugee—"

"A refugee? A Vranian?" Glynholly's voice was harsh in the stillness of the room. Ulian groaned.

"Leave me to my work," Lennan said tersely, and even Glynholly knew better than to argue. "Abisina," he called as they left the room, "your sweet balm tea is better than mine. I'll need some—if he makes it through the night."

When Glynholly and Abisina stepped out of Ulian's door, the hamadryad was gone, and several humans, dwarves, and centaurs had joined the fauns.

"How is he?" Bevan asked.

"Lennan is doing everything he can." Glynholly was Keeper again—cautious, politic.

Glynholly and Abisina passed silently through the crowd, but as they reached the edge of the ward, one of the dwarves spoke up. "What about these attacks, Keeper? Tesia spotted überwolves on the banks of the River Lesser last night—a few paces from Watersmeet."

"They get bolder each day," someone added.

"Their numbers are growing!"

"It's these Vranian refugees," a young faun said angrily. "They're leading the beasts right to us—easy prey. Then *our* folk have to go out and search for food to feed the Vranians."

"Farron—" Bevan began, with a glance at Abisina.

"I'm going to say it, and I don't care who hears me," Farron continued. "The refugees are the problem."

"They killed Rueshlan!" a centaur shouted. "Why should we help them?"

Abisina caught her breath as a murmur of assent rippled across the gathering. *Charach killed Rueshlan. The Vranians who fought beside him were little more than slaves.*

Glynholly stepped forward, and the crowd quieted. "I will keep Watersmeet safe, no matter what," she said. "The Council is discussing the issue now, but I can assure you that we will no longer put ourselves at risk for refugees."

What does she mean?

Not waiting for a response, Glynholly left. The ward buzzed with excitement.

"Bevan," Abisina said, "please let me know if Ulian's condition changes." The faun nodded, and Abisina ran out of the ward to catch up with Glynholly.

The Keeper had not gone far. Abisina found her staring moodily into the waters of the Middle River. She approached the faun slowly, suddenly not sure what to say.

"I knew you'd come," Glynholly said. She sounded bitter, mocking—so unlike the faun who had welcomed Abisina to Watersmeet. "You think you should be Keeper, but you don't know what it's like. Are you ready to send out patrols, not knowing who will come back? Are you ready to have Ulian's death on *your* head? The food stores are dwindling every day, and foraging groups have to go farther and farther. The risks they take! And they all expect me to protect them. Do you think you could do better?"

When Abisina said nothing, Glynholly held up the necklace from around her throat. *"Here,"* she said.

The necklace hung between them. Twisting metal filaments, beginning as many and winding into a single strand. For an instant, the light of the Obrium flashed, the metal blazing like a Midsummer bonfire. Abisina stared at it. *Could I use the necklace to help Watersmeet?*

As if hearing Abisina's thoughts, Glynholly snatched the necklace away and tucked it inside her tunic. But even before it dropped out of sight, the light extinguished and the necklace looked tarnished and cold.

"I will not let these refugees destroy my home," Glynholly declared.

"It's my home, too!" Abisina cried.

She hadn't meant to say it. She'd meant to reassure Glynholly that she didn't want to be Keeper.

"Your home? You've been here less than two years!"

"Yes, but—"

"I've lived here all of my life! And generations of my family before me."

"Of course." Abisina tried to steady her voice. "But Watersmeet means more to me than you realize. My life in Vranille was . . . unlivable. Watersmeet saved me. These refugees come with the same hope I did. You think you're threatened now?

If we shut folk out, we'll be besieged. If Watersmeet can be home to only a few, it will no longer be Watersmeet. I beg you: don't close out the refugees."

"It's the only way Watersmeet can survive," Glynholly said.

"But my father—"

"I advised your father for years, Abisina. I'm trying to save the home he died for." She fixed her eyes on Abisina. "I *will* save Watersmeet."

Glynholly stalked down the path, and this time Abisina didn't try to follow.

Haret was pacing in front of the hearth when Abisina entered. He took one look at Ulian's blood on her under-shirt and the überwolf scratches on her neck, and a frown replaced the relief on his face. "Kyron said you weren't hurt! Thank the Earth that Grandmother isn't here to see you."

"It's just a scratch," Abisina insisted. She'd forgotten all about her wounds. She sank into a chair. Only then did she see that Haret's friend Alden sat in another chair. Alden had the same brown skin, wiry hair, and thick beard as Haret, though Alden's hair was ginger colored, while Haret's was black.

"What's happened?" Haret asked. "Did Ulian—"

"No," Abisina said quickly. "But Lennan isn't sure he'll make it through the night. And Glynholly's threatening to close Watersmeet to the refugees!"

"Hmph," Haret said.

"You're not surprised?"

"There were rumors," he said tersely.

"Why didn't you tell me?"

"I didn't understand the extent of it—until now. That's what Alden's come to tell me. Folk know how you stand on this and assumed that I would agree with you. Which I do, human."

"Abisina, you're still mourning the loss of your father," Alden said soothingly. "Your friends didn't want you to get upset over rumors."

"Can Glynholly do it?" she asked Alden, who was a member of the Council. "Close Watersmeet?"

"It's due to come up at our next meeting," he admitted.

"The Council will never agree to isolate Watersmeet," Abisina insisted.

"Tell her, Alden, as you should've told me—as soon as you heard it." There was an edge to Haret's voice.

"It's hard to say," Alden said cautiously, and Abisina clenched her fists. "Some think going to fight Charach was a mistake—not to speak ill of your father," he added. "They blame our current problems on the battle. You saw little of Watersmeet before then. It was a different place: completely peaceful. Plenty of food. Parties and celebrations. Überwolves rarely attacked foraging parties. Minotaur sightings were even more unusual."

"But you had arms, toughness, skill," Haret commented.

"Rueshlan insisted we stay in fighting form," Alden

explained. "He remembered the days when Watersmeet had to fight to survive. But he was the only one; the rest of us knew only peace and abundance."

"When Charach threatened, my father refused to sacrifice the south, even to preserve Watersmeet's peace," Abisina said. "Are folk willing to do that now?"

"They didn't know war then," Alden argued. "They didn't know want or hunger. They want their old lives back."

"The world has changed, Alden," Haret said. "The Green Man took care of that after the battle when he blasted his Cleft through the Obrun Mountains."

"I wish we knew why!" Alden exclaimed.

As the refugee problem had grown worse, it was a question many in Watersmeet were asking. The Green Man had always been viewed as mysterious but benevolent. Perhaps even divine. He had created the Sylvyads and the vast forests carpeting the land north and south of the Obruns. So when the folk of Watersmeet first saw the Green Man's Cleft—the only practical passage through the Obrun Mountains—they assumed it was a gift. But now, as the refugees and überwolves poured through, it seemed more like a curse.

"It doesn't matter why he made it, Alden," Abisina said. "Watersmeet is not about food and parties. I would rather starve here than have a feast in a Vranian village."

Alden dropped his gaze and rubbed his forehead. "It's not that I disagree with you," he said. "But it's hard to fight for an ideal when you're hungry."

A knock on the door made them jump. Without waiting for an answer, Findlay walked in, followed by Neiall, a human who served on the Council with Alden.

Findlay was a familiar figure in Abisina's home. Blond with brown eyes, he had grown tall and broad—no longer a gangly boy. He'd been Abisina's close friend almost since they met. She had thought their friendship was on the brink of becoming something more. When grief had consumed her, Findlay stayed by her side. He never let her be alone too long, took her to target practice, and brought his little sister, Meelah, over as a distraction. But he seemed content to remain her friend.

Findlay knelt down in front of Abisina and took her hands. His usually ruddy face was pale.

"Ulian's dead."

CHAPTER III

ABISINA SANK INTO HER CHAIR.

"We ran into Bevan on our way here," Findlay said.

Alden stood. "I'll leave you," he said, bowing. "Ulian was a friend—and one of the best patrollers we had."

"Good night," Haret said softly.

As Alden opened the door, the room filled with the distant keening of the fauns. Images of her friend played through Abisina's mind—on patrol, dancing in moonlight, laughing around a bonfire during Midsummer.

Findlay squeezed her hand. "I'm sorry, Abby," he whispered.

There was a loud thudding of hoofbeats, and then Kyron entered. "I heard the keening. I wonder how long it will take for the Keeper to act."

"That's why we're here," Neiall said. He was young, twenty-five winters, but his coloring made him look as if he were at the brink of death: skin and hair white as bone, his eyes barely touched with blue. "We need to be prepared."

"Prepared for what?" Abisina asked.

"I—I hardly know," Neiall admitted. "Coming over here—the tension on the pathways, the threatening stares. We've all heard the grumblings. But it's gone much further than I would have imagined."

"As friends of Abisina, we've heard less than others," Findlay said. "Folk assume our allegiance is to her."

"Allegiance!" Abisina stared at Findlay. "My allegiance is to *Watersmeet*."

Neiall went on, "Anwyn came to me tonight. She was nervous. She said Glynholly's been meeting with Council members individually, getting a sense for how much they will support isolation. The Keeper didn't meet with me. She knows where I stand. But now, with the loss of Ulian, most of the Council will support her."

"Ulian would not support closing Watersmeet," Abisina said.

"Glynholly will want to observe the full mourning period," Findlay noted.

"You're right," said Neiall. "She won't call the Council for six days."

"Can we get to the Council members? Try to convince them that this will be a mistake?" Findlay asked.

"Abisina can," Kyron boomed. "They'll listen to her."

Neiall shook his head. "If folk think Abisina is working

against Glynholly, it's going to drive them farther apart."

"Not the centaurs. They'll always support Rueshlan's daughter," Kyron pronounced.

"Maybe," Findlay said. "But a lot of the centaurs blame the Vranians for Rueshlan's death and want nothing to do with them."

"No one would dare say anything like that to me," Kyron asserted.

"Or to any of us," Neiall said. "But you should have seen how nervous Anwyn was when she came to me. It seemed that, as a faun, she felt like a traitor to her kind, talking to a human about Glynholly."

"Do you hear yourselves?" Abisina asked. "Her 'kind'?"

"We have to offer folk some hope," Haret said. "Give them something practical to hold on to."

"We can step up the patrols," Findlay suggested. "Make sure we lose no one else."

"We need to train the refugees for patrols and forage. Send more of them out," Kyron added. "I'll train them myself."

"All of those things have to happen," Haret agreed. "But I don't think they're enough."

Abisina was only half listening. This talk of divisions and allegiance—it couldn't go on! And then it came to her.

"The fairies!" she said. "They came to us for help when Charach threatened them. Now they could help us control the überwolves. They can move through the treetops like birds, and they're expert archers. They could drive the überwolves away. Our foragers could build up the stores. The refugees need time to get used to all the differences in Watersmeet. They'll work hard. They can feed themselves, if we show them how."

She remembered how her own hatred for the Vranians had blinded her, and her father had insisted that they were worth saving. *Now it's up to me.*

The others looked at her skeptically.

"What is it?" she asked.

"There's a lot of mistrust for the fairies in Watersmeet," Findlay explained. "Folk blame them for drawing us into the battle with Charach. They couldn't protect their Motherland alone."

"But we have a long history with them," Abisina said.

"*Rueshlan* had a long history with them." Neiall ran his hand through his white hair. "He's the only one who's even visited the Fairy Motherland. He worked tirelessly on building an alliance, and Watersmeet was happy to have him do it." Neiall sighed. "But the truth is that the folk here are not comfortable with the fairies."

"The fairies danced at Midsummer—just a few days after I arrived in Watersmeet. The folk couldn't wait!" Abisina was pleading, needing to convince them—and herself—that the picture of Watersmeet she held in her mind was true.

"The fairies dancing here was a rare event. It hadn't happened in generations," Neiall said. "And remember how hard it was to get folk to agree to an alliance with them? If

Watersmeet didn't come to their aid, the fairies said they would negotiate with Charach to protect themselves. The fairies will support us only if there's something in it for them. And they have one goal in mind—keep their Motherland safe."

"But there *is* something in it for them," Haret insisted. "The northern side of the Cleft comes out close to the Motherland. They have to be affected by the überwolves and refugees—even more than we are."

"That's true," Findlay said. "Talking to them might be worth a try."

"It buys us time, nothing more," Neiall argued. "There's simply not enough space, not enough food for the refugees. This will just delay the inevitable."

"A delay would help," Abisina said. "If we can teach the Vranians another way to live, show them that the Vranian way is not the *only* way, they could return to the south with skills to help them start over. They wouldn't need to come north."

Neiall still seemed doubtful. "It will take you almost two weeks to get to the Motherland, and that again to come back. The decision of the Council will already be made!"

"Then we'll have to delay it," Findlay said. "Talk to all the members who have lingering doubts, keep the debate going."

"For two months?" Neiall was incredulous.

"It's our only choice," Haret said. "Even if we can't delay the Council, we need the fairies."

The truth of his words settled over the room.

"If we have any hope of convincing the fairies to work with us," Neiall finally said, "you'll have to go to them, Abisina."

"Me?"

"You're hoping to renew your father's alliance. Of course, your trip should be approved by the Council and the Keeper. . . ." Neiall hesitated.

"We can't wait for the Council's approval," Findlay said decisively, "even if they'd give it."

"If Abisina goes, I go," Kyron said. He had promised her father to protect her, and he took his oath very seriously. "I can carry her. We'll go faster."

Abisina could hardly believe what she was about to attempt. *But if there's a chance this will help Watersmeet . . .*

"I'll go," she said. Across the room, Haret smiled. Findlay looked worried, but he nodded at her.

Haret got to his feet and rubbed his hands together. "Let's get to work."

Kyron went to pack his gear. Haret would ready Abisina's while she caught a few hours of sleep.

Abisina followed Neiall and Findlay outside. The fauns' keening ripped through the night. *I'm going to miss Ulian's funeral pyre*, Abisina thought. In Vranille, she had watched her mother's body burn along with the other outcasts. Then she had stood at her father's pyre on the battlefield. *Will there be an end?*

Neiall hugged Abisina. "Good luck. And be careful. We will do all we can here while you're gone." He headed to the ward entrance. "Coming, Fin?"

"I'll catch up." Findlay waited for Neiall to leave before taking Abisina's hands in his.

They stood in the shadows. "I wish I were going with you," Findlay said, caressing her hand. Abisina could hardly see his face in the darkness. "Abby, I—" Findlay began, but approaching footsteps made them break apart.

Abisina would know those footsteps anywhere: the uneven pat-shuffle-pat-shuffle of Hoysta's bare feet.

"Oh, dearies," the old dwarf rasped. "I've just heard about poor Ulian. Such a fine young faun. And—oh!" Abisina had stepped into the light coming from the window. The dwarf's ancient face creased with concern as she saw the scratches on Abisina's neck.

How could I have ever thought her ugly? Abisina wondered. Like all Vranians, she had been taught to hate the dwarves.

"We knew *you'd* want to look after her," Findlay said.

Hoysta smiled, exposing her few teeth.

"I'll need some of your wintergreen salve," Abisina said, "for this and because I'm going on a journey."

"I just made a new batch," Hoysta said, hurrying to the door. "A journey? Is Haret going?" She kept talking as she entered the house.

Abisina turned back to Findlay, suddenly embarrassed. She put her hand on the door. "I—I guess I'd better go."

"Good-bye, Abisina," Findlay said quietly. He started to walk away, but came back and grabbed Abisina's hand again. "You *have* to be careful," he said in a rush. "I—I—Come home as soon as you can." He pulled her to him, kissed her on the lips, and strode out of the ward.

Abisina's cheeks were red and her eyes shining when she went inside. Haret raised his eyebrows at her and growled, " 'Bout time, human." She could hear Hoysta digging through her pots of healing salve.

Abisina headed to bed, hoping to get a little sleep before her journey began.

CHAPTER IV

ABISINA AND KYRON SET OFF SHORTLY BEFORE SUNRISE. Kyron's hooves thudded dully as they crossed a root bridge, mixing with the fauns' funeral song rolling across Watersmeet. Abisina looked back. The Sylvyads were gray in the dusk, their broad flat needles silvery with dew. Lights glowed across the misty water as the community rose to say good-bye to Ulian. *Ulian would want me to do this,* Abisina thought. *He would want me to do whatever I can to help Watersmeet.*

But would the fairies listen to her? Was being Rueshlan's daughter enough? *And even if I do convince the fairies to help us, will it change Glynholly's mind?*

Kyron and Abisina were traveling light. They brought essential foods—smoked rabbit, salted fish, thin travel bread, hard cheese—though Abisina had seen Kyron slip a few honeyed buns into his sack. They each had a water skin, their bows and arrows, and a cloak to sleep in. Abisina carried a packet of herbs for injuries and a small knife in her belt. Kyron had a sword strapped on his back and a knife on his upper arm. They hoped to get to the Motherland in ten days.

Abisina had traveled near the Motherland when she and her father had marched with Watersmeet's army. But then they had gone to the southern side, closer to the Obrun Mountains. This time they took a northern route, following the River Fennish east before abandoning it to head south. The river was swollen with spring rains. Later in the summer, it would move sluggishly, carrying the smell of rot and decay. It was fed by the Fens, a marsh that spread across the northern territory.

The folk of Watersmeet visited the Fens to harvest reeds for weaving baskets and mats, and to collect the delicious cattail roots that could be boiled and eaten or ground into flour. But the Fens were dangerous, even at their edges. Abisina had never been there, but she knew the stories: Islands of grasses floated in the black water, appearing solid and stable until you stepped on them and sank out of sight. Pathless bogs drew you in; sucking mud held you fast. In the Watersmeet library, books told tales of outlaws who hid in the Fens for years, but more told of innocent folk who had gone in and never came out.

They had taken the northern route to avoid überwolves, but Abisina spotted plenty of tracks. She worried far more when she saw the massive footprints of minotaurs, followed by the diminutive prints of the hags who held the beasts in their power. These creatures must be remnants of the Worm's army, but she had seen few signs of them since the battle ended. Luckily, no minotaurs or hags crossed their path, and the only überwolves were solitary ones, unwilling to challenge a large centaur with an archer on his back.

Galloping through forests and splashing across streams, Abisina often thought of Ulian. On patrol, he was serious and tough. But off patrol, he'd been quick with a joke or a song. Was he really gone?

She also thought of Findlay, remembering the feel of his lips against hers. At times, she dismissed his kiss. *We're friends, and he was worried about me going on this journey.* But other times, she saw it differently. *We've always had feelings for each other.* There had been years when she wouldn't have dared hope for such a thing. *An outcast like me—kissed!*

But mostly, she thought about the Motherland. She had to admit to herself that the fairies scared her. They were graceful, otherworldly beings, so different that she couldn't imagine sharing any of the same concerns or feelings with them. *But the fairies respected my father,* she reminded herself. A few had stayed to mourn at his funeral pyre. Lohring, daughter of the Fairy Mother, was one of them.

Abisina tried to compose a speech to deliver to the Fairy Mother—something about the long alliances between the Motherland and Watersmeet, and Watersmeet's present need.

She thought of Neiall's words: "The fairies will support us only if there's something in it for them." Would the fairies—so powerful and independent—really see something to gain by helping Watersmeet?

She tried her speech out on Kyron. She got through the first couple of lines, paused for effect, and Kyron applauded: "It's perfect! How can they say no?"

"But Kyron, I haven't presented my argument yet!"

"I can hear Rueshlan in you. The fairies will, too."

"You can't hear Rueshlan in two sentences! Oh, the Earth," Abisina moaned, adopting Haret's favorite phrase. *It's Haret I need. He'd never be that easy on me.*

"Stop worrying. They'll listen to you."

Kyron's belief in her made it hard to be angry with him. He would do anything for her. But he wasn't the best source for advice on diplomacy.

On the sixth day of their journey, Abisina thought constantly of the Council meeting going on in Watersmeet. Had Neiall, Findlay, and Haret managed to find any members to oppose Glynholly?

Kyron seemed to be thinking of it, too; he galloped harder than he had on previous days, and didn't stop until long after sundown.

They had decided to catch a few hours of sleep when Abisina spotted a light ahead. She knew it at once: the glow of a Seldar grove. They went toward it. Soon she could make out the bark of the slender trees, the trailing leaves, and the supple branches. The trees of this grove, like the Seldar groves around Watersmeet, grew in roughly concentric circles and bathed the center clearing in their soft light.

Abisina recalled the moment the Green Man had appeared at her father's funeral pyre, towering over all the creatures that had drawn together to bid Rueshlan farewell. As the flames died, the Green Man had gathered the ash and spread it on the winds, sending it spinning away with his breath. Wherever the ash settled, groves of Seldar trees sprang from the earth. For Abisina, these groves were living eulogies to her father. And while the Sylvyads were Watersmeet's trees, the Seldars belonged to everyone.

She wasn't alone in her love of the Seldars. The groves had become sacred places to the folk of Watersmeet, places to wander in silent contemplation. Before the überwolves had started attacking in such numbers, some folk had even gone on pilgrimages to the more far-flung groves.

The refugees from the south shared this awe for the Seldars. They called the groves "Rueshlan's Balefire." Abisina first heard the term from a Vranian man who arrived in Watersmeet with his frail grandson clutched to him. As she dabbed horseradish ointment on his wounds, he said, "I know you." Abisina's heart had raced. Was he from Vranille? Would he call her outcast?

"I knew at once," the man continued, now smiling. "You have Rueshlan's Balefire in your eyes."

Abisina gasped.

"Oh, we know his name," he said confidently. "And we know what he did for us. He gave us those trees, the Seldars—burning like his pyre burned, leading us to freedom."

After that, she heard tales of Rueshlan's Balefire from many refugees. Some reported that they had a friend saved from an überwolf's claws by leaping into a grove. Others insisted that sleeping in the groves cured hunger pains or that Rueshlan spoke to them through the trees. "I was headed into an überwolf ambush when I turned aside to visit the trees. I heard a voice telling me to take a different route, and I haven't seen an überwolf since," a young man claimed.

Abisina told herself that these tales were from people desperate for refuge, but the truth was that she wanted to believe them.

Vigar—the founder of Watersmeet—dead for generations, had once spoken to Abisina, telling her how to get to Watersmeet and reassuring her at her most difficult moments. Perhaps, through his trees, Rueshlan spoke to those in need. *When my need is enough, maybe he'll speak to me.* But each time she entered a grove, she heard only the rustle of the leaves.

As she and Kyron approached the trees, Abisina wanted more than ever to hear her father's voice, to have something more than the dreams she had almost nightly of him—the two of them racing across fields and meadows, she on his back, the wind streaming through her hair. Those were just images, and each night his image grew more insubstantial. But his voice! That would be real. He could tell her what to do.

"I'll stand guard outside, Abisina. You go in alone," Kyron said. He understood what these groves meant to her.

She stepped between the trunks, running her fingers along the cool bark, letting the branches trail across her back. As she moved to the center, the light increased.

"I need you, Father," she said softly. "Watersmeet needs you. The fairies—how can I make them listen to me?"

She waited and waited. But no voice came.

A few nights after finding the Seldar grove, Abisina woke suddenly. The campfire smoldered, and she could see Kyron's shadow in the low light. He was on watch. She strained to listen. The wind whispered in the trees, but the night animals were silent. Then she heard it: a rustling to her left. She sniffed. There was no stink of überwolf musk. *And a minotaur could never be that stealthy.*

She picked up her bow, strung and ready.

The rustling continued. Then a twig snapped.

Is it a refugee? Abisina wondered. Few came this far north.

At the next snap—closer now—Abisina nocked her arrow and drew the string back to her ear.

A third snap—

"I have my sword at the ready. Don't move," Kyron rumbled through the dark.

"My weapons are down!" a male voice answered.

I know that voice.

"I'm from the south—seeking Watersmeet."

Abisina remembered a blond boy with a shock of hair covering one of his blue eyes. "Corlin?" she whispered.

Kyron kicked the fire to life, and the reddish light showed a grubby figure stepping from the trees. His hair was long and snarled. His clothes were rags. The bones of his face protruded as if ready to split the skin. But his eyes told Abisina that this was indeed the boy who had helped her escape the mob in Vranille, the young man who had joined forces with the folk of Watersmeet to defeat the White Worm.

Abisina lowered her arrow. "It *is* you! What are you doing here?"

"I—I found you," Corlin managed before sinking to the ground.

"Here," Kyron said, rummaging through his satchel and handing Corlin the last of his honeyed buns. "It's a bit stale," he apologized.

Corlin startled as Kyron stepped into the light. Corlin had known centaurs during the battle, but he was Vranian. His people had fought centaurs for generations.

He swallowed the bun in two bites. Kyron followed up with pieces of travel bread and salted fish.

Finally, Corlin had satisfied his hunger enough to talk. "I came north, headed to Watersmeet, but überwolves attacked my group. We got separated. The track from the Cleft to Watersmeet has become too dangerous to go alone, so I continued north, figuring I could make my way west eventually. But I lost all my gear and food in the attack."

"You're a refugee?" Abisina was astonished. After the Worm's defeat, Corlin was determined to return home and help his people start over.

"I came to get *help*," Corlin said. "The south is in chaos. Before the battle, the Worm killed most of the women and children and forced the men to fight for him. Some people survived in the woods. There are überwolves and minotaurs everywhere and very little food. You know the Worm destroyed Vranille, but there's also nothing left of Vranberg, Vrandun, or Vranhurst. Only the two original villages are still standing."

Abisina had never been to any village except Vranille, but she knew the story of each one's founding. Vranham was the first village, sometimes called Home Village, because Vran, founder of the Vranian way of life, had lived there. Vranlyn was second.

"Those who didn't go north went to those villages. Theckis has taken over Vranham."

Abisina's chest tightened. "The refugees don't talk much about the villages and never mentioned Theckis," she said. He had been an Elder in Vranille, punishing Abisina for every breath she took.

"Theckis is leading the village as if he were Vran himself," Corlin said. "He's gathered to him those Elders who survived the battle, but he calls himself the *Eldest*. For men, the life there is just livable. But it's slavery for females and outcasts. Death to anyone too different. No one gets out of Vranham."

During her months of mourning her father, Abisina had

one comfort: The Vranians had been released from the power of Charach by an army of centaurs, fauns, dwarves, fairies, and humans who had almost none of the qualities the Vranians valued. How could they continue to believe that their rescuers were demons?

"Does Theckis have many followers?" Abisina asked.

"Maybe two or three hundred. I don't know how many are true followers. Theckis offers them something familiar and at least the hope of survival."

"What about Vranlyn? Is another Elder in charge there?"

"No, Abisina," Corlin said. "Vranlyn is the hope of the south—well, it's my hope. We're trying to build a new kind of community. One like—Watersmeet." He hesitated and glanced up shyly. "We're just beginning," he continued. "There are a group of us—mostly people who saw the evil of the Vranian way—outcasts, women, and those who lost loved ones to the cruelty of the Elders. We welcome all and share what we have."

"You welcome *all*?" Kyron sounded doubtful. He was preparing a rabbit stew that had been planned for breakfast.

"Right now, we're just humans," Corlin admitted. "It's been hard to convince people that reaching out to fauns and dwarves will make us stronger."

"What about centaurs?" Kyron demanded.

Corlin looked down. "That will be harder still. The Vranians cannot imagine befriending centaurs. People are thinking only of survival. We returned from the battle to fields destroyed by the White Worm and soaked with his poison.

He didn't want to leave his army anything worth returning to. That winter we lost many to disease and hunger. When spring came, most were too weak to plant. We were short on seed. We had no tools and few people to use them. Theckis's men, centaurs, and gangs raided what we did manage to plant."

"What gangs?" Abisina asked.

"They're Vranian men who came home from the battle determined to follow their own law. They live together in the forests, stealing, hunting, and fighting other gangs or each other. We've tried to bring some of them into Vranlyn to help with the work. Our wall is down in places, a troll has been seen nearby—"

"Have you always had trolls in the south?" Kyron broke in.

"We think the Worm brought them—from wherever he came from."

Kyron gave a low whistle.

"We did try to reach out to nonhumans," Corlin added. "Dwarves have returned to the ruin of Vrandun—they call it Stonedun. Do you remember the story? They tried to destroy the human village by building under it?"

"The dwarves say that the humans tried to destroy *their* community by building on top of it," Abisina said.

"That's what they told me," Corlin said. "I went to ask for help, but they refused. Like everyone in the south, they have their own problems."

"Would the humans in Vranlyn have worked with the dwarves?"

"Most, no," Corlin acknowledged. "But I had to try. During the battle, I fought beside dwarves; they dressed my wounds. I tried to explain that this was another way the Elders had lied to us." He shook his head. "The Vranians have no experience outside the Elders' teaching about the 'demons and beasts.'" Corlin sighed.

The rabbit meat was boiling, and they heard the soft pop of water bubbles and the hiss of the fire.

The south needs Vranlyn, Abisina thought. *If it survives—and thrives—the Vranians would see that the ideals of Watersmeet can exist in the south.*

"What kind of help do you need from Watersmeet?" she asked.

"With planting. With labor to repair the wall. With any tools or clothing you can spare. But, that's not all. They need to see you—a free people—free *folk,*" he corrected himself, "working as one."

"Didn't they see that on the battlefield as you did?" Abisina said.

"Some did. That's why a place like Vranlyn exists at all. But it's not enough."

The stew was ready. Kyron ladled it out and handed a bowl to Corlin.

"I know you'll need to go to your Council to make my request," said Corlin. "But . . . wait. Why are you out here alone?"

Abisina had to tell the truth. "Watersmeet's in trouble. We can barely feed ourselves. We're going to the fairies to ask for help."

Corlin paled. "If Watersmeet can't help us, I've come all this way for nothing."

"No!" Abisina insisted. "Watersmeet needs Vranlyn, too. The fairies' help will only delay our problem. There is a limit to how many refugees Watersmeet can take in. Vranlyn will give the humans of the south a reason to stay in the south."

"But will the fairies help you?"

"They owe us." Abisina sounded sure, but she doubted this argument would work with the Fairy Mother. "Come with us, Corlin," she suggested. "You will get a better hearing in the Council if we have an alliance with the fairies."

"There's no point in continuing to Watersmeet if the Council will say no to me," Corlin agreed.

They wrapped up in their cloaks to sleep through the few remaining hours of darkness. Abisina closed her eyes but couldn't sleep. She could see the answer before her. *Save Vranlyn to save Watersmeet.* But her task had gotten harder. *If* she convinced the Fairy Mother to help Watersmeet, she still had to convince Glynholly to help Vranlyn.

As Abisina lay there watching the approach of dawn, she wondered again if being Rueshlan's daughter would be enough.

CHAPTER V

IN THE MORNING, THE THREE ARRIVED AT A WIDE PLAIN. Maps in the Watersmeet library had shown the Motherland on the other side of that plain; they hoped to be there in two days.

Corlin, worn out from his travels, rode on Kyron's back. Abisina was quiet, but when Corlin spoke about his journey home after the battle, she got drawn in.

"What happened to Lilas?" Abisina asked.

Lilas had tormented Abisina in Vranille. She'd been with Corlin's group of deserters when they met the Watersmeet army. And she was as cruel to Abisina as ever. But Abisina also pitied her. Lilas continued to believe that she would be rewarded for her loyalty to Vran.

"She didn't make it back. You saw what she was like. Centaurs attacked us, and she didn't have the sense to save herself. She stood her ground, screaming that she was an heir to Vran and could not be touched by their demon hands. I just hope her end was swift."

Abisina felt sick. No one deserved to die like that.

The first day on the plain, they discovered a broken spear, a trail of blood, and many überwolf tracks. Kyron gave his knife to Corlin, who was weaponless. They slept for a few hours in the darkest part of the night, and then kept on.

The Motherland appeared on the horizon: a forbidding line of dark trees rising from the rocky plain. They tramped and tramped beneath the hot sun, but the trees refused to get closer. The überwolf tracks increased, and they fought a few skirmishes.

The rough and rutted plain ended about fifty body lengths from the line of trees. Between where they stood and the forest was a margin of land swept bare—no stray branches or leaves, no stone or hump of dirt. The smooth corona was sinister in its perfection.

Corlin climbed down from Kyron's back.

"What do you make of that?" Abisina whispered, though the only living things in sight were two black birds wheeling overhead.

"I don't like it," Kyron grumbled.

Abisina took a deep breath and said, "There's nothing to do but go in."

"No!" Kyron cried, but before he could stop her, she stepped into the ring of even ground.

Nothing happened. She let out her breath.

"It's all right," she called. But the instant Kyron crossed the boundary, the earth began to shake.

"Get back!" Abisina yelled too late. Snaking roots, some as thick as her arm, shot from the ground, looped around Kyron's hooves, and brought him down hard. More roots burst forth and twisted across the centaur's body, binding him so tightly he could not lift his head or reach for his weapons.

Corlin bolted forward, drawing his knife, but the roots jerked it out of his hand and pinioned him to the earth. Abisina raced to help her friends as Kyron roared: "Stay back!"

She ignored him. She reached Kyron first and pulled out her dagger. Before she could hack through his bonds, a slender root snatched her dagger out of her hand and dangled it maddeningly out of reach. While Abisina jumped at her dagger, two more roots hooked her bow and quiver, and these, too, swung teasingly close to her outstretched arms.

"Your sword, Kyron." Abisina squatted next to the centaur and reached between the bars of root to pull his sword free.

"Stop," Kyron rasped as the bands tightened, pushing the air from his lungs and grinding his face and torso into the dirt. "Get back," he wheezed, and Abisina leapt away. Immediately, the roots loosened, taking Kyron's sword and arrows, but allowing him to tuck his hooves under him and sit upright. His cheek and chest glistened with bloody abrasions. Corlin fared little better. The roots had built a cage around him as solid as Kyron's.

"The fairies are doing this," Abisina fumed.

"They know we're out here," Kyron agreed, pointing to the sky where the black birds rode the air currents. "They've probably known since we left Watersmeet."

Abisina knew the fairies could speak to birds, but she hadn't expected them to spy on Watersmeet.

"Why didn't they capture me?" she asked.

Kyron looked toward the trees, as if hoping to find an answer, but the wall of trunks gave nothing away.

"I'm going in," Abisina said again.

"Absolutely not!" Kyron bellowed from his cage. "You cannot risk it. I won't allow it!"

"They could've done the same to me, and they haven't. I think they want me to go in."

"Abisina!" Kyron tried to get to his feet, but the woody bars of his cage clamped down. He struggled, kicking out with his hooves, driving his shoulders into the roots, until he was again laid out on the ground, his spine painfully twisted.

"Fairies!" Abisina called. "I am Abisina, daughter of Rueshlan." She waited. Were they listening? She groped for diplomatic words. "This centaur, Kyron, was Rueshlan's herd brother. This man, Corlin, fought next to the fairies at the battle with the Worm. In the name of Rueshlan and his long friendship with the fairies, we want to—we request permission to—enter the Motherland—"

Abisina had thought she was doing well, but at these words, the roots around Kyron and Corlin twitched and closed in farther. Kyron began to yell—

"Just me," she called frantically. "*I* would like to come in."

The roots stilled. Abisina took a step forward, and the cages expanded slightly.

"I'll return as soon as I've seen the Mother," she promised Kyron.

Abisina turned, squared her shoulders, and stepped into the trees.

She walked into night; the thick branches of the firs blocked the sun. No wind or birds moved through the heavy foliage. The smell of rotting meat hung in the air, and Abisina gagged. She wanted to run! But as she took a step, vines materialized out of the forest floor and dragged at her feet. She tried another direction, but again plants tied her feet to the ground. There was no break in the trees. In every direction, moss hung on immense evergreens. Trunks grew so close together she could not squeeze between them. Where was the plain? Where should she go? Had they lured her in here just to imprison her? Abisina kept trying to move. She didn't care where. The reek was unbearable. She pulled her tunic over her nose and breathed in the fresh air and sunshine that clung faintly to it.

She must have finally hit on the direction the fairies wanted her to go because she managed a few steps. Branches scratched her face, pulled at her hair, snagged the embroidery Hoysta had so caringly done on her tunic. Each time Abisina strayed from the invisible path, the vines stopped her. After what felt like hours, she came to a dead end. With every move, more vines gripped her. Soaked with sweat, she tried again and again. "I didn't come all this way for nothing!" she shouted. Then she felt the tiniest give, and she threw herself in that direction. With a grunt, she burst through a web of branches and fell into open space, her feet still wrapped in vines.

Here she had room to stretch her arms between the trees that surrounded her. Beech, aspen, and birch replaced the gloomy evergreens. Light from the setting sun filtered onto her face, and the air lifted strands of her hair, cooling her sweaty neck. A nightingale sang somewhere in the dusk.

I've made it to the Motherland.

She sat up, untangled her feet, and pulled leaves and twigs from her hair.

"Go no farther," a voice spoke. "One step, and my arrow flies."

Abisina scanned the trees. "I am Abisina," she called into the tense air.

"We know who you are." The voice was now near her right ear, but when Abisina turned, she saw no one.

"What do you want?" Same voice, left ear. She looked, but again—nothing.

"I—I want to speak with Lohring," Abisina said, grasping at the only name she knew, furious at her stammer. "I know Lohring."

"You *know* her." The voice came from behind her now. She didn't bother to turn. "How?"

"I met her on the campaign against Charach."

"*You* went to battle against the Worm?" Abisina felt breath on her face, and a rustling in the leaves that may have been laughter.

The sound died away. Had she been left alone? "Wait!" she called.

"I am here." And there was a fairy—standing before her on the very tip of a branch, not more than a twig, though the fairy was as tall as Abisina. *Short for a full-grown fairy,* Abisina thought. Light eyes stared out of a dark face; a slight smile pulled at the fairy's lips. Abisina hadn't thought fairies smiled. The fairy had its arrow trained on Abisina's chest.

"I am Reava, Lohring's daughter." As if on cue, six fairies leapt from the branches above and landed noiselessly on the ground on either side of Reava. These fairies were taller, and like all the fairies Abisina had met, they had blue-black skin that shone even in the low light. They wore loose black tunics and pants. Their hair grew in tight curls well past the middle of their backs. Each aimed an arrow at Abisina.

Abisina hoped the fairies couldn't see the goose pimples on her arms or hear her heart pounding. It wasn't just the arrows. As usual, she couldn't read their faces or even tell if they were male or female. Their haughtiness unsettled her, as did their ability to leap through trees in complete defiance of gravity. For all she knew, hundreds of fairies glared down at her from the foliage.

Reava sprang to the ground and approached Abisina, stopping when her arrow was a breath away. Abisina tried not to flinch. As the fairy's light eyes raked over her, Abisina recognized the tilt of her chin and her insolent look. *She's a bully,* Abisina realized. *Like Lilas and all the children in Vranille who called me "demon." I know bullies.* She stared back at Reava, and the fairy slowly dropped the point of her arrow to the ground.

"The Farewell will begin soon," the fairy said. "We will take you there."

"What's—"

Reava cut her off. "The Fairy Mother is dead. We bid her farewell tonight."

"I . . . I'm sorry," Abisina said. Reava ignored her.

"Lohring—who will be the new Fairy Mother—may decide to give you an audience. But not now." Reava turned away from Abisina and began to walk farther into the Motherland. With their arrows, the other fairies motioned that Abisina should follow.

The news that Lohring would be the new Fairy Mother gave Abisina more confidence. "Am I to come as a prisoner?" she called to Reava.

The fairy stopped. "You need us, Abisina of Watersmeet. You would not have made the journey otherwise. You will come however we decide, or we will send you back into the boundary forest." She set off again.

Abisina blushed. Reava was right.

The six fairies vaulted into the trees and out of sight, but Abisina knew they were there, arrows ready.

After walking for half a league, Abisina could hear high,

ethereal voices—fairy song that wept out of the sky. She didn't understand the words, but the beauty of it, the pain, brought tears.

Reava had almost left Abisina behind. In the fading light it was harder and harder to see the fairy, and she ran to catch up.

Abisina reached Reava at the base of a beech trunk. "Up," the fairy commanded.

Abisina peered at a platform high above her. There was no ladder, no branches to climb. The tree was too wide for her to shimmy up it. "I can't," she said.

Reava narrowed her eyes, but she kept walking. Abisina followed in frustration. *She knows I can't leap like they can.*

At the base of a second tree, Reava stopped again. It was almost night now. The moon had not yet risen, but Abisina could just make out a slender ladder hanging from another platform. "The ladder is used for *children* who are too young to leap," Reava scoffed.

Without a word, Abisina stepped onto the ladder.

At every rung she was sure it would break. It seemed to be made of grass or reeds, and it swung wildly under her weight. But she said nothing. Reava was testing her, and she planned to pass.

Reaching the platform wasn't much comfort. It was woven of twigs, and several snapped as Abisina stepped onto it. "You can watch the Farewell from here," Reava said in her ear, but again, when Abisina turned, she couldn't see the fairy. "Do not try to leave. We will know."

Abisina turned her attention to the flimsy platform, longing to crouch down and spread out her weight as she would on thin ice, but somewhere in the darkness, the fairies watched her, and she would not show her fear. Instead she groped with her feet for the supporting branch and stood on it, as close to the trunk as she could. The singing continued in the dark around her.

What will the Mother's death mean for the fairies? Abisina thought. *Will Lohring talk to me?* The fairies had let her in. That was something. She tried not to think of her friends trapped at the edge of the Motherland.

Night grew deeper. The fairy dirge went on until it became as natural as the wind sighing in the trees. Abisina sat down and leaned her head against the trunk. She must have dozed, because she dreamed of galloping across fields with her father, the necklace thumping against her chest at each footfall. When she woke, the singing had stopped.

Then, as the full, yellow moon rose on the horizon, a low note rang through the trees.

Below the rising moon, another circle of light appeared, as if the moon were reflected in a still lake. Slowly, the reflection grew in size. The fairies had danced at Watersmeet with glowing orbs of moonlight. Is that what she saw now?

Another "moon" appeared. And then another. Soon there were many. Smaller orbs arose on each side of the central lights, rippling like waves. The low note beat on: a pulsing heartbeat.

Then a much larger, more brilliant circle joined the procession—this one so bright, Abisina had to look at it through half-closed eyes. A single fairy carried the light balanced on its head, and below, a dozen more fairies supported a bier. On the bier lay the Fairy Mother, her white hair spread like a halo around the moon. She was draped in black, shiny cloth. Lohring stood at the head of the bier, ebony hair streaked with silver. Though she held her head erect and moved regally, grief radiated from her.

The bier came to rest, and the music turned from the throbbing note to a cacophony, the fairies wailing out their loss. The night vibrated with it, and Abisina's own sadness rose. How could they seem such hard, cold creatures and express such sad beauty?

The keening ebbed until there was only one voice left, breathy and uneven but unwilling to give in to silence: Lohring. The fairy choked out a final sound. Abisina held her breath.

Thrum! Thrum! Thrum!

She knew the noise but couldn't place it. The fairies remained motionless as the thrumming grew louder. Abisina spotted them at last, hundreds of owls swooping to the Fairy Mother. Abisina now noticed the silver threads hanging from the bier; the owls took the threads in their beaks and lifted the bier into the air. They cleared the trees and flew upward, as if bearing the Mother's body to the moon.

Abisina watched the owls fly out of sight. Where were they taking her?

The fairies continued to stare after them, seeing what Abisina could not. Then a small speck appeared against the moon, growing steadily larger. It wasn't until it was quite close that Abisina recognized a single, enormous owl with something clasped in its talons. As the owl neared them, the object gathered the orbs' light.

Obrium! Abisina's hand went to her throat, feeling for the Keeper's necklace that she wore in her dreams.

The object was a crown, and as the owl flew low over the fairies, the bird let the crown fall, turning end over end. Lohring raised her hand and caught it, then lowered it to her head.

The wood burst with song. Fairies left the trees, dark shapes leaping past Abisina. They danced, Lohring at the center, while the rest of the fairies spun out from her like spokes on a wheel, moving first one way, then the other. The dance went on and on, bewitching Abisina until moonset when the fairies melted into the trees.

The Farewell was over. The fairies had a new Mother.

Chapter VI

Abisina awoke feeling energized and hopeful. Today she would talk to Lohring.

First, she had to get past Reava. The fairy came to her as the birds were warming up their song. "It is time to go."

"Go?" Abisina forced herself to sound calm. "I have to speak with Lohring."

"Who are you to request an audience with our Mother?"

"I am the daughter of Rueshlan," she said, "friend of the fairies for generations. He stood with you on the battlefield and died to defeat our common enemy. I, too, fought to defeat Charach and protect the Motherland. *That* is who I am."

"Reava!" A deep call echoed around Abisina. The birds hushed. "Bring her to me. As I asked you."

Reava's been playing with me, Abisina seethed.

As Abisina made her way down the reed ladder, two rungs

broke beneath her feet, and she had to jump off to save herself from a fall.

Reava was waiting for her, and there was no mistaking the hostility on her face. "Follow me. And keep up." She leapt away, landing high in a tree where the leaves hid her.

Abisina clenched her teeth. *She's going to make this as difficult as possible. But the Fairy Mother said to bring me to her. I don't need to play Reava's game.* She set off after the fairy at a steady but unhurried pace. Reava was almost out of sight and could easily have lost Abisina, but she didn't.

They seemed to skirt the center of the community. Through the trees, Abisina could spot what must have been the fairies' homes. They stood against the sky like huge bee-hives built of sticks, woven to a point at the top. Each had an archway at its base. A few lithe figures leapt from one to another, and Abisina thought of Watersmeet in the morning as children played or neighbors shared an extra loaf of bread. She couldn't imagine the fairies' daily lives—chores, friendships, conversation. But seeing their homes made them less mysterious, and Abisina relaxed slightly. They had to have some sense of fairness, camaraderie, sympathy that she could appeal to when she talked to Lohring.

Then a familiar sight beckoned through the trees. *A Seldar grove!* She headed toward it without checking if Reava followed.

A fairy sat on a branch close to the top of a Seldar. Another wove among the branches as if performing a ritual dance. A few sat and gazed upward at the foliage.

Abisina stayed outside the grove, not wanting to interrupt. Love for the Seldars was another element of the fairies she could understand.

Suddenly Reava stood in front of her, arms spread wide. "The Fairy Mother waits," she said through tight lips.

Abisina nodded and turned away from the grove.

A few moments later, she came face-to-face with Lohring, and all hope of camaraderie vanished. The Fairy Mother stood beneath an enormous oak, flanked on either side by eight of the biggest fairies Abisina had ever seen. Lohring's Obrium crown washed the Fairy Mother with light. The crown was woven of thousands of tiny metal threads and was alive with figures—flowers and birds, naiads and hamadryads, fairies and fauns—looking as if they were in motion as the light played off them. Beneath her brilliant crown, Lohring's silver-streaked hair hung free. She wore the crown as if she had always worn it. Abisina remembered how Lohring had commanded the Council House when she had been in Watersmeet. She was even more powerful now.

Reava leapt from the trees and sank onto her knees, head bowed. "Mother," she said. She did not address her as a daughter—Reava spoke to *the* Mother.

The Fairy Mother glared at Reava. "Leave us."

Reava raised her head to meet Lohring's eyes.

She's brave, Abisina admitted to herself.

"Mother, you said I could—"

"*Reava.*" Lohring's tone made Abisina want to cover her

ears, and even Reava couldn't stand up to it. She leapt away, brushing against Abisina as she did so.

Did Reava whisper a threat to me? Abisina couldn't be sure, but words echoed in her head: *You will regret this.*

Abisina began to kneel, but then thought better of it. *I am not Lohring's subject.* Respect was important, but she needed the fairies to respect her, too. Abisina bowed.

"Welcome to the Motherland," Lohring said. "I apologize for my daughter's rudeness." Lohring didn't look at Abisina when she spoke.

"I am sorry for your loss, Fairy Mother," Abisina said, bowing slightly again. *What do I know of diplomacy?* she worried, but she steadied herself.

"The Mother was old, and it was her time." Lohring's words were clipped. "You have honored the Motherland with your presence."

They were speaking from a script, and Abisina kept up her end. "I was honored to be part of the Farewell."

Lohring took a seat on a carved chair at the base of the oak. The chair was simple—a broad seat with saplings bent to form the back—but it added to her majesty. Abisina remained standing, which put her at a disadvantage: she was a petitioner.

"What brings you here, Rueshlan's daughter?" Lohring's tone changed as she moved to business.

Now the real discussion begins. Abisina tried to remember the speech she had rehearsed. "Watersmeet is—" She was going to say, "in trouble," but she saw her error. *Don't show weakness.* "Watersmeet has long been an ally of the Motherland. When you came to my father for aid two years ago, he gave it." *Better.*

"We are again in need," Lohring broke in. "Perhaps more so. Like Watersmeet, the Motherland is the Green Man's creation, and we celebrate him here as you do. His Seldars, too, we see as a gift. But his Cleft threatens to destroy us." Lohring's voice shook. "When the Green Man provided a road through the mountains, he put the Motherland directly in the path of every überwolf, minotaur, or troll that comes north. We are prisoners in our own land. On the plain, with no trees for cover, we are vulnerable. Some can cross—the young and strong. But our elders, our children cannot. And we lost many in the battle. We cannot risk losing more."

Were the *fairies* admitting to a weakness? "You can't cross the plain?" Abisina asked. "But for the battle, you crossed the mountains."

"That was my mother's choice. And there were no überwolves then. Or not enough to worry about. We have few children, and their youth is long. The battle with the Worm was very costly.

"Watersmeet is in a similar position," Lohring continued. "The Sylvyads are your protection and your prison." She leaned forward. "Once again, we have something to offer each other."

Abisina fought the urge to smile. The fairies were willing to work with Watersmeet! She would return to Glynholly with a solution.

"We must close the Cleft," Lohring said firmly. "It is our only choice. With the Cleft open, the migration will get worse. We need the folk of Watersmeet to build a wall across the mouth of the Cleft. Your dwarves can do the work. In the meantime, with Watersmeet's protection, we can move a contingent of fairies across the plain to the safety of the trees where we can then hunt down the überwolves. Once we have wiped them out, your folk can return Watersmeet to the community your father built."

Abisina struggled to take in Lohring's plan. A solution to both the refugee and the überwolf population. It could save Watersmeet. Wasn't that why she had come here?

But walling the Cleft was no different than closing Watersmeet. Watersmeet would survive, but Vranlyn would not. Corlin's villagers would have to return to Theckis's village. War between humans and the southern folk would continue.

"It's not right." Abisina hadn't meant to speak this plainly, but now that she had, she didn't stop. "My father saw it as Watersmeet's responsibility to free the Vranians. Charach's defeat is meaningless unless the folk on both sides of the Obruns are at peace. There is a community in the south struggling for survival, free from Vran's beliefs. *That* is where the solution lies, Fairy Mother."

"The fairies are not concerned with the folk in the south," Lohring said, leaning back.

"You will be, when the fighting spreads here. And it will, wall or no wall."

Lohring stood up. "So you think your Keeper will agree with you? That you will return with that Vranian we have locked up out there, and Glynholly will lead her folk across the mountains, leaving Watersmeet to the überwolves and the trolls?"

Abisina wanted to protest, but she couldn't.

"I had hoped to convince you," Lohring said, "but in the end it does not matter. I have sent fairies to Watersmeet to make our offer. Your Keeper may have already said yes."

Abisina's fury rose. "Then why bother with me? Why let me into the Motherland at all?"

"Despite what you might think, Abisina, I respected your father. Deeply. I see him in you." The fairy paused and Abisina glimpsed something in her face. Regret? But it was gone in an instant.

"In honor of him, I wanted to make our offer to *you*. I assumed you would see the logic of our plan—as your father certainly would have." Lohring took a step closer. "It is nice to think that he would want to save your mother's people, but you cannot lead a folk for as long as Rueshlan did and not be logical. To the Vranians, he was a monster. I do not think he would be willing to see Watersmeet destroyed for them."

Abisina wouldn't show how much the words had stung her.

"Return to Watersmeet," Lohring said. "Talk to the folk there. Talk to Glynholly. She knew Rueshlan as well as anybody. You will see that I am right. If you persist in your goal of helping the south, you will find yourself very much alone."

With that, Lohring took to the trees, and in one leap, she was out of sight, followed by her retinue.

Abisina stared at the empty chair. Had Lohring really offered to help Watersmeet? And she had refused? What was she thinking?

The Fairy Mother wants to preserve the Motherland at the expense of the south. I could not have agreed to that.

But Glynholly will. She probably already has.

Abisina had to get back to Watersmeet.

She hoped someone—even Reava—would appear to lead her out of the Motherland. But the clearing remained empty. She would have to go alone. *Will the trees let me through? And what about Corlin and Kyron?* Panic started to choke her, but she forced herself to think.

If she walked in any direction, she should come to the boundary; if she walked north, she should come out on the side where Corlin and Kyron were held. She checked the direction of the sun and set off. She was sure the fairies were watching her.

Abisina hadn't walked more than twenty steps when a tall, black figure dropped out of the sky. "This way!" With a hard yank, her new guide led her more to the west, and Abisina had to follow.

She could barely keep up and had no breath to ask who this fairy was or where they were going.

Finally the fairy slowed down and said, "I'm Neriah." The fairy spoke so quietly that Abisina felt more than heard the words. "Lohring's daughter."

"Another daughter?"

"I'm Reava's older sister. But we should not talk here." Neriah scanned the trees and picked up the pace again.

What is she up to? Abisina considered breaking free, but how could she outrun a fairy? And they were heading in the direction Abisina wanted to go.

Abisina stole a few glances at Neriah as they hurried along. She was taller than Reava and wore her hair long and free under a ring of silver leaves. *Is she Lohring's heir?* Abisina hadn't seen a band in Reava's hair.

Neriah was graceful and mysterious—but different from the other fairies somehow. Three Seldar leaves were caught in her hair, making her look almost disheveled—and more human.

Neriah stopped and pulled Abisina around to face her. Her eyes were touched with brown; every fairy Abisina had ever seen had eyes of the lightest blue. As the two looked at each other, Abisina knew she could trust Neriah.

They had reached the ominous darkness of the boundary trees. "As long as you're headed *out*, the trees will let you through."

Abisina nodded. "My friends. Will they—"

"I'll release them, but you all must leave immediately. I

cannot hold the trees back for long. Once my mother realizes what I've done . . ."

"She didn't want to let me out?"

"She wouldn't have held *you*."

Abisina swallowed. "Thank you for helping me."

"I knew your father, too, Abisina. Better than my mother did." She clutched Abisina's hand. "Now go!" She gave Abisina a shove toward the trees.

Abisina spun back to ask Neriah more. *How* did she know Rueshlan?

But the thick trunks surrounded her. The Motherland was gone.

Chapter VII

As Abisina emerged from the trees, the root cages around Corlin and Kyron began to retract. The slender shoots that held their weapons released, and the knives, bows, and sword dropped into the dust.

Beyond the cages, a cluster of überwolves waited on the plain.

Abisina started to run.

Kyron and Corlin scrambled up, stiff and awkward after a night in their cramped cages. Abisina reached the weapons just as the überwolves' spears flew. She rolled to one side to avoid a missile, and Corlin did the same. Kyron was not as lucky. He dodged one spear, but stepped into the path of another. As Abisina watched, a root bristling with fibers shot from the ground, caught the spear intended for Kyron, and snapped it in half.

Neriah?

Corlin gaped at the broken spear. "Here!" Abisina tossed them weapons. "Run!" she shouted, as the ground came alive beneath her feet, boiling with roots. Abisina grabbed the packs and sprinted toward the plain, her friends hobbling after her. A root caught her right ankle, and she went down. A second root pulled at the first, and Abisina managed to snatch her foot away. She got to her feet and kept running. Roots snaked over the ground, twisting in and out as some fought to catch hold of Abisina, Kyron, and Corlin, and others fought to free them. Neriah's roots seemed to be winning.

But we're running toward überwolves! Abisina clutched her knife, stepped onto the plain, and took a defensive stance. The wolves had lost their spears, but still had claws and teeth.

Corlin thrust his knife into the belly of one wolf. Another flew at Abisina. She crouched down, and it sailed over her, tumbling into the sand. A root lassoed out of the ground and wrapped around the wolf's middle. The wolf twisted and clawed as the cord drew it along the earth. With the snap of bones, the root yanked the wolf underground, as if forcing a fat piece of wool through the eye of a needle.

A sharp yip pulled Abisina's attention back to the fight. An überwolf fell beneath Kyron's sword. The centaur's shoulder bled. Corlin stood over two unmoving bodies, and the rest raced away.

Once Abisina caught her breath, she went to Kyron to check his wound.

"It's not deep," he assured her. "You all right there, Corlin?"

Corlin grunted as he wiped his knife on the ground. Abisina bound Kyron's shoulder with her extra under-shirt and then helped Corlin drag the bodies to the sand. Roots appeared and pulled the corpses underground. Abisina tracked the bulge of the wolves' bodies into the trees, which shifted and then resettled. Is that what she had smelled in the forest—rotting corpses? What, or *who*, else had been snared by the fairies' trees?

"Let's get out of here," Kyron said. "I've had enough of the fairies' hospitality."

"Me, too." Abisina wiped the sweat out of her eyes.

No one pressed Abisina for details about her visit to the Motherland, but she could feel their expectation growing as they walked north. "You need to know what happened," she said when the Motherland's boundary trees were far behind them.

"At last," Kyron exploded, bringing a smile from Abisina. But she sobered as she described the Fairy Mother's Farewell, Reava, and Lohring's request for help.

"That's what we wanted!" Kyron jumped in. "To work with the fairies!"

"I rejected Lohring's offer," Abisina said. "We might not have gotten away, but her eldest daughter helped me." She told them about meeting Neriah.

"But you had to tell them no," Corlin said vehemently. "Closing the Cleft would destroy the south."

"It doesn't matter. Lohring has sent fairies to Watersmeet.

By now, Glynholly has probably accepted their offer."

"No!" Corlin cried.

"I know it's not what we wanted," Kyron said, "but the Fairy Mother's plan will take care of the überwolves. We won't have to close Watersmeet to the refugees who have already come north."

"But now that we know about Vranlyn . . ." Abisina began.

"I'm not saying we should close off the south permanently," Kyron argued. "But if we can get a handle on things in Watersmeet, we would be in a better position to help Vranlyn."

"It would be too late," Corlin said dully. "We won't survive the winter. The south is on its own."

Abisina wanted to comfort him, but as she reached toward him, he stiffened, and she let her hand drop.

But then he said to her, "Will you come back with me?" He was almost begging. "They're your people, too. It would mean so much to them to see Rueshlan's daughter."

Abisina had gone to the Motherland because she was "Rueshlan's daughter." What had she achieved? And what about Watersmeet? Didn't she owe them more than the villagers who had made her an outcast?

If we close the Cleft, the Vranians in the south will continue to kill humans like me, Abisina thought.

I don't have the answers! But somehow, she had to find them.

"I have to go to Watersmeet first," she said finally. "I have to try to convince them not to close the Cleft. But I can offer them a different solution now: Vranlyn."

Corlin's face became stony.

"I have to try, Corlin," she pleaded. "If I fail, if Watersmeet insists on working with the fairies, I'll come to Vranlyn myself. Alone, if I have to."

"Not alone," Kyron said.

Abisina knew Corlin didn't believe her, but she clasped his hand to seal her promise.

Corlin handed the knife back to Kyron, but he refused it. "You'll need it on the way back," Kyron said. He grasped Corlin's arm in the centaur farewell.

Then, without a backward glance, Corlin walked south.

"You had to, Abisina," Kyron said gently. "You can't abandon Watersmeet."

"What would my father have done?"

"I don't know," Kyron admitted.

"It's strange. Lohring and Neriah both said they 'knew my father,' but it sounded different coming from Neriah."

Abisina shook her head. The fairies confused her more than ever. *I can't think of them now. I have to concentrate on Watersmeet.*

With Kyron's shoulder wounded, Abisina couldn't ride. They would lose precious time. It took them two grueling days, with one stop for a few hours of sleep, before they stumbled off the plain and into the relative safety of the forest. It was dawn, but they had to sleep.

Abisina woke from dreams of galloping. She had a

headache and a parched throat. A groan nearby told her that Kyron felt the same.

"Do we have any water?" she croaked.

"Nope. I'll go," he replied. He started to rise, but bellowed as he tried to stand, and sank back to the ground.

"I'll go," Abisina said, crawling out of her cloak.

"I hear a stream that way." The centaur pointed to the right. "I'll work on breakfast."

Abisina's stomach answered with a grumble. When had she last eaten?

She gathered up the empty water skins, accompanied by another yell from Kyron. "Vigar's braid! I hurt from my hooves to my head."

Abisina had left her bow leaning against a tree, close to where she slept. She reached for it, but it was gone! It wasn't on the ground. It wasn't tangled in her cloak. A touch to her waist told her that her knife was gone, too.

At that moment, Kyron shouted, "My weapons!"

They searched frantically, emptying packs, strewing food and cloaks and cooking pots this way and that. Nothing. Two bows, two quivers of arrows, Abisina's knife, and Kyron's sword had vanished. They found no footprints.

"Fairies," Kyron spat.

"Reava," Abisina added. This was retaliation for humiliating the fairy in front of the Fairy Mother. "We'd better fill up on water and get going. The farther we get from the Motherland, the safer we'll be."

"Safe from the fairies? Ha!"

Unarmed, they had to proceed with more caution than ever, avoiding thick brush that might hide an überwolf ambush. Kyron insisted that Abisina ride. She stayed alert for signs of wolves or minotaurs and scanned the sky for birds spying for the fairies, but saw nothing suspicious. *Reava assumed the überwolves would take care of us. She all but insured they would.*

When they reached the edge of the Fens, Abisina and Kyron relaxed a little; überwolves seemed to avoid the boggy land. The water from spring rains and snowmelt had receded from its high mark, leaving stagnant pools that were the perfect breeding ground for mosquitoes, gnats, and flies. The constant buzz drove Abisina and Kyron mad. Abisina broke off branches to fan their faces, but between each swipe, more bugs clustered around her eyes and mouth, whined in her ears, and flew into her nose.

They were walking close to the Fens, the mud soothing to Kyron's sore hooves, when they heard the bawl of a minotaur. Kyron wheeled as the beast thundered out of the long grass, horns lowered, bearing down on them. Kyron had no choice but to run.

The soft ground slowed the centaur. Before they had gone ten lengths, the minotaur attacked. Abisina smacked at the beast's head with her pitiful branches. She braced herself as its horns neared her belly, but the minotaur stumbled and fell in the slick mud.

Kyron veered into the water. For a few steps, the bog supported Kyron's immense weight. But the fallen minotaur lunged after them, knocking Kyron and Abisina farther into the marsh. The minotaur grabbed onto Kyron's back, dragging him under more quickly. Abisina struggled away from them, half crawling, half swimming to a small island of grass.

Let it hold me, she prayed. The grass cut her palms as she pulled herself up. The island dipped but didn't sink, and she clambered onto it.

The minotaur had lost its grip on Kyron and was sinking faster now. But the mud continued to creep up Kyron's flanks as he groped for solid ground.

On the shore, a hag slipped from the tall reeds and shrieked at her charge. The minotaur's eyes were wild as it floundered, its thrashing only ensnaring it deeper. It bawled once, before the mud moved into its mouth. Its eyes rolled, then it steadied them on the hag, as if pleading for help. Or comfort. The hag's face was impassive.

Abisina cringed as the black mud covered the minotaur's eyes, leaving only its fat nose and the tips of its horns visible. With a final sucking sound, the mud closed over the minotaur's head.

The hag stared at the spot. Then, without looking at Kyron or Abisina, she disappeared into the grass.

Abisina searched for a stick—anything—she could give Kyron to grab onto, but all she saw was the flimsy grass nodding in the breeze.

I have to get to him! She threw herself flat on her little island, plunged her hands into the mud, and paddled.

"Kyron!" she yelled. "Don't move. I'm coming!"

It felt as if she were pushing herself through something solid, but with each thrust of her arms, the island inched closer to Kyron.

"Get out of here while you can!" he yelled.

She kept paddling.

"Abisina, get to shore! You can help me more from there!"

It was a ruse to get her to safety, but Abisina agreed that she needed firm ground to help him. She shifted her position and propelled herself toward the edge of the marsh.

When Abisina reached the shore, the black mud was halfway up Kyron's chest. "Throw me your satchel," she called. Kyron began to argue, then changed his mind and did as she asked. Abisina threw the contents of her bag on the ground, then did the same with Kyron's. "Keep your arms free," she told him.

"I'm trying," he muttered.

By looping the bags' straps together, Abisina managed to create a makeshift rope. "Catch this."

"It's no use—"

"Do it!" Abisina screamed.

She flung the satchels to him, keeping hold of one of the straps. It took several tries but finally, with Abisina ankle deep in the mud, Kyron caught his end—a weak victory. Kyron's shoulders and head were the only parts of him above the mud, and Abisina didn't think she'd have the strength to pull him out.

"Hang on," she called. She started to pull and went down; she couldn't get traction on the mud and slick grass. She needed to stand on the dry spot just out of reach of their rope.

"Get back to Watersmeet," Kyron said quietly. "Follow the river. And Abisina—"

"Try again," she interrupted, as she scrambled up.

Please, Father! Vigar! Anyone! Help me! She steadied her feet.

She stepped toward the anchor of dry grass, digging in.

"Pull!" she shouted. Muscles and sinew tightened along her arms, down her legs, across her back.

The leather satchels strained. She took two steps back, and Kyron followed, his chest beginning to rise. *It's working!* It was hard, but not nearly as hard as she expected. A few steps more and Kyron was freed to the shoulders. Then the waist. Another step. And another. *All of my feet on dry ground,* she thought, but didn't pause to consider what she meant. Kyron's front legs pawed the shore.

One more gut-ripping pull and the satchel straps tore. Kyron stumbled free of the muck—and he and Abisina collapsed in a tangle of hooves and arms and legs. She lay on the grass, tasting mud and sweat and exhaustion. She didn't know how she'd done it.

When Abisina opened her eyes and got up, it could no longer be ignored.

She stood on all four of her own hooves.

She *was* her father's daughter—a shape-shifter—a centaur.

CHAPTER VIII

KYRON SMILED THROUGH HIS TEARS, ARM EXTENDED IN the traditional centaur greeting. Abisina could not look at him, could not grasp his forearm in the gesture she had seen her father do so many times.

This can't be me!

She wanted to get away—run away. But now that she was aware of her centaur body, it refused to obey. She stumbled over her hooves, painfully nicking her front heel with a rear hoof, slipping on patches of wet grass. Her knees wobbled beneath her like a newborn centaur finding its legs. She made it into the tall grass and kept going, desperate to be alone.

"Abisina!" Kyron cried.

"Leave me," she yelled over her shoulder. "I need—just leave me!"

The sound and feel of her body moving through the reeds was all wrong: the dull thud of her hooves, the swish of grass rubbing against her sides long after she should have passed through it.

She picked up her pace, desperate to put distance between herself—her *real* self—and this other self, and suddenly she was galloping, like she had in all those dreams about her father, the breathless rides they took through forest and field, up mountains, across plains.

It's just a dream, she told herself.

But the dreams had changed lately—she hadn't allowed herself to acknowledge it—her father was no longer in them. *She* was the one galloping, glorying in the speed and rush of the wind.

Now she was haunted by what she would have to face when she stopped.

Her breath gave out, and she slowed to a walk. Her sides heaved. Her front hooves ached from being kicked by her rear ones, but she closed off these sensations.

Her fear was so big in her chest, it left no room for breath. She hugged herself for comfort.

What will Findlay say?

She sobbed as the thought came to her. She had been so happy when he kissed her. How could she be an outcast if Findlay could like—even love—her?

He couldn't possibly love her now.

She heard Kyron approach. She ran, nicked her front hoof and stumbled.

"Abisina—"

She didn't let him continue.

"Demon." A word she'd thought she left behind in Vranille rose to her lips. She had used the word herself when she learned of her father's shape-shifting. It came back to her now with all the strength it once held.

"No, Abisina," Kyron said. "You should be proud."

"You can't understand, Kyron. My father told me this was possible. I thought I could handle it. I told myself it would be fine. Even wonderful. Oh, the Earth!" she sobbed. As she turned away, she caught a glimpse of her rear legs, as black as her hair, and her tail. They disgusted her.

"Abisina," Kyron said softly, "you're beautiful."

His gentleness stopped her. How could she tell Kyron that all of her Vranian beliefs about centaurs were surfacing again?

In the south, the centaurs had done terrible things to any Vranian they captured—taking toes, feet, leaving bodies broken and unrecognizable. Icksyon, a herd-leader, decorated himself with the human toes he collected, including one of her own. She had escaped, with Haret's help, before he could take the rest.

Now she *was* Icksyon.

Or even Charach. He, too, was a shape-shifter.

She knew Kyron was waiting for her to speak, but she couldn't say what he wanted to hear. "Please, I can't talk about this now."

With a sigh, Kyron started to prepare for the coming night. The sun hung low in the sky, and they would need supper. He set down the satchels he had repacked after tying the ripped straps together and rummaged for the cooking pot. Her job was to gather fresh greens and roots since they could no longer shoot game. When she bent to pick up her satchel, she transformed again, back into her human shape.

Though her tunic reached her mid-thighs, she was naked from the waist down, barefoot, and humiliated. She self-consciously knelt and dug in her bag for her spare pair of leggings. Pretending to see something of interest in the grass, Kyron turned away while Abisina dressed.

"Finished," she muttered. "Did you see my boots?"

"Yes—but they're, ah, split."

Abisina nodded and snatched up one of the water skins. "I'll be right back," she said miserably.

She was just out of Kyron's sight when she heard the rip of leather and knew she had transformed again. Her last pair of leggings lay shredded on the ground.

The next week was unbearable for Abisina. She had no control of her own limbs. At times she could manage to trot or canter, but at other times, she struggled to coordinate the new parts of her body. Her front heels bled from being kicked, the bottom of one rear hoof was bruised from stepping on a sharp stone, and her stomach muscles ached as she worked to hold her torso upright atop her horse legs. Her human feet were equally sore. With no boots, her toes were stubbed and her heels criss-crossed with cuts. She couldn't ride Kyron to give her feet a rest, because she never knew when the change would come.

If she stayed completely focused, she could maintain one shape. But if she were trotting along and a stray thought of Findlay flitted across her mind, she'd find herself rolling on the ground, her human legs unable to keep up with her centaur speed. Sitting at the edge of the River Fennish in her human form, she might startle at the snap of a twig and leap to her hooves, ready to run. Each morning her sleeping place was gouged and rutted from shape-shifting in her dreams. By the time they made camp on the second night, she counted that she would've gone through thirty-four pairs of leggings.

Their pace, already slowed by their loss of weapons, was now even slower, adding to Abisina's frustration. They had to get back to Watersmeet! At the same time, Abisina dreaded returning. Watersmeet meant facing them all—Elodie, Haret, Hoysta, Glynholly. And *Findlay*. She had made Kyron promise that he would not tell anyone until she was ready. But even if he didn't, her body would betray her. How could she pretend to be the same Abisina if she changed shape twice before she got up in the morning?

She couldn't get the image of Icksyon out of her mind: the giant centaur with a dirty white beard, rolls of fat, red-rimmed eyes, blackened teeth, and a necklace of toes. She tried to study Kyron instead: his powerful legs, accentuated muscles, and shining reddish coat. His chest was straight and proud. *He's beautiful, just like my father. Why can't I think of myself like them?*

But the word was right there: *Demon.*
Will I ever leave it behind?

They were just days outside of Watersmeet, roasting roots in the coals of the fire, both preoccupied with their own thoughts.

"Abisina," Kyron began tentatively.

"Mmm?"

"Have you thought about how your shape-shifting might affect Watersmeet?"

She looked up at him. "What do you mean?"

"Well . . . if folk see that you're a shape-shifter like your father, they'll follow you anywhere."

"No!" She leapt up. "No one can know. Not ever! You promised, Kyron!"

"I know, but I've been thinking—"

"No!" she cried again.

Her need to run was so strong she transformed instantly and galloped off down the bank of the Fennish. *I can't do it! I won't!* Her hooves pounded the rhythm of her defiance.

She had gone several leagues before she outran her anger. If she stood in the Council House as a centaur, they might listen to her. They might agree to help Vranlyn.

But I can't do it.

"Am I really that selfish?" she asked out loud. "I would sacrifice Watersmeet and Vranlyn to keep my secret?"

She started the long, slow walk back to Kyron.

Kyron found her at dawn cooling her battered hooves in the river near their camp.

She looked at him guiltily. "I'm sorry. I know you were worried."

"I'm sorry, too. I shouldn't—"

"No." She gave him an apologetic smile. "No" seemed to be all she could say to him lately. "You're right," she continued, "but this . . . change is really hard for me."

"Oh, Abisina! If you could see yourself—how magnificent you are!"

Abisina sighed. He was doing his best, but he wasn't helping.

"I'm just frustrated," she said. "If I had some *control*. The worst part—well, *one* of the worst parts—is that I never know which shape I'll be from moment to moment. I feel like I did in Vranille, when the Elders decided what I ate, where I lived, *if* I lived! The only time I made my own choices was in the forest. With my bow. Then I could feed myself, protect myself."

"You're a mean shot with your bow," Kyron agreed. "Better than Glynholly." She saw the hint of a grin.

"You think I do everything better than Glynholly," Abisina pointed out.

"That's true." Kyron nodded.

"I did let her win that last tournament," Abisina admitted.

Kyron laughed. "Stay here. I'll get our gear."

As she waited for him to return, she thought about how her father had controlled his shape so effortlessly. The first time she had seen him, addressing the whole of Watersmeet, he had worn boots and leggings. Clearly he had known that he would not transform. Many more times, however, he strode through the forest or through Watersmeet with bare legs and feet. She hadn't understood it then, but now the significance was clear: he needed to be ready to change shape. *I wonder how many boots he went through before he figured it out?*

She picked up a stone and skimmed it across the river. It bounced, two, three, four times before sinking to the bottom. She picked up another. She had skipped stones with her father one precious evening when he had left the preparations for battle to stroll with her along the River Deliverance. She remembered that evening vividly: her father, as a centaur, standing midstream, while she sat on a rock on the shore.

With a shriek, Abisina sat in the cold river, her human knees poking above the water. "Vigar's braid!" She slapped the water and sent some up her nose. "I give up!"

Kyron trotted up. "What are you doing sitting in the middle of the river?"

"Sitting!" she snapped. But then she cried, "That's it! I'm *sitting* in the middle of the river! Centaurs don't sit!" She scrambled to her feet and ran up the bank.

"Of course centaurs sit," Kyron said. "I sat in that fairy

cage for an entire day and night—I've got the stiff knees to prove it."

"The horse part of you *lies down*," Abisina explained.

"So?"

"It's different for humans. That's how my father learned to control his shape! He told me once how hard it was when he first became a shape-shifter. I forgot—it was all so overwhelming to me then. He said he learned to think about *sitting* in order to became human again. We have to try it!" Abisina stepped away from Kyron. "Humans don't gallop. So, first, I'll think about galloping."

She closed her eyes and imagined open space, speed, wind in her face, hooves churning the turf.

"You did it!" Kyron exclaimed.

She looked. Her slender, black centaur legs stretched below her. "I did!" A smile lit up her face.

"Okay, now sitting." She shut her eyes again. She pictured her favorite chair next to the hearth in her home in Watersmeet, with the special cushion Hoysta had made. *Sitting back, warming my cold hands after a patrol. Resting my weary legs.*

"Open your eyes, Abisina."

"Feet!" She wiggled her toes.

Kyron beamed at her. "You're a natural."

"No, I *expected* it to be natural," Abisina said. "But I need to practice. Like I did with my bow."

For the rest of the day, Abisina practiced. She took three steps as a human and then thought, *Gallop.*

Centaur.

She took three more steps and thought, *Sit.*

Human.

Hooves!—centaur. *Toes!*—human. *Speed!*—centaur. *Find-lay!*—human. She tried trigger after trigger—words, images, sounds—as she learned what worked and what didn't. She pictured two halves of herself: the human-self and the centaur-self. Her two selves stood on either side of a wall. Each trigger secured the wall. Stray thoughts weakened it.

"It's time to switch tactics," Abisina announced after they had stopped to eat. "Now, I want to stay in one shape, no matter what I think or see."

When they set off, Abisina walked behind Kyron in human form. Her brow furrowed in concentration. She thought of racing over a downy meadow, tail streaming out behind her. In the next instant, she galloped past Kyron at a full clip.

"Whoa!" he yelled.

"Sorry," she muttered.

Remaining a centaur, she built the wall again as she thought of squishing mud between her toes on a warm summer day. This time, she stayed a centaur for a full five minutes before losing her concentration.

CHAPTER IX

THEY WERE A DAY OUTSIDE OF WATERSMEET. ABISINA'S ability to control her shape had improved markedly, but it wasn't perfect. As she worried less about her shape, she worried more about the situation in Watersmeet. Surely Glynholly and the Council had accepted the Fairy Mother's offer. How much debate had there been? Did folk even *think* about what it would mean to close off the south?

If I have to show them what I am, I will, she told herself, but she hoped it wouldn't come to that. She reminded Kyron that he had promised to keep her secret. *Will he?*

Kyron stopped abruptly in front of her. Abisina, in human form, almost walked into him. "What's that?" he said.

Six rough lean-tos—the barest shelters built with branches and pine boughs—stood in a ring. In the center, a fire smoldered, a blackened cooking pot resting next to the coals. A broken bow, a pair of boots, and a ragged shirt littered the ground. The camp looked deserted, but as they walked up, a woman carrying a baby came around the side of one of the lean-tos and shrieked at the sight of them. She had Vranian blonde hair and washed-out blue eyes.

"We won't hurt you," Abisina assured her. "We're from Watersmeet."

The woman's face hardened. "My baby is starving, and what has Watersmeet done?"

"They're not letting you in?"

"As if you didn't know," she snapped. "Winter will be here before we can get back to the south—and we have nothing to go back to. People talked about Watersmeet like it was some kind of haven. I didn't half believe them. How could it be with all—well, with *your* lot there?" she said accusingly. "But I didn't think we'd be turned away!"

"Demma!" A man rushed toward them, a small rabbit tied to his waist, bow in hand. "Please, please—my wife means no harm. She isn't used to the ways of the north. We're anxious to show the people—*folk*—of Watersmeet that we want to be here. We will work for our keep. Hard. Vranians are known for their strength." The man yanked up the sleeve of his undershirt to show his muscles.

"How long have you been here?" Abisina asked.

"We arrived two days ago," the man said, "but they closed the bridges before Midsummer."

"Before Midsummer!" Kyron spoke for the first time, and the woman jumped.

"Before we left the Motherland," Abisina murmured.

"We'd better get going," Kyron said grimly.

"Can you take us with you?" the man asked. "Just us? The rest are out searching for food. If we came now . . ."

Demma's lips closed in a hard line, but she waited for their answer.

"We've been away," Abisina tried to explain. "We need to see what's happening ourselves, before we can bring you in." Demma exhaled sharply and turned away. "We're here to help the refugees," Abisina continued. "I'm Vranian, too—well, my mother was."

"Ha!" Demma cried, without turning around.

"Quiet," the man said harshly.

Abisina's cheeks burned. "I'm sure there will be a way to work this out."

"Remember us!" the man called as Abisina and Kyron left.

"They hate us, but they want us to save them again," Kyron grumbled when they were out of hearing.

Abisina sighed. "They don't make our job easier, do they?"

The first wave of refugees were outcasts and those disillusioned with the Vranian way. They had struggled with getting used to dwarves, fauns, and especially centaurs, but were committed to learning the ways of Watersmeet. The later refugees were driven north out of desperation. It was much harder to imagine them becoming part of Watersmeet.

"Glynholly closed the bridges!" Kyron shook his head.

"How are they getting out to forage?"

"Whatever they're doing, things can't be good inside."

At least I stayed human, Abisina thought. She had passed her first test.

They met many angry refugees that day. After a while, Abisina transformed; the refugees were less likely to approach two centaurs. As they neared Watersmeet, she changed back to her human shape. She expected to see someone she knew, but there were no folk on the banks, no foraging teams, no patrols. *Have they shut themselves up entirely? Like the Motherland, trapped behind its boundary trees?*

Then Abisina saw a Seldar grove. She stopped. "I'll be quick," she told Kyron, who said he'd keep watch.

Abisina passed through the first layers of trees and found a small faun standing with her forehead resting against one of the trunks. *Someone from Watersmeet!* The faun spun around.

"Abisina?"

"Erna?" Abisina knew this faun well. She and her mate, Darvus, had escaped the Worm's terror in the south and sought refuge with the Watersmeet army. After the battle, Erna had come to Watersmeet at Darvus's insistence. He had returned to their home to hunt for survivors, especially Erna's mother. He'd promised he would come to get her as soon as it was safe, but Erna was still waiting.

"A-A-Abisina." The faun stumbled, and Abisina caught her. Erna was trembling.

"Erna, what is it?"

"Elodie sent me to check here each day," she managed, tugging on her dark curls. "She knew you'd stop at the grove when you got back. She wanted to warn you. It was too dangerous for her to come, but she didn't think anyone would follow me." Erna's eyelids fluttered, and Abisina worried she might faint.

Although Erna was typically timid, Abisina had never seen her so frightened. "Warn me about what?" Abisina asked as gently as she could.

"That—that the Keeper has called you a . . . traitor," Erna whispered and then cast a fearful look at the trees as if the Seldars themselves would attack.

"A traitor? That's what Glynholly said?"

Erna nodded.

"What could she possibly mean?"

"The fairies have been here. They said you came to them to overthrow the Keeper!"

Kyron entered the grove.

Erna gasped. "They want to arrest him, too!"

It took a lot of calming and coddling from Abisina before Erna would say more, and a look or word from Kyron would close her mouth.

Glynholly and the Council had closed the bridges right after Abisina and Kyron left for the Motherland. Foraging teams went out heavily guarded against überwolves and refugees. Sentries patrolled all paths in and out of Watersmeet. For now, the refugees already in Watersmeet were allowed to stay. Some folk had grumbled at this. Neiall had called a meeting to protest the closing of the bridges, but the low food stores scared Council members and most accepted Glynholly's decision.

From what Erna said, it seemed that the fairies had arrived in Watersmeet after Abisina and Kyron left the Motherland.

Lohring made me think that she'd already sent them, Abisina realized. *But she must've sent them only when I said no to her.*

When the Keeper emerged from meeting with the fairies, she had called a secret Council session. Afterward Glynholly summoned all the folk of Watersmeet to the Gathering Place. She told them of Abisina's "treachery" and how the fairies wanted to work together to solve the problem of the über-wolves. Glynholly's supporters quickly shouted down those who stood up for Abisina.

"I can believe that the fairies would betray me," Abisina said. "But Glynholly and the others—"

"We've no choice but to go in there, confront the Keeper, and rally those loyal to Rueshlan," said Kyron. "They need to *see* you. Especially now." He looked pointedly at Abisina.

"We need to talk to our friends *first*," Abisina insisted, "before we do anything. Erna, you said Elodie sent you here?"

"You're supposed to hide near the grove. She's going to meet you. I—I'm supposed to tell Elodie that you're here." Erna's slender fingers wandered nervously from her hair, to her mouth, and back to her hair.

"How soon can she get here?"

"I don't know," Erna said. "They're watching her. They know you're friends." The faun began to shake. "What if I can't get back in?" she whispered, wringing her hands.

Abisina tried to be patient. "You're from Watersmeet now. They'll let you in." *Wouldn't they?*

"What if someone asks me where I've been? What then?" She wrung her hands faster.

"You can tell the truth," Abisina soothed. "You've been in the Seldar grove."

"Yes," agreed Erna. "But won't they wonder why I'm going to Elodie?"

"You often visit Elodie, don't you?"

Erna nodded sorrowfully. "She's very kind."

"So there's nothing odd in that."

Erna's hands stopped moving. "No." Her eyes widened. "You have to hide!" she said to Abisina. "I shouldn't have kept you talking."

"We will hide as soon as you leave. Please hurry," Abisina urged, but there was no need. Erna left the grove and lit out for Watersmeet as if a pack of überwolves chased her.

Abisina followed Kyron out of the grove and took cover in the trees nearby.

"Not one soul in Watersmeet believes the fairies—not if they know you," Kyron muttered. "You're a threat to Glynholly, plain and simple. She's losing control, the folk are scared. She's as desperate as the refugees. And when you come galloping across the bridge—"

"Stop, Kyron."

"But Abisina—"

"I told you, I'll do it if I have to. But not yet."

Knowing she could never sleep, Abisina offered to take the first watch. She settled in a tree with a view of the grove and leaned her head against the trunk. *I should never have left. If I'd stayed, no one could have accused me of anything.*

Or what if I had agreed to Lohring's proposal? I would've been welcomed home. If we solved the überwolf problem, folk might relent and accept the refugees. She thought of the mother and baby she had met. *To the mother, we're monsters, but if that child grew up in Watersmeet—*

Her trip to the Motherland had been a fool's errand. Now she was worse than a fool: she was a traitor.

When Kyron came to relieve her, she told him to go back to sleep.

Chapter X

The moon set, leaving the night black except for the glow of the Seldar grove. *Perfect for Elodie to get out of Watersmeet.* Abisina stared at the trees, desperate to see a shadow stealing among the trunks. Even when it was clear that no one was coming, she kept her eyes fixed on the grove.

"What if Erna was caught?" Abisina asked when Kyron relieved her after sunrise.

"If Erna gives us up, we'll know," he said as she climbed down.

Abisina was in her perch again right after noon, when she spotted two überwolves slinking toward the Seldar grove. Her hands itched to string an arrow, but she had none. The wolves stopped, noses to the ground, ears swiveling. Luckily she was downwind of them.

She heard the unmistakable whiz of an arrow, and the lead überwolf fell. With a yip, the second wolf raced into the trees.

Two centaurs cantered over to inspect the body. She knew them: Morrell and Gabra. She had done archery practice with Gabra a few days before she left for the Motherland.

"I couldn't get a clear shot at the other one," Morrell said as Gabra removed her arrow from the first überwolf's back.

"We have to move the body," Gabra said. "It shouldn't be this close to a grove." She looked into the trees and sighed. "Being near one always makes me think of him."

Morrell nodded. "Me, too."

"Do you think she really did it? Would Rueshlan's daughter betray Watersmeet?"

"She's part Vranian, you know," Morrell said angrily. "Those Vranians want power. If she thought she could take over Watersmeet . . ."

Abisina bit her lip and tasted blood.

"She went on the campaign against them," Gabra noted.

"I see no reason to question Glynholly. At least she's stopped the refugees."

"Here, help me with this," Gabra said. "We'll throw it over there." She pointed past the Seldar grove.

"There's a bog a bit farther," Morrell suggested. "That'll take care of it." He grabbed the überwolf under the shoulders while Gabra picked up its ankles. With a few groans and the shuffle of hooves in the leaves, the centaurs moved out of sight.

Abisina gripped the branch she sat on, fighting the urge to go after them, to yell that they were betraying Rueshlan *and* Watersmeet.

Kyron arrived a few minutes after the centaurs had gone. She knew what he would say if he had heard them: *If they could only see you.*

The next night, a few hours before dawn, Elodie still hadn't come. Abisina was in her tree, tired and stiff. It seemed ridiculous now that they had entrusted such an important errand to Erna. *I should have tried to sneak into Watersmeet myself.*

She woke from a light doze with a start. There, against the glow of the Seldars, were two figures: one tall, willowy girl and one short, stout dwarf. *Elodie and Haret!*

Abisina slid from her branch, wanting to run to them—and immediately became a centaur. She carefully rebuilt the wall between her selves and stood again as a human.

Thankfully, they had slipped into a clump of bushes. After checking that no one was following them, she edged toward their hiding place.

"Elodie," she whispered. "Haret. It's Abisina."

"Thank the Earth!" came Haret's voice, and the two emerged. Abisina hugged them tightly.

"I'm glad you're back, human," Haret said.

Abisina knew he'd been worried. *But what will he call me when he finds out I'm not just human?*

Haret handed her a new bow and quiver. She recognized his workmanship and saw that he had a much larger one with him for Kyron. The bow settled on her shoulder like an old friend.

"Erna said you didn't have a bow," Haret whispered. "I know how much you hate not having a bow."

Abisina led them to Kyron. The centaur began to vent his anger the instant he saw them, but Haret's sharp, "Wait for the meeting!" hushed him. Haret led them farther into the woods, keeping away from the refugee fires that burned in the distance. Finally, he grunted, "Torch." Elodie passed him one, and they paused to light it.

"They'll assume it's a refugee's," Elodie explained.

When did Watersmeet become "they"? Abisina wondered.

A growl to their right stopped their whispers. Each readied an arrow. The crunching of bones and the wet swallow of meat got them moving again. An überwolf was feeding nearby, its unlucky victim keeping them safe as they crept on.

They stopped when they reached several large rocks in a circle among the trees. Charred logs, trampled pine needles, the broken haft of a knife, and other debris showed they were not the first to meet here.

As they entered the ring, a tall man appeared from behind a rock. *A refugee?* Abisina worried. But the torchlight shining off the man's white hair reassured her: Neiall.

"Abisina," he said, grasping her hand. "It's good to see you."

"I'll stand watch, Neiall," Elodie said.

Then Findlay stepped from behind another rock. He tried to look serious, but he couldn't erase his grin. Abisina could hardly breathe. He rushed to embrace her, and she met him halfway. As he held her, she knew he'd thought of her as constantly as she'd thought of him—that he loved her as she loved him.

"What have you got for weapons? How many folk are ready to take a stand?"

Kyron's words broke Findlay and Abisina apart sooner than either would have wished.

"A few others are on their way," Neiall said.

"A *few?*" Kyron's voice rang against the rocks, and Neiall tried to quiet him.

"Will Hoysta be here?" Abisina asked Haret.

"It was all I could do to keep her away," Haret said. "Elodie and I crossed in boats, and you know how Grandmother hates water. She would have done it for you, but we didn't want too many here."

Another figure entered the small circle of light: Anwyn, a faun with nut-brown skin. Next arrived Moyla, a bay centaur with a black tail and long black hair in a braid. Kyron went to her immediately, and they grasped each other's arms. Abisina didn't know Anwyn or Moyla well. She was humbled that two relative strangers would take such a risk for her. *No,* she corrected herself, *for Watersmeet.*

"Is this all we expect?" Neiall asked, glancing around.

"Macklin planned on coming, but his patrol was called up for a predawn forage. He didn't want to risk it," Anwyn explained.

"I spoke to two who wanted to come," Moyla put in, "but they didn't show."

"Where are the centaurs?" Kyron grumbled.

Moyla shook her head.

"She's Rueshlan's daughter," Kyron insisted. "His heir. She—"Abisina held her breath. "She deserves their loyalty!"

"I agree with you," Moyla said. "But they also see her as the one who brought us Charach and war. Some believe that Rueshlan was willing to save the Vranians because he had a Vranian daughter. We know it's not true," Moyla continued with a glance at Abisina. "But that's how some see it. They keep saying that the Vranians killed Rueshlan."

"The *Worm* killed Rueshlan," Abisina said. "I've no great love for the Vranians—as they had no love for me—but they were victims, too."

"We can't convince the others to see it our way," Haret said.

"Folk are supporting Glynholly's pact with the fairies, even if they don't really believe that Abisina turned traitor," Anwyn added.

"The fairies are liars! The faun is a usurper!" Kyron cried. "Why are we here if not to fight?"

"I will not attack Watersmeet," Abisina said. "No matter what."

"Not Watersmeet—Glynholly," Kyron countered.

"At Ulian's funeral there wasn't just weeping," Findlay said. "There was anger, and all the fear and anxiety that had built up since Rueshlan's death. And the fact that Abisina left—well, folk questioned it. I've never seen anything like it.

Keep the refugees out. Make them pay. It was like we were back on the battlefield."

"What happened with the fairies?" Haret asked Abisina. "Why did they turn on you?"

She told them about the Motherland, about meeting Corlin, and about Vranlyn.

Haret frowned. "You said no to the Fairy Mother. I'm surprised the fairies let you go."

"Corlin and Kyron got out only because Neriah helped us."

"I don't think the fairies wanted to make you a martyr," Neiall said. "They need Watersmeet. It could alienate folk if they took direct action against you."

"They all but killed her when they stole our weapons," Kyron muttered.

"*They* took your weapons?" Haret raised an eyebrow.

"It must have been them," Abisina explained, "but we have no proof. One morning we woke up, and the weapons were gone. Nothing else."

Neiall nodded. "It would've been easier for them if the überwolves got you."

Haret shook his head. "They made their offer to Glynholly, and she saw the answer to all of her problems: the wolves, the refugees, *and* her rival."

"So what do we do now?" Abisina asked.

She never got an answer.

From the darkness, Elodie screamed, "Fly!"

CHAPTER XI

NEIALL DOUSED THE TORCH, AND EVERYONE RAN. FOR A few steps, Abisina and Findlay stayed together, but then Abisina tripped. Regaining her feet, she paused. *Where's Findlay?* But she was afraid to call out.

I have to keep moving! The thought made her transform. She broke into a gallop, praying that Findlay had already gotten away. She ran, smacking her shoulder into a tree, stumbling against a rock. Shouts and cries echoed on all sides. Had any of her friends been captured? She risked a glance back. A line of torches came through the trees.

"Hey, you there!" A voice on her right—deep, male. A centaur. "Have you found any?"

"Not yet," Abisina growled, trying to disguise her voice.

"If we're lucky, we won't find *her*," the centaur replied. "I don't relish the idea of arresting Rueshlan's daughter, even if she has forgotten him."

"Me, neither," Abisina agreed. *Forgotten my father? Is that what they think?* They walked side by side. The torches were getting closer, but Abisina was afraid to gallop away.

Then a shout—"I've got one!"—and the other centaur took off. The torchbearers raced toward a central point. Abisina headed the opposite way, wanting to get as far from the torchlight as she could. But who had been captured?

She stayed in her centaur form, alone in the dark. If she stumbled into someone else from Watersmeet, they would also assume that she was one of them. But as dawn colored the sky, she could hide better as a human. She transformed and tucked herself high in the crook of a tree.

Who'd gotten away? Who hadn't? How would she find any of them if they were scattered throughout the wood, afraid to show themselves? She wanted to go back to the circle of stones, the last place she had seen her friends, but it was too dangerous. The Seldar grove where she'd met Elodie and Haret also seemed risky.

Someone was coming through the woods. *Is it one of us?* She held very still. She saw the legs of a faun between the leaves, but they were too dark to be Anwyn's. The faun paused and gave a whistle. To Abisina's left came another whistle. Then a third, farther off. *They're searching the whole wood.* Findlay and Elodie might get into the trees, but what about Kyron, Moyla, and Anwyn? Their hooves prevented climbing. And Haret hated heights so much he wouldn't consider hiding in a tree.

She had to find her friends! She decided to wait until dark, transform, and head to the Seldar grove at the southern end of Watersmeet. It was a popular grove, close to some of the central bridges. Maybe someone would turn up there.

The sun hung in the sky that day, hardly moving as Abisina waited for sunset. Two more patrols passed her way, and she recognized a centaur and a dwarf. She knew them from celebrations, archery contests, and Gatherings. *Do they really believe I'm a traitor?*

At last, the light faded, and she dropped from her perch, transforming into a centaur as she touched ground. Her control was improving.

First she would go toward Watersmeet. The rush of the rivers would cover the drumming of her hooves, and the patrols wouldn't expect her to risk going so close. She skirted several refugee encampments on her way—and the smell of cooking fish nearly drove her mad.

Abisina reached the Seldar grove and found a pine that would hide her while giving her a view of the grove. Transforming back into a human, she began to climb. Without boots, her feet had become tough. The scratchy bark and sharp branches didn't bother her. But halfway up she regretted choosing a pine; pitch coated her hands, legs, and feet.

The day had been hot, but once the sun went down, the air felt more like early spring. *The cold will keep me awake.* When had she last slept? She listened to the rush of the river, the scurry of raccoon and possum, and the wind in the branches. She toyed with the idea of going into Watersmeet itself. What if she swam over as a centaur, transformed—

The animals of the wood went quiet. Someone was coming.

Abisina peered at the forest floor, the bank, the river, the grove. She saw no one. Any of her friends would stay hidden. The night animals were still silent, and her hope grew.

The lower branches of her pine moved slightly. A very stealthy someone had chosen the same tree to hide in.

This someone did not climb up. Instead, he must have been lying on the ground, watching the river.

Maybe it's Haret, she thought. Abisina tried to wait, but she had to know.

Carefully, she climbed down the tree, shifting her weight from branch to branch. Six feet above the ground, she stopped and strained to see who was below her. Whoever it was stayed concealed beneath the tree, where the Seldars' glow and the moonlight did not reach. But he—or she—had to move sometime.

The noises of the night creatures slowly resumed as Abisina and her visitor remained motionless. Her hands and feet tingled and then went numb. If she didn't move soon, she would fall. She went lower. The perch she found was precarious, feet on two small branches half a length apart, hands on two other branches, like one of the bridges arching from Watersmeet to the distant bank. She couldn't stay this way for long. Should she go back up? The decision was made for her. One of the branches she held cracked, and she pitched forward. If this wasn't a friend, she had no hope except to surprise her opponent.

Breaking branches on the way down, she landed hard.

"Argh!" a voice yelled.

Abisina lunged at the voice. A hand grabbed at her, and she caught it, twisting hard.

"Oof!"

"Findlay?" Abisina whispered.

"Abisina?"

"It's you!"

"Get in here." He scooted farther under the tree to make room.

"Did anyone hear us?" she asked breathlessly.

Findlay peered out between the branches. "I don't see anyone. Vigar's braid!" he said, turning to her again. "You're all right. I thought they'd gotten you." He pulled her to him, embraced her, and then kissed her. A soft, tender kiss. The warmth spread down Abisina's body. Findlay drew back a little and sighed. "I thought I might never get to do that again."

Abisina nodded, unable to speak. Held to his chest, she could feel his heart beating against her cheek.

But they had no time to linger. They separated, holding hands.

"The others—do you know what happened to them?" Abisina asked.

"They got Neiall. He distracted them, giving us all a chance to get away. I wasn't far from him when it happened. I wanted to *do* something. It was horrible to just lie there hiding while they took him. But I would've been captured, too. I looked for any signs of you or the others but found nothing."

Abisina swallowed. *He wasn't looking for hoofprints.*

"I couldn't think of any place to go but here." He squeezed her hand. "I guess we think alike."

"I hope the others think like we do."

"We can wait here through the night. See if anyone comes," Findlay said. They both knew they were putting off a harder conversation—what to do if no one showed—but it was enough to have a plan for the next few hours.

Findlay sat up against the tree trunk and pulled her to him again. "Abisina! What happened to your clothes?"

"We got caught in the Fens," she said. "My boots were pulled off . . . and I had to swim out of my leggings." In the dark, he couldn't see her blush.

"I didn't notice at the meeting. Aren't you cold? Here," he added, slipping off his own boots. "Take mine."

"Then you'll be cold. I'm used to it now."

"We'll take turns," he insisted, unlacing his leggings where they tied at his ankles.

"Okay, but just the boots," Abisina said. "My cloak covers my legs, and you don't have a cloak."

The boots felt extravagantly warm and soft. Abisina yawned.

"Go to sleep, Abby. I'll keep watch. I'll wake you if I see anything."

Abisina didn't have the energy to refuse. She laid her head in his lap and closed her eyes.

What if I transform while I'm sleeping? She jolted awake and startled Findlay. "What is it?" he asked.

She glanced down at her feet in Findlay's boots. She was human. "Must have been a dream," she said.

Findlay leaned against the tree. "Go back to sleep. You slept only an hour or so."

She shook her head. "You need to sleep, too. I'm wide awake now. Did you see anything?"

"Not even an überwolf." Abisina's stomach rumbled, and Findlay reached into a pocket in his tunic and pulled out some smoked meat. "I meant to bring more. I figured you had run out of food. But Meelah distracted the faun watching our house, and I had to go."

"Meelah knows that you came to meet me?"

"I needed her help. Of course, she wanted to come, too." Findlay's younger sister was headstrong, energetic, and a dear friend of Abisina's. He must've had a hard time keeping her home.

Abisina chewed the gamey meat as slowly as she could; it didn't last long enough to satisfy her hunger. She did doze after her snack but kept startling awake. Her control was weakest when she slept.

"I'm going to look for food," she told Findlay as the sky began to brighten.

"I'll come with you."

"Someone needs to watch," Abisina said. "You stay here."

"Abby—"

"If I wait, it will be too light," she said as she crawled out of their hiding place.

"I think we should stay together."

"One is less noticeable than two, and I really think we need to keep watch."

Findlay hesitated, but he ducked back under the boughs. Abisina knew she had been too insistent. But she would be less recognizable as a centaur and couldn't have Findlay with her.

Abisina almost transformed while wearing Findlay's boots. She would have ruined them! She took them off and hid them in a tree. Once she became a centaur, she trotted even farther away before searching for breakfast.

The folk of Watersmeet had picked the surrounding forests clean. Abisina had to content herself with raiding a squirrel's store of nuts and picking a few bitter herbs. She filled her water skin at a stream and was about to return to Findlay when she felt a presence nearby. She checked the sky for fairy birds. She saw nothing. But she didn't like being watched. Not watched—*sensed*. By what?

Abisina suddenly knew there was a bit of moisture in a leaf near her shoulder and had the strange desire to nibble it. She knew that the stick in front of her would snap loudly if she stepped on it. And the sensations in her nose! The forest had new dimensions and new shadows, warnings and havens and deliciousness. What was going on?

The picture—not the right word, but words were losing meaning now—sharpened, and she saw the forest with a peculiar vision that this foreign presence gave to her. *Handsandhooves*, it spoke to her without words or sound. *Handsandhooves*.

The presence receded, and Abisina gasped for air, as if she had been suspended without breath while she was *with* this other being.

What did it mean? Ahead the trees thinned, and the light increased. She took a step and—snap! The stick was there. She got her answer in the soft mud at her hooves: tracks of a large deer—probably an adult buck. Few deer were left near Watersmeet. The überwolves had seen to that. As she straightened up, she realized what was happening. Centaurs could communicate with hoofed animals. She had sensed the deer. And the deer had sensed her.

She transformed back to a human. Tears filled her eyes, and she wiped them away quickly, though no one was there to see. She had known centaurs had this ability—why should it surprise her that she, as a centaur, had it, too? The tears kept coming. She'd thought she was getting used to this new self. But her control was an illusion. This intrusion—so raw, so foreign—had come out of nowhere.

She raced back to Findlay, wanting only to be reminded that she was human. She almost forgot his boots.

"What is it? Were you chased?" he asked as she threw herself down next to him.

"No," she croaked through gulps of air.

"Are you all right?"

"I'm fine. Sorry. I just need to catch my breath."

"What happened?" he asked again as her breathing slowed.

She almost told him. She wanted somebody to talk to, someone to help her make sense of what was happening to her.

But it was too strange. Too strange for her, and too strange for Findlay.

If only my father were alive. Why had he told her so little? Why hadn't he prepared her for this possibility? She rested her head in her hands. She knew Findlay's eyes were on her, could imagine the lines of worry on his face.

"Abisina, tell me. What is it?"

She couldn't. Instead she forced a laugh. "I scared myself," she said. "I—I thought someone—or something—was after me. I don't think it was anything, really. I'm just worn out." She tried to keep her tone light. "Really, I'm fine."

She offered him some nuts and herbs. He ate but kept watching her. Abisina flopped onto her belly, peering out from under the branches as if totally absorbed by what she saw. "Try to sleep," she said casually. "I'll watch."

Findlay tilted his head back and shut his eyes. He didn't relax.

He opened his eyes again. "Abby, I want you to know that you can trust me." She opened her mouth to protest, but he cut her off. "I'm not asking you to tell me anything. I just want you to trust me."

He leaned against the tree again. Eventually, his breath evened out and got deeper. He was asleep.

Abisina looked fixedly at the river. In her head, she knew she could trust Findlay. It was her heart that beat uncontrollably when she thought about saying the words to him: I am a shape-shifter, a centaur.

On the far bank, a buck with eight-point antlers stepped from the trees and stared at her.

CHAPTER XII

THE BUCK SHOWED UP THREE MORE TIMES THAT DAY. Several überwolves had loped toward the refugee camps upriver, and as the sun went down, Findlay said, "That buck is back. Doesn't it sense the überwolves?"

Abisina had just woken up, driven to sleep by sheer exhaustion and hunger. She realized what she had been denying all day: the deer had a message for her, had tried to tell her before, but she'd refused to listen. She sat up. "We have to follow him."

"What?" Findlay gaped at her.

Abisina ignored Findlay's surprise. "You're right. He must sense the überwolves, but he keeps coming to the river. The buck is trying to tell us something. I think Kyron sent him."

Findlay considered. "I hadn't thought of that."

"Let's go." Abisina put on her cloak. She peeked between the branches. The buck stood poised at the edge of the river, waiting for her. She started to crawl out, but Findlay stopped her.

"Let's wait until it's darker."

"He's here now. We have to go. Who knows when an überwolf might show up?"

"At least put your hood over your hair," Findlay said. "I look like a refugee, but everyone will know you're from Watersmeet."

As they neared the river, the buck tensed, ready to run. *He's not sure it's me,* Abisina thought. She needed to reach out to him, but could she do it without transforming?

She fought to keep her inner-wall firm, as her centaur-self reached toward the buck. *Handsandhooves.* She used the same thought he had used earlier.

The buck startled, and Abisina thought she had frightened him, but almost immediately, a foreign presence touched her mind. She tensed, and the presence darted away. She tried to relax, and it neared again. The forest filled with stronger smells and sharper sounds. Not as powerful as before, but strong enough to make her cringe. The buck pulled away as Abisina struggled. Her wall had slipped.

Don't fight it, she told herself. She grabbed Findlay's hand and used it as an anchor: *You're human AND centaur.* She tried to open herself again to the buck.

Picture-words flew through her mind: *Handsandhooves, sun-on-the-side, cold-that-kills, life-wet, sun-on-the-side.* Her mind clamped down in frustration.

I'm sorry, she pleaded. *I just don't understand.*

New picture-words. *Nose-nuzzle. Milk-warm.* She relaxed and opened her eyes, not realizing that she had closed them. The buck had crossed the river and stood in front of her, rubbing his head up under her free hand. She was vaguely aware of Findlay frozen next to her, his hand clutched in her own.

Findlay, she said to herself, strengthening her wall. She reached forward again, inviting the picture-words. Images began to flow, but now they had more depth, motion, color.

The sun on the left, and Watersmeet on the right. Into the water, the cold racing up her leg. She noticed her foot on the pebbled riverbed—slender, mottled brown, cloven. *This is what the buck sees, has seen,* she thought. The cold moved onto her belly. She gasped when the water covered her back. Swimming now, powerful legs pushing the water until her hoof knocked against the gravel of the bottom. The cold receded as she came out again, on the far bank, the sun blissfully warm, driving out the killing cold of the river. Leaping then into the forest—*ground-air, ground-air, ground-air.* The brush snagged at her sides, briars pulled at her fur. She fought her way deeper and deeper, far from the river, out of sight of Watersmeet. She reached a tangle of brambles. Kyron and Elodie turned to greet her. . . .

Abisina wanted to ask about the others, but before she could give the buck a picture of Haret, Anwyn, and Moyla, the image ripped in two. Pain exploded behind her forehead.

"Abisina!" Findlay was yelling.

The buck plunged into the river. *Where are you going?* she called, but when she tried to open her mind to him, noise and pain and fear and flight filled her senses.

"Run!" A new urgency in Findlay's voice.

Behind them, two ragged refugee boys came through the trees, bows in their hands, victory on their faces.

"We got it! We got it!" the one in front shouted.

"It's getting away!" the second called.

Across the river, the buck scrambled onto the shore, an arrow sticking out of his rear haunch, blood streaming down his leg.

In Vranille, Abisina had hunted, brought down deer, gutted, and eaten them. She had been proud of her skill. When she first arrived in Watersmeet, she'd learned that to the folk there, killing deer was barbaric. Once you communicate, you cannot kill.

The smell of blood washed over her. "We have to help him!" She waded into the River Deliverance.

"Abisina!" Findlay yelled.

"We can't let him die!"

As she neared the middle of the river, the current took her cloak, and she lost her balance. The water pulled her down. The buck's picture-words came to her, *cold-that-kills*, as the air was pressed from her chest.

Then a strong hand grabbed her.

"Hang on to me!" Findlay called.

She clamped her arms around his waist, drawing air greedily into her lungs as he pulled her across.

She reached the shore, but the buck was out of sight. Her acute sense of smell was gone. Her connection to the buck had been severed. Findlay paused to catch his breath. The two young refugees stayed on the far bank, unwilling to brave the stiff current.

It wasn't hard to find the buck's trail—blots of blood leading straight for the woods. She took off, Findlay right behind her.

Abisina despaired as the blood trail became heavier, but somehow the buck kept going. The brush grew thicker, snagging her cloak, scratching her cheeks.

"Wait! Where are you going?" Findlay called, but she couldn't stop.

She raced through a bramble patch, ignoring the stabs of pain. "They should be close," she called.

"Who?"

"Kyron and Elodie. He showed me—after the brambles. There they are!"

Elodie came toward them. "You're here! I didn't think it would work."

Beyond Elodie, the buck lay on the ground. Kyron bent over him, a bloody arrow in his fist.

"Is he alive?" Abisina asked softly.

Kyron shook his head. "The wound was deep. If he had stopped, or slowed—but he must have spent all his energy, kept his heart pumping to get here." He looked at her. "So he found you—"

"Yes," Abisina cut in, shaking her head slightly at Kyron.

Kyron sighed. "I sent him. Hoped he would—somehow—lead you to us."

"That's what Abisina thought," Findlay said. "I—I don't understand it."

"It just seemed that he wanted . . . to tell me something. Didn't you feel it?" she said.

"He did act differently than most deer," Findlay admitted.

Abisina knelt next to the buck's head and closed his eyes. She tried to open her mind again. She imagined sun, green leaves, speckled fawns—anything the buck might have taken pleasure in, hoping that in some way she was expressing her gratitude.

They dragged the body away from where Elodie and Kyron had set up camp. Though the Watersmeet custom was to burn bodies, Kyron said it would be best to leave the buck for the forest to reclaim.

When they had returned to the camp, Abisina asked the question she dreaded: "Does anyone know what happened to the others? Any news of Haret?"

Elodie shook her head. "We were hoping you knew something."

"How did you find each other?"

Elodie explained that she and Kyron had run in the same direction and then slipped away in the confusion after Neiall's capture.

"It was Elodie's idea to come to the western side of the river," Kyron said.

Although Watersmeet was a good distance from the Mountains Eternal, the mysteries and legends of the mountains had made generations of folk prefer the eastern bank to forage, gather wood, take picnics, or go exploring. The western side was seen as dangerous, the realm of the unknown. Refugees coming from the Cleft arrived to the east and stayed there, where more paths and cleared places allowed them to set up camps. Überwolves tended to follow the food; they stayed near refugee camps, bridges, and pathways. On the western bank, Abisina and her friends would have more places to hide and fewer folk to hide from.

"We need to find the others," Abisina said.

"Of course." Findlay nodded. "But where should we look? What if they've been caught? Or—or killed?"

"Killed?" Elodie echoed.

"No," Abisina said firmly. "Glynholly would never kill them. Is there any way we can get into Watersmeet—or get a message in? Haret would go to Hoysta if he could."

"There's a way in," Kyron said, eyeing Abisina. "Right across those bridges."

"Kyron, we've been through this," she said.

"How about boats?" Findlay asked. "That's how we got over when we came to meet you."

"By now they've taken our boats," Elodie replied. "And Hoysta will be watched."

"What about Alden?" Findlay suggested. "His daughter is sweet on Haret."

"But is Alden on our side?" Abisina asked.

"I don't know," Findlay admitted.

"Centaurs! We should be talking about the centaurs!" Kyron bellowed. Elodie hushed him, but he continued in a lower voice. "There have to be centaurs we can trust—who will ride with us, with Rueshlan's daughter."

Abisina knew what he wanted.

"Kyron," she said, facing him, "it's not going to work. It's—*I'm* not enough. Not now."

"You could *lead* us," he insisted.

"They think I'm a traitor—even the centaurs! I heard them talking about me. What you want . . . it's not the answer."

Kyron stared at her stubbornly.

Klee-klee-klee.

Abisina looked up and caught sight of a small bird. A kestrel.

A louder screech split the air: *Cack-cack-cack.* Two other birds, much larger, swooped overhead.

Peregrine falcons, Abisina noted.

The falcons dropped down on the kestrel, the first striking with its talons, the second sinking its hooked beak into the kestrel's neck. The kestrel plummeted to the earth and landed with a sickening thud. The fight over, the peregrines soared up and out of sight.

Abisina ran to the bird and gently picked up its broken

body. Bright blood streaked its snowy neck, but it was beautiful: red back, slate-blue wings peppered with dark spots. The kestrel was small enough to lie in the palm of her hand. She turned it over. Its head lolled to one side, and something fluttered to the ground.

A perfect, golden Seldar leaf.

"Neriah," Abisina whispered.

"What?" Findlay said. He had come to her side.

"Were the fairies in Watersmeet when you left?" she asked.

"Yes. They stayed to help organize the dwarves going to the Cleft."

"They sent the falcons as spies. This one," Abisina stroked one of the kestrel's wings, "was sent by Neriah to warn me. We need to go," she said. "The fairies know we're here. They'll alert Glynholly."

"They already have."

CHAPTER XIII

GLYNHOLLY STRODE FORWARD, FLANKED BY REAVA AND A faun. Behind them stood several more folk from Watersmeet with arrows ready.

"Take them," Glynholly said curtly.

"Don't fight!" Abisina told the others. Kyron was ready to bring his hooves down on anyone who came near him, and she didn't want to prompt a volley of arrows.

Glynholly's guards grabbed them, held their arms, and took their weapons. Abisina stared at the fauns who were her captors, but they wouldn't look at her. Kyron cursed the centaurs who held him.

"You don't need to fight. We're here to make you a bargain," Glynholly said to Abisina, then motioned the fauns to let her go.

Abisina tried to mask her surprise. "What's your offer?"

"You have many friends in Watersmeet, Abisina. I want

to welcome you back into the community. We all do."

"You'll let me—all of us—back in?" Abisina asked.

"Yes. If you give me, as Keeper, your unwavering support. And make a public avowal that your father would have worked with the fairies to close the Cleft, that you were misguided in thinking he wouldn't. That's all."

That's all. "If I refuse?"

"And do what? Fight us? Would you really attack the home your father built?"

We have an alliance with the fairies. Watersmeet will survive. My friends can return to their families and loved ones. Glynholly's offer might be the best she would get. *It's not what I wanted. But isn't it better than nothing?* She was so tired. *I could rest, find a way to help Vranlyn.*

"We have the rest of your friends," Reava said impatiently. "Neiall, Anwyn, and Moyla." She paused and then added, "The dwarf and his grandmother."

Haret and Hoysta! "What will you do to them?" Abisina demanded.

Reava shrugged. "If you will not work with us, there are plenty of überwolves in the forest."

Abisina saw Glynholly flinch.

She caught sight of the Keeper's necklace around Glynholly's neck, black against the white of her tunic—nothing like the brilliant ornament that still wove in and out of her dreams. Noticing Abisina's gaze, Glynholly hastily slid the necklace under her shirt.

For a short time, Watersmeet had been the answer to all of Abisina's dreams: a father, friends, love, respect. But that was gone now.

"No, I will not support this new Watersmeet. I would be a traitor to my father. I will go south."

"You'll leave Watersmeet? Forever?" Glynholly looked stunned.

Clearly they had expected Abisina to agree. A few of the guards murmured to themselves.

"What about the other traitors?" Reava asked.

Going to Vranlyn was a risk Abisina could take, but she couldn't ask the same from her friends. "If they agree to . . . swear loyalty to you, will you let them stay?" she asked Glynholly.

"I won't stay," Findlay said through clenched teeth.

"Nor I!" Kyron shouted.

"They all have to go," Reava answered without waiting for Glynholly. "And the others we are holding."

"No." Glynholly turned to Reava.

"We cannot take the risk," Reava said fiercely.

"I will not have anyone *native* to Watersmeet forced to leave," Glynholly said, with a nervous glance at the guards gathered behind her. "I am still Keeper, Reava." She said to Abisina, "You, Haret, and Hoysta will be exiled but not the others."

"I choose exile," Findlay said.

"Me, too," Kyron added.

"And me. Erna's not *native*, either," Elodie said bitterly. "You can bring her with Haret and Hoysta."

Abisina's heart sank. Kyron had no family, but Findlay might never see Meelah again or Elodie, her mother. And Erna was still waiting for her mate, Darvus, to arrive from the south.

"Enough," Glynholly said. "The rest will stay."

"If they agree," Kyron grumbled.

"There will be no changing your minds," Reava warned.

"Findlay . . . Elodie . . ." Abisina begged. "You can't—"

"Enough," Reava repeated. "It is done."

Abisina had exiled herself—and her closest friends. Haret, Hoysta, and Erna would meet her group at the southern Seldar grove at first light. Guards would accompany them south for two more leagues. Then the outlaws would continue on their own.

"We will be watching you," Reava reminded them. "Our birds are everywhere. We will know if you take one step north."

Glynholly, Reava, and their escort returned to Watersmeet, leaving a few guards behind.

Turning to her friends, Abisina saw their stricken faces.

"I'm sorry," she said. "I never meant for you to have to leave. I'll be okay if I go to Vranlyn; I'm used to their ways." *Not as a centaur*, she couldn't help thinking. "But it will be unlivable for you there. They'll treat the rest of you like demons—if they let you in."

"But they've left Vran's teachings," Findlay said.

"They have a long way to go. The conditions in the south are horrible. I don't know if Vranlyn will survive."

"So what are you going to do down there, Abisina?" Elodie asked.

"I can teach them to forage—as you taught me. I can help them talk to dwarves, fauns, and centaurs. I don't want my father's death to be for nothing."

"It seems to me," Kyron said, "that I know how to talk to centaurs better than you do."

Findlay nodded. "My mother has been in charge of foraging teams for longer than you've been alive, Abby."

"And Erna knows fauns very well," Elodie said.

"I know what you're trying to do—" Abisina began.

"You have no choice," Kyron boomed. "We're going."

"You didn't really think we'd let you go alone?" Findlay said.

Abisina couldn't help but smile. If her friends came, there was a better chance they'd succeed. She could not let Watersmeet become like Vrania—even if it meant she would have to save Vrania to do it.

The mood was far more somber the next morning as they waited outside the Seldar grove. Abisina leaned against one of the Seldars, the slender trunk comforting at her back. Up the river, the dawn touched the towering Sylvyads, pulling them from the shadows. In the cool morning, were her friends regretting their decision?

I could go to Glynholly, she thought. *Give in. No matter what Reava said, Watersmeet would take us back.*

What if I had transformed? The thought had kept her up all night. *Would coming to the folk as a centaur have changed anything?*

Findlay sat, his head tipped against a tree, staring at the sky. *With his blond hair and fair skin, he will be welcomed by the Vranians. But Elodie?* Elodie sat a few feet away, arms around her knees, rocking back and forth. Her midnight skin, hair, and eyes would mark her instantly as an outcast—or worse.

And Kyron? Could the Vranians ever accept a centaur?

The trip itself was dangerous. Überwolves, minotaurs. The difficulty of crossing the mountains. Reaching the other side brought more dangers: centaurs at war with humans. The gangs of Vranians that Corlin described who preyed on anyone or anything with food. Trolls.

With a sigh, Abisina recognized the truth: she *wanted* her friends to come. For all her brave talk, she dreaded being back in a Vranian village. There would be people there who had known her as an outcast. Her friends would remind her that she'd been accepted and loved in Watersmeet.

And Findlay. Could I really say good-bye to him?

"Abby?" Findlay put his hand on her shoulder. "They're coming." He pointed to two centaurs leaving the southernmost bridge out of Watersmeet. They led Haret, Hoysta, and Erna with hands bound, legs shackled. No one else came with them.

Abisina got to her feet. Reava leapt from one of the Syl-vyad branches far above and landed right in front of Hoysta, startling her. The fairy walked toward Abisina, her chin raised, her eyes taunting.

Abisina met Reava's stare.

"Fleeing south." Reava's voice whispered in Abisina's ear. "Back to your *people*."

Abisina looked past Reava to Haret.

"Trip over the Obruns wouldn't be the same without me, eh, human?" he said.

"Talk on the trail," Reava cut in.

"Release their bonds," Abisina responded.

"They'll be released when you are two leagues from Watersmeet." Reava lifted her chin higher.

"They are no longer your prisoners," Abisina said.

Reava hesitated. Then she smirked and flicked her head toward one of the centaurs, a palomino with hair as white as his tail. He moved to cut the prisoners' bonds.

Kyron pawed the gravel of the riverbank. His anger rolled off him like summer heat. "How can you call yourself a centaur?" he spat. The palomino said nothing, but his fair skin went pink.

"Glynholly wanted you to have supplies and weapons," Reava said. Abisina noticed that the palomino carried several bows over his shoulder, one of them the bow Haret had given her.

"Are these to replace the weapons we 'lost' while leaving the Motherland?" Abisina asked.

Reava ignored her. "Guards, hold these weapons until you get the traitors safely away."

"That's enough!" the palomino spoke suddenly. "Our Keeper said nothing about holding their weapons from them. This forest is dangerous. I know these folk. They have pledged to go south, and they will."

The palomino gave the bows he carried to Haret. The other centaur held out a satchel with Findlay's sword poking out of it.

With bows in hand, Haret brushed past Reava and came to stand next to Abisina. Hoysta, rubbing her wrists, followed.

"At my age! I was baking bread when they took me. I don't treat my badgers like this!" Hoysta muttered. Erna scurried over. They were each handed satchels bulging with provisions.

"Neiall and the others?" Abisina asked.

"They have *decided* to stay," Reava said.

Abisina turned and led her company away from Watersmeet.

For the first few hours, they went due south. Above them, two falcons wheeled in the sky, crying out at intervals as if to remind them that they were watched. Not knowing if the birds understood speech, the group spoke in whispers. Findlay walked with Elodie. Abisina sensed that they were talking about the families they'd left behind, and her throat tightened.

Haret, Hoysta, and Erna, on the other hand, seemed almost cheerful.

"Just think, Grandmother," Haret said. "We'll actually see Stonedun. The dwarves of the south are rebuilding it."

"To think I've lived this long. . . ." Hoysta sighed.

"I didn't know you longed to see Stonedun, Hoysta," Abisina said.

"We'd never have left you, dearie. Not while you needed us. But Stonedun! It's not the ancient Obrun City under the mountains, of course. That's closed off to us forever. But it will do my old eyes good to see Stonedun."

Abisina had been surprised when Elodie insisted that Erna leave with them, but Erna was beaming. "I'll see Darvus again! And my mother!" For a short time the little faun set a pace that had Abisina panting to keep up.

Abisina fell into step with Haret, and Kyron trotted up to join them. "What about the others?" Abisina asked. "Are they all right?"

"I don't know much," Haret said. "Neiall was injured when they took him. Moyla and Anwyn must've been captured."

"How did they get you?"

"Hmph. They didn't at first," Haret grumbled. "I hid in a crevice beneath the roots of a fallen tree. The next night I headed toward the southern Seldar grove."

"That's where Findlay and I went. Kyron and Elodie crossed to the other side."

"I thought of that," Haret said, "but I wanted to keep track of Grandmother. I went to the riverbank and saw no light in our home. I got worried, came out too far on the bank, and got captured. A couple of centaurs. We fought the Worm together, but it was as if they didn't know me."

Kyron swore under his breath.

"What did Glynholly say?" Abisina asked.

"She wanted me to give you up. Said it was best for Watersmeet. She promised me that you would be treated well."

"Then why did she have us ambushed?" Kyron asked.

"That's what I said, and that ended the conversation. I thought she'd parade me through Watersmeet, showing all the folk that she had put the 'insurrection' down. I was looking forward to it, actually. Instead they took me to Alden's before dawn. Didn't want anyone to know I'd been captured."

"Why?" Abisina asked.

"I wondered the same thing, but from what Breide told me—"

"Breide? When did you see Breide?"

"Alden had her bring me food. He knows how she, er, feels." Haret's cheeks grew red. Though he denied it, Abisina was convinced that he liked Alden's daughter as much as she liked him. "I don't think Alden would act directly against the Keeper, but sending me Breide was his way to support you. The two of us started planning my escape right away."

"There must be others like Alden," Haret continued. "Why else did they keep our capture quiet? Glynholly doesn't want the folk to know that we've actually dared to take a stand against her. Especially you, Abisina. Most don't believe that you're a traitor."

Abisina refused to catch Kyron's eye.

"Reava worries me." Haret shook his head. "Breide said she's always at Glynholly's side."

Abisina told Haret about Neriah's kestrel.

"Neriah is the Fairy Mother's heir?" Haret asked.

"She wears the silver leaf crown," Abisina said, "like Lohring did once."

"There must be divisions in the Motherland as well," Haret mused. "I wonder how deep they go."

As if they'd heard Haret, the falcons dived at him. At the last moment, they pulled up, skimmed over the treetops with a raucous shriek, and soared away to the north.

Everyone spoke at once, relieved to be rid of the fairy spies. There wasn't much to be cheerful about, but Abisina felt lighter. Some folk in Watersmeet believed in her. The memory of her father was not dead. If they could make a difference in the south, Watersmeet might be saved.

CHAPTER XIV

AFTER THE FALCONS LEFT, THE PARTY CHANGED COURSE TO head southeast to the Cleft. Abisina briefly considered going through Vigar's garden, a notch between Mounts Sumus and Arduus. Even if they could get into the mysterious garden, Kyron could never climb down the cliffs on the other side. Going through the Cleft—heading to the east, crossing the mountains, and then heading back northwest across the piedmont—would take them weeks, but it was their only choice.

Though she barely admitted it to herself, there was another reason she longed to go through the garden. Vigar was buried there and it was there that Abisina had first heard her voice. Wasn't it possible that her father would speak to her there as well?

Erna trotted along at Elodie's side with hardly a whimper about überwolves or minotaurs. She also had an uncanny skill for finding edible plants, no matter how hidden.

When Abisina asked Erna how she did this, she said: "I ask the trees."

"Ask them? Can all fauns do that?"

"I—I'm unusual," Erna said, and then squeaked as if alarmed by her own boasting. "I thought others could, too, but they can speak only to hamadryads. I can speak to *trees*. It's gotten much easier since the Seldars came. They've been waking up the other trees and their spirits. You saw what that hamadryad did to help poor Ulian. He couldn't have done that before."

"How do the Seldars wake up the trees?"

Erna frowned and scratched around one of her horns. "I don't quite know how to explain it. The trees went to sleep—put themselves to sleep—after the massacre."

"Massacre?"

"Long ago. The first time the White Worm attacked Watersmeet." Erna quavered. "He killed thousands of trees to dam up the rivers. Scores of hamadryads perished along with their trees. When the dams broke, some of the Sylvyads came down." Erna shivered as if speaking of a recent event, not one that happened three hundred years before she was born. "But when the Green Man brought the Seldars, the trees began to wake. The Seldars are . . . guardians of the other trees. They reach out to them somehow."

It amazed Abisina to think that timid Erna was comfortable with the powerful hamadryads.

"Elodie asked me to help forage on this journey. Is that all right?" Erna asked.

"Erna, you've been a huge help," Abisina reassured her— perhaps too strongly because Erna squeaked again. "Thank you," Abisina said softly. Erna smiled.

Five days later, the weather was overcast, and the mood of the travelers matched the sky. They'd had three tough fights with überwolves. The smoked meat and travel-bread were already getting boring. Except for Kyron and Abisina, no one's bodies had adjusted to the demands of the trek. Abisina tried to convince Findlay that she didn't need to share his boots, but he insisted, despite his bloody, aching feet. They trudged through forest that was the same league after league, with only a downed tree here and there to break the monotony. For Findlay, Elodie, and Kyron, the sense of excitement had worn off, and the reality of leaving their families, their home— everything that they had ever known—had settled in. At least once a day, a pair of falcons flew over them, circled, and then flew back to the north.

The mood of the others fed Abisina's worries. Every day she wondered if she could have done more to convince her friends to stay in Watersmeet. *What if Vranlyn hasn't survived?*

She had few chances to get away from the group to practice shape-shifting. She felt her centaur-self getting restless and wondered how long she could sustain her human form. During the days, someone was always near her. If she wanted any practice at all, she had to ask Kyron to wake her whenever he took night-watch. So when he suggested that she go ahead with him to scout terrain, she was eager to accept. *A chance to gallop!*

But Elodie spoke up before Abisina could. "Can I go with you?" she asked with a glance at Erna. The faun rarely left Elodie's side and chattered mostly about Darvus.

Abisina had lost her chance.

At midmorning, Kyron and Elodie came racing back.

"Troll!" Elodie pointed behind her. "Down that slope! We almost stumbled into its lair. Vigar be blessed, it was asleep, and it didn't come after us."

"Didn't see it until we got close," Kyron explained.

"The stink!" Elodie added. "I almost got sick."

"Did it follow you?" Erna peered behind them, but no boulderlike creature came through the trees.

"Should we go around?" Findlay asked.

"It will delay us," Kyron said, "but it's better than facing the troll."

They hadn't gone more than half a league to the north when the familiar snarls and howls of überwolves rang from several directions.

The archers had arrows ready, Findlay unsheathed his sword, and Hoysta gripped her axe. Erna had a dagger around her waist but didn't touch it. She was whimpering.

"Pull yourself together, Erna," Elodie said.

Abisina saw the weakness of their position: they stood in a natural depression. The wolves had the high ground.

The howls continued to echo around them. *At least fifteen*

wolves, Abisina guessed. She had never faced that many. *There are seven of us—six.* Erna would be more of a hindrance than a help. She spotted a large boulder. *That's what I need!* "Erna, that rock. Get behind it."

A small female wolf leapt from the trees. "Mine!" Abisina yelled. Her arrow caught the wolf in the neck and threw it backward. "Now, Erna!" she cried.

Abisina and Erna sprinted toward the boulder. Behind them, Kyron shouted out in pain, and Findlay called, "To the left, Elodie!" As Abisina jumped onto the boulder, Erna scurried behind it. *Good girl!*

Abisina reached the top and spun, another arrow ready. Kyron bled from his left flank, an überwolf dead beneath his hooves. Findlay pulled his sword from the midsection of another, while Elodie took aim at a third headed for Findlay.

More wolves broke from the trees. Abisina shot a huge, silver male that had its spear set to gore Haret in the chest. Her arrow found its mark, and the big male stumbled, its spear falling inches from Haret. She sent another arrow at a female bearing down on Kyron. Hoysta fought two überwolves at once, landing a blow in one's belly. Abisina didn't have a clear shot at the second; Hoysta stood in her way. "Hoysta—go!"

Without pause, Hoysta ran, giving Abisina her shot. She took full advantage, bringing down the wolf that Hoysta had injured. But Abisina rushed her next shot, and it struck the ground short of the second wolf.

Hoysta spun, swinging her axe. With one last push, the wolf clawed Hoysta's shoulder as it died.

"Grandmother!" Haret yelled, but Abisina's attention was on Kyron, locked in battle with two more. Findlay rained blows on one; Kyron was choking the other, but its jaws were locked on his upper arm.

A scream from Erna made Abisina turn. Something gray streaked by. But now more überwolves headed toward Hoysta! Elodie was there. Abisina had to help Erna. She reached for an arrow as the überwolf lifted Erna from her hiding place and ran, cutting behind trees. There was no shot!

Abisina leapt from the rock and took off after them.

I'll never catch up, she thought. The wolf wouldn't stop to feed until it found shelter, but it might bite Erna at any time. She let herself transform. With centaur speed, she had a chance.

Abisina raced after them, leaping fallen trees, dodging stones and downed branches, just keeping the wolf in sight.

Then, a scream filled the air. The überwolf was ready to feed, and Erna knew it.

"I'm coming!" Abisina shouted.

The überwolf rose up before her, leaping from a thicket of brush. Abisina barreled into it and knocked it over. It was like running into a wall. Her wrist snapped, her head crashed into its skull, and she trampled it. She reeled back, ignoring the pain as she sank an arrow into its heart.

The world spun around her, and she stumbled against a tree. She transformed again and fell.

Abisina woke to Erna's concerned face inches from her own. *Am I still—* She thought of her toes and wiggled them. *I'm human!*

"Erna," she croaked. "You cannot—"

"Is she talking?" Kyron's loud voice hurt Abisina's ears.

Beyond Erna, Abisina saw hazy shapes. With effort, she focused on Kyron, Elodie, and Findlay, staring down at her, silhouetted against the sky so that she couldn't see their faces.

What did Erna tell them? "I—I—"

"Don't worry," Elodie said soothingly. "Erna told us what you did."

Abisina's eyes flew to Findlay.

"Kyron got here first." Findlay—concerned and gentle. Nothing else.

"I'm afraid I tore the place up, tramping around in a frenzy," Kyron rumbled.

The hoofprints. He covered for me. And Vigar be blessed, Findlay's wearing the boots. Abisina's panic ebbed, and she closed her eyes.

They flew open again. "Haret? Hoysta?"

The silence that followed hammered in her skull.

"Oh, Vigar!"

"We don't know what happened," Elodie said. "The wolves took them—but they could still be alive."

"They're fighters," Kyron reassured her, as Findlay took her hand.

"Do they have their weapons?" Abisina asked.

"We found Hoysta's axe where she was fighting," Findlay said quietly. "But not Haret's bow."

Abisina closed her eyes and turned away.

Hands softly touched her face, her neck. Findlay—checking her injuries. "The cut on your head is bad." His hand moved to her shoulders, then worked down her arms. A touch on her wrist made her suck in her breath.

"Broken," she murmured. She had known it as soon as it happened.

"Mmm." Findlay continued to probe her injuries: a few cuts and plenty of bruises, but nothing as severe as her head or wrist.

"You—and the others. You're all right?" Abisina asked.

"Kyron has a bad bite on his arm, and a cut on his flank. When you've rested, I'll need you to do some mending, if you can."

Abisina saw Hoysta's wrinkled hands, so skilled with a needle. *She taught me to stitch wounds.* "We have to find them." Abisina tried to get up, but her head spun, and she fell back.

"Elodie and I are going," Findlay said. "You, Kyron, and Erna will stay here. We just waited to see if you were okay."

Abisina tried to get up again but knew she couldn't. She listened as Elodie's and Findlay's footsteps retreated.

"Thank you," Abisina said to Kyron. "Erna?" She squinted up at the faun. "Can you understand why I don't want anyone to know about me?" Erna shook her head. "I need some more time to get used to this myself . . . before I ask anyone else to accept it."

"Accept it?" Erna whispered. "They love you, Abisina."

If only it were that easy. "Please, I want to tell my friends when the time is right. Will you let me? Will you keep my secret for me?"

"You saved my life," Erna said. "I'll do anything for you."

CHAPTER XV

FINDLAY AND ELODIE RETURNED AT NIGHTFALL. "WE tracked them for a few leagues," Findlay told Abisina, kneeling next to her. "But we couldn't catch them."

"Did you see—blood?"

He shook his head.

"They're alive!"

"Abby, I don't think—"

"I'd know if they were dead," she said. "If Haret were dead."

"I found this," he said reluctantly, handing her Haret's bow.

She took it, held the grip worn smooth by Haret's hand.

"Abisina, there's almost no way—"

"I would know," she said again.

Haret! Her thoughts reached out to her best friend. *Keep fighting! You have to stay alive. I cannot do this without you.*

Abisina would have gone after Haret and Hoysta the next morning, but Findlay wouldn't let her. "We need to splint your wrist. You can hardly stand. And look at the others! They're worn out."

"Haret and Hoysta are out there!" She clenched her fists, sending pain radiating through her wrist.

"I want to go after them, too, but we can't fight right now, Abby. If we run into more überwolves, they'll finish us."

She talked Findlay through splinting her wrist. She could sew up Kyron's arm and flank with her right hand, but she couldn't handle a bow. Elodie had gashes on her neck and back that would leave scars, as would a cut on Findlay's thigh.

"I need some horseradish to make a salve for those to stop the infection," Abisina said.

Erna jumped up and wandered among the trees, trailing her fingers along the trunks and humming. In a short while, she returned. "There's horseradish in that direction. It's not far." She pointed south.

"I'll go," Elodie said. "Can you show me, Erna?" The faun nodded.

Findlay stood, too. "I'll go with you." He drew his sword.

The three disappeared among the trunks, and Abisina lay near the fire, wanting to sleep, to get away from thoughts of what Haret and Hoysta might be going through.

"Abisina?" Kyron interrupted. "You have to tell them. How

are Elodie and Findlay going to react if they find out the way Erna did? Erna's right. They love you. We all do."

When Abisina didn't answer, Kyron continued, "What are you afraid of? You have a great gift! You saved Erna's life. How can you be ashamed?"

"Great gift!" Abisina exploded. "Haret and Hoysta could be dead! The rest of you are exiled! All of that is *my* fault. My father was a leader, a visionary. Watersmeet has crumbled without him. You think *I* can take his place? Just because I can become a centaur? And this—this *thing*—lives in me, a constant reminder of what's expected of me. Do you think if I told them it would get easier?"

"Yes, I do!" Kyron shot back. "We *chose* to come on this journey with you. Your gift has responsibilities, it's true. But you don't have to shoulder them alone."

Kyron stalked away from her.

But they'd never have left Watersmeet if I had stayed. And now it's too late to turn back.

Findlay returned to camp alone. "Abby, you need to come with me. And Kyron."

"Why? What's going on? Where are Elodie and Erna?"

"We found Frayda."

Frayda, her father's companion, had vanished over a year ago, unable to stay in Watersmeet after the death of Rueshlan. "Where? How is she?"

"You'd better see for yourself," Findlay said. "And bring your healing pouch."

Abisina and Kyron followed Findlay through the woods.

"We're almost at the troll's cave," Kyron said.

"That's where we found Frayda—or, I should say, she found us."

A scream shattered the stillness.

Abisina started forward, but Findlay stopped her. "Go slowly. You'll scare her."

Abisina approached Elodie and Erna, who knelt on the ground, each holding the arm of—she was barely recognizable as a woman, much less as strong, lithe Frayda, a celebrated archer in Watersmeet. Elodie was whispering to her.

Frayda looked as if she had been beaten, kicked, and dragged through the muck. Her dirty, matted hair had fallen out in clumps across her skull. One eye was swollen shut and the other was red and sunken. Her skin hung on her frame as if it were made for a larger woman, and she was all but naked. Her bone-white skin, once beautiful, was now spectral. As Abisina stood there, the figure on the ground gave another hollow cry, arched her back, and tried to shake free, lifting Erna off the ground with a strength that seemed impossible in one so wasted. Elodie continued whispering to her.

"What's happening?" Abisina breathed to Findlay.

"She wants to go to the troll. She thinks it's sick, and she wants to help. We had to stop her or she would have gone right up to it."

Listening to Elodie, Frayda's body had gone slack again. Abisina took a few steps closer. Elodie was singing:

Sparks dancing to the sky,
A summer day, the sun is gone,
Winter has been sent away,
Burn the holly and the pine.

Abisina remembered the song from the fires at Midsummer. She knelt down beside Elodie and began humming along. As Abisina took hold of Frayda's arm, relieving Erna, Frayda's eyes opened slightly. Her head lolled over, she saw Abisina, and gave a heartrending wail.

Abisina tensed, waiting for Frayda to resume her struggle, but the howl had emptied her, and she crumpled, weeping. Abisina pulled Frayda to her, cradling the woman in her arms like a child.

Frayda's sobs quieted, but she clung to Abisina. After a whispered conference with the others, Elodie said, "Abisina, do you think you could bring Frayda with you to our camp?"

Abisina helped Frayda to her feet, but before they could take a step, Frayda's head snapped up. "No! Heal it!" She stared accusingly at Abisina.

"The troll?" Abisina asked.

Frayda nodded, and her tears flowed again.

"I have my medicine pouch right here." Abisina touched her waist. "But we'll upset the troll if we all go. You stay with Elodie, and I'll see what's wrong."

Frayda nodded. "No more killing!" she cried.

Elodie put her arms around Frayda and resumed humming, while Abisina backed away. Reaching Findlay, she asked under her breath, "Where's this troll?"

"You're not really going to help it?"

"Well, I have to go in that direction. Are you coming with me?"

Findlay led the way. "What do you make of her?"

"I have no idea." Abisina shook her head. "She seems to have gone mad."

Kyron joined them. "She's been away for so long," he said. "If she's been out here alone this whole time . . ."

They walked through the forest until the smell of rot grew so strong, Abisina knew they were close.

"It's over there, below that rise," Kyron said, pointing to a swell in the land.

"Let's go," Abisina said, heading to the rise.

"What are you doing?" Findlay asked.

"Frayda said it was hurt. I should at least *look* at it."

"It's a troll, Abisina. You can't help it," Findlay said.

"Nor *should* you," Kyron added.

"I can see it from up there, can't I? That's a safe distance." She knew it was crazy, but it was one thing she could do for Frayda.

She went up the slope. Near the top, she lay down and scooted forward to peek over. Kyron had an arrow ready. Findlay had his sword out. Abisina was unarmed.

Raising her head, she peered down the rocky slope dotted

with a few thin, almost bare trees. Everything was quiet but for a slight gurgle from a stream running at the bottom. She didn't see the troll. Bits of bone were strewn about—mostly small game—and there were gashes in the earth where the top layer of soil had been ripped up. A large boulder blocked the entrance to a crudely dug hole in the far side of the steep valley. Abisina's eyes watered from the stench.

"Do you see it?" she mouthed to Findlay.

He shook his head.

Abisina was ready to give up. Then she saw it. The lump blocking the cave was no boulder but the hulking mound of a troll as it lay on the ground. Its head looked like a smaller stone.

It was as still as death.

She pointed it out to Findlay. "Do you think it's dead?"

He studied it and shrugged. "I'm not going to find out. Let's get out of here. The smell is unbearable!"

Abisina couldn't look away. "I'm going closer."

"What? Why?"

Yes, why? she asked herself. Why would she go any closer to a troll—even a dead one?

Because she felt like she owed it to Frayda. *No more killing,* Frayda had said.

Abisina inched farther up the slope. She heard Findlay following behind her. Some animals played dead to avoid predators. Did a troll play dead to trick prey? But the more she watched it, the more sure she was that this was no act.

The troll had fallen on its face. Chains across its back, massive links of iron, bit into its flesh. The Vranians had used chains and the lash to control trolls as weapons on the battle-field. This troll had survived the battle but died anyway, apparently from the wounds inflicted by the Vranians. Not too long ago, by the look of its corpse. Whatever state of good or evil this creature lived in, it had died in pain.

Abisina turned away. "Let's go," she said to a relieved Findlay and Kyron.

When they returned to the camp, Abisina went straight to Frayda, who was using her fingers to scrape the last bit of slippery elm gruel from a bowl.

"We saw your troll," Abisina said.

"Did you heal it?" Frayda asked.

"It will not suffer anymore," Abisina told her, and Frayda smiled.

Abisina had to force herself to stay two more days at their camp. Kyron couldn't travel and Frayda's wounds had to be treated. She wanted to yell, "Haret might be alive!"

He has to be! Abisina knew she was holding onto the thin-nest of hopes.

She ground her teeth when Reava's falcons made their daily appearance. How Reava must be enjoying word of their troubles! She wondered if Glynholly, too, was pleased.

Listening to Frayda's murmurings, Abisina tried to learn what had driven her to madness. She repeated the refrain "no killing, no killing" constantly and was obsessed with healing—from the troll, to broken branches, to nibbled mushrooms, to the scratches on Elodie's arm. When Findlay shot a rabbit, her screams echoed through the forest until he left the camp entirely. Once, Abisina returned from getting water to find Frayda weeping over an arrow. Elodie had retrieved it from a tree after a skirmish with the überwolves. Discovering a thin split in the shaft as she repaired it, Elodie snapped it in two. When Abisina approached, Frayda, clutching the arrow, lifted streaming eyes to her and said, "The world is broken." They took to preparing food away from Frayda, lest she see them slicing greenbrier roots or breaking open nuts. Abisina marveled that Frayda had survived at all. What had she eaten? And how had she escaped the überwolves?

They couldn't bring Frayda on their journey, but they couldn't leave her, either. On the second night, when Frayda had fallen into a fitful sleep, they huddled together to figure out what to do.

"Maybe one of us should take her to Watersmeet," Elodie said. "It would mean turning ourselves in . . ."

Abisina watched her friends closely. Would she see a spark of longing? She braced herself. "That may be best," she said. "Then we would know that Frayda was cared for."

They looked at one another uncomfortably. Kyron spoke first. "Most of the time, she's convinced I'm ready to skewer her, so I don't think I could take her."

"She's not comfortable with me," Findlay quickly put in.

"Well, Erna wants to go south," Elodie said, "and since I got her into this, I should see it through—for her sake."

"I guess that leaves me," Abisina said. Everyone stared at her in shock before they realized that she was teasing them. It felt strange—but good—to laugh together.

"But where can we take her?" Elodie asked. "The fairies are the only community between here and the Cleft."

"There's one other possibility," Abisina said, "but it means separating."

"No!" Kyron said immediately.

"Where?" Findlay asked.

"Vigar's garden," Abisina explained. "It's safe, and there's plenty to eat. If any place can heal her spirit, it's there."

"Why would that make us separate?" said Findlay.

"The path goes down a cliff. The trail's too narrow for a centaur."

"Then you'll have to come through the Cleft with me, Abisina," Kyron insisted. "I won't leave you. Elodie and Findlay can take Frayda."

"Abisina has to go to the garden," Elodie pointed out. "She knows how to get in."

"Fine," Kyron said. "We'll all go: take Frayda to the garden and then head back to the Cleft."

"We don't have time for that," Findlay argued. "The Watersmeet dwarves may already be on their way to the Cleft to begin the wall. Once they're there, we won't be able to get through."

"I don't mean to be a bother," Erna piped up, "but I have to go through the Cleft. Darvus is that way. And my mother."

"Erna and I should go with Kyron through the Cleft," Elodie concluded.

But Kyron wasn't ready to give in. "We need Abisina to get us into Vranlyn. If I trotted up to the village, they'd shoot me on sight. Erna, too."

Erna squeaked.

"You're right, Kyron," Abisina said. "But the journey from the garden is shorter; I'll get to Vranlyn first."

It took a long time to convince Kyron that separation was the only plan. He was still inventing reasons to stay together while they divided their gear. In the end, he had to satisfy himself with keeping Abisina up far too late to give her every bit of advice she might need before they saw each other again.

Chapter XVI

The next morning, Kyron stamped around the camp growling at anybody in his way. Erna stayed inches from Abisina's shoulder until Abisina snapped at her—and then had to apologize and soothe the faun to stop her crying. Findlay and Elodie barely spoke to anyone. Only Frayda was unaffected. With two days of rest and plenty of food, she seemed less like a hunted animal. She sat calmly watching the others break camp, plaiting a small bit of her hair over and over again.

The short tempers and grouchiness disappeared when it was time to part. They all hugged more than once. Erna wept, and Elodie's voice shook as she said good-bye. For Abisina, the hardest good-bye was to Kyron.

"We had no idea how far this journey would take us," Abisina said as they clasped arms in the centaur way. "I'm sorry that all of this has happened, Kyron."

"I'm sorry, too," he said gruffly. "But we're doing what your father would want. I'm not sorry about that."

She hugged him one last time.

"Remember," he whispered before he let her go, "we all love you for who you are, not *what* you are. You can trust Findlay."

Abisina nodded. "I—I'll try."

It was a relief to Abisina to be back on the trail; she would finally have a chance to search for signs of Hoysta and Haret.

They had few challenges on the trip to the base of Mounts Arduus and Sumus, where they would begin their ascent to the garden. The weather was hot, but there were plenty of streams, and forage was easy. Abisina made a new splint for her wrist so that she could handle her bow, but most of the überwolves they saw were alone and avoided a fight. Frayda went along at a pace only slightly slower than they would have set themselves. The fairy falcons continued to follow them.

The days in camp, with both Erna and Kyron in on her secret, had given Abisina more opportunities to transform. She could slip away with one of them to gather firewood or forage. Now Abisina worried that she'd have no chance to practice shape-shifting. She had as much control as ever and feared losing that. But she found she was able to transform every night while Findlay and Frayda slept. She was careful that Findlay never woke up to a centaur standing watch where a girl should have been.

As they neared the base of the mountains, Abisina and Findlay discovered how Frayda had survived. They met über-wolves ready to attack, and Frayda scampered up the nearest tree like a squirrel. Her speed and the height she reached were amazing. It took some time to convince her to come down, however, even after they had killed two of the wolves, and the third had fled. Frayda's cries of "No killing!" rang from the tree until Findlay dragged the bodies out of sight. When Frayda did come down, she refused to speak to Findlay, but in a few hours, she had forgotten the incident.

They saw no tracks, abandoned fires, or anything that might feed Abisina's hope that Haret and Hoysta had escaped the überwolves. Abisina refused to believe that they were dead. Not yet. She knew Findlay did, but she also knew he would keep searching as long as she did. Her last hope was that, somehow, they had made their way to the garden.

As they began the climb, Abisina thought about how to get into Vigar's garden. The first time, some property of the necklace had pulled Abisina and Haret through solid rock into the warren of caves and tunnels that led to the garden. The second time, she had fled Watersmeet when she'd discovered that her father was a shape-shifter. But then the necklace had gone dead around her neck. Abisina had spoken to it, yelled at it, pleaded with it. The garden refused to let her in. After hours of trying, she finally squeezed through a tiny fissure.

I'll do it again.

She didn't think beyond that. She ignored the questions

that waited on the other side of the mountains, and refused to consider the pain that would come if Haret and Hoysta were not there. *Get into the garden first,* she told herself and kept climbing.

They reached the rugged cliffs of black-and-white stone. Findlay threw himself down on the gravel, wiping the sweat from his forehead. Frayda also sat down, tucking her legs under her.

"Isn't this the place, Abby?" Findlay asked when she didn't sit down.

"Mmm," she murmured, studying the wall.

"Should we plan to sleep here then?"

She shrugged. "Probably."

Findlay didn't untie the bundles right away. They'd brought a bit of firewood, and he soon had a blaze going up against the cliff wall. "Why don't you sit down and eat," he said, touching her shoulder. "We can wait until morning."

Abisina nodded but kept studying the rock. Findlay left her alone, returning with a cup of yarrow tea—a true gift as they had limited water with them. She smiled her thanks, and he let his hand rest on hers. As Abisina sipped her tea, Frayda curled herself into a ball and fell asleep. Findlay settled down against the cliff and closed his eyes. The final rays of the sun made his hair a reddish gold. Abisina continued tracing the wall's cracks and recesses for some kind of pattern or sign.

The sunlight died, leaving the cliff in darkness. She sat

next to Findlay, and he put his arm around her. "Any luck?" he asked without opening his eyes.

"Not yet."

"We can always get in the way you got in last time, right?"

"Last time, I got in *despite* the garden. It was closed to me. Vigar wasn't there, and I felt none of its peace. It needs to be different this time. For Frayda."

The wind started to howl, and the fire leapt to several times its size, flooding their little camp with light and waking Frayda. They scrambled to their feet.

A glow emanated from within the rock wall.

"Hang on to Frayda," Abisina yelled to Findlay as the wind increased. "And to me! We have to stay together!"

A finger of light reached toward Frayda, looping around the haggard woman's waist and drawing her toward the rock, as if into an embrace.

Abisina grabbed her bag and Findlay's. Findlay reached Frayda and snatched her hand. Abisina threw her arms around Findlay's chest, and the three of them were drawn into the rock.

The wind increased again, and Abisina felt like she was being ripped apart. Findlay gasped.

"Don't let go," Abisina managed. She strained to keep her grip on Findlay, the pain in her wrist unbearable. Her legs screamed with effort, her muscles ready to snap, but she held on as she felt an ancient coldness surround her.

The wind died suddenly. Abisina and Findlay were panting, but Frayda was untouched: her hair unruffled; her clothes, which had looked ready to disintegrate, intact.

They had been drawn inside the mountain.

Abisina expected to be in the center of the caves, a round room with branching tunnels. Instead, they were in a single tunnel with a few alcoves dug in the walls. "This is where we sleep," she whispered, afraid to disturb the silence. Each alcove was outfitted with soft mattresses and warm blankets, as they'd been when she was last here.

She took Frayda's hand and led her to one. Frayda lay down and smiled wearily as Abisina pulled the blanket over her. A small window chiseled into the wall above Frayda's bed let in the sweetness of ripe fruit. The moon had risen, and the rest of the sky was studded with stars.

"Let's go out there, Fin," Abisina whispered, pulling him farther down the tunnel. "We'll let Frayda sleep."

Abisina strolled through the garden, hand in hand with Findlay, and its unique peace settled on her. Plucking fruit, drinking water from the icy spring, lying on the grass to gaze at the full moon—for now, Abisina was happy just to be here. She knew where Vigar's grave was but didn't seek it out. The ache of Haret and Hoysta's loss was there, but muted. She had seen no sign of them in the sleeping alcoves, but she would search tomorrow. Tonight, she wanted to forget her worries.

Findlay kissed her as they lay beside each other. "So you did get us in," he said.

"Not me. Frayda. It's because of her that we're here."

"What a place," he said. "I've never felt like this before."

"Me neither," Abisina murmured. Lying next to Findlay made the garden even sweeter.

Findlay kissed her again. "Abby, I've loved you for so long."

Abisina had once avoided meeting his gaze—*an outcast cannot look at a Vranian*. Now she drank in his soft brown eyes and knew that he was lost in her green ones.

I can tell him, she thought. But she let his lips stop her words.

In the morning, before she opened her eyes, Abisina knew that Vigar was waiting for her. She left the others in their beds and slipped down the tunnel to the garden. Her bare feet left footprints in the dewy grass, but she hardly felt the mountain chill. She had so many questions! Was she right to leave Watersmeet? How should they help Corlin? Was their any hope for Haret and Hoysta?

Will I ever speak to my father again?

She broke into a run. *Maybe today. Maybe now. He could be with her!* Like Rueshlan, Vigar had been killed by Charach. They had both been wearers of the necklace and Keepers of Watersmeet. If Vigar could speak to her here, why couldn't he?

She arrived breathless at the ring of white stones marking Vigar's grave. *Laid there by my father.* She knelt down and put her hand on one of the stones.

At the top of the ring, a rowan tree grew, heavy with white blossoms though it was high summer. Abisina could see scars on the rowan's bark where she had witnessed a minotaur rip off its branches. *The garden is not impregnable,* she reminded herself, but the thought faded away. *It is today.*

Water bubbled from a tiny spring. Abisina sat between the spring and the grave, waiting for Vigar to speak. She was there. Abisina could feel it.

Frayda is welcome here, said a familiar voice.

The hair on Abisina's arms rose, as if a breeze had passed, but the leaves of the rowan didn't quiver. She fought the urge to ask all of her questions at once.

The silence returned.

Vigar was leaving her!

"Wait!" Abisina cried. "Please! I need to talk to you."

The presence continued to recede, and Abisina leapt to her feet. "What about my father? Will I ever speak to my father?" Vigar was almost gone. "If you weren't going to talk to me, why did you let me in here?" she shouted.

I let Frayda in.

And Vigar was gone.

Abisina spun around, glaring at the grave, the rowan, the orchard's wall in the distance. She wanted to lash out—at what? How do you lash out at a sensation? A spirit?

How can she do this to me? I need her! Abisina screamed inside.

She strode away through the trees. "It's like last time," she muttered. "When I most needed help and answers, I got nothing from her. We shouldn't have come. We'd be halfway to the Cleft by now." She was being irrational, but it felt good.

If I had the necklace! The longing she felt for it in her dreams became almost physical. She started to run, but a glint of silvery bark stopped her. A Seldar.

This Seldar stood alone. She'd never seen that before. Its slender trunk grew above most of the fruit trees, before it bent back down, trailing its yellow leaves on the grass.

Abisina sat down next to it, letting the leaves caress her face.

She saw herself standing by Vigar's grave, smugly expecting that Vigar would give her the answers. *I threw a tantrum when I didn't get what I wanted. Just like a child.*

And do I really need her help?

She sighed. *I may not need it, but it would be nice.*

A long drink from the spring refreshed her, and her skin tingled as she splashed her face. She dunked her whole head in the icy water—as she had done with Haret on her first visit to the garden.

Even without Vigar, Abisina knew what she had to do. She would never entirely give up hope for Haret and Hoysta. But once they got Frayda settled, she and Findlay had to continue to Vranlyn.

When Abisina returned to the cave entrance, Findlay was sitting on a patch of grass munching a green fruit, juice dripping down his chin and onto his tunic. More fruit was piled to his right—red, yellow, orange, and, a new one, blue. To his left, a growing pile of pits.

He grinned at her. "These are good," he said around a bite and then swallowed. "You look like you could use one. No sign of Vigar?"

"She was here," Abisina said, joining him in the grass. "She said Frayda was welcome—and not much else."

Findlay sobered. "I'm sorry, Abby. I know that's not what you were hoping for."

She shrugged, but her tears rose. *Stop it,* she told herself.

"So what's next?" Findlay asked.

"We go south," she said. "We'll have to get Frayda settled first, make sure she understands that she can stay here."

Findlay nodded but said nothing. He seemed to sense that she didn't want to talk about Haret and Hoysta.

"Where is Frayda?" Abisina said.

"She was asleep when I came out."

"I'll check on her."

"With no breakfast?" Findlay tossed her the blue fruit, flat on the ends and thick in the center.

Abisina returned to the alcoves. Frayda breathed deeply in her sleep. Abisina grabbed their satchels, thinking they could go through them on the grass and figure out what to leave for Frayda. She also wanted to wash more thoroughly in the spring. *Though the grime on my ankles and neck would make Hoysta proud,* she thought with a pang of sadness.

By the time the sun was directly overhead, Abisina and Findlay had finished all their chores. Findlay had explored the tunnels while Abisina bathed, and Abisina had taken a nap in the sunlight while Findlay bathed. Despite the disappointment of the morning, the garden worked its magic; Abisina felt content. Even her centaur-self behind the wall seemed at ease.

She was considering taking another nap—Findlay was already asleep next to her on the grass—when she sat up quickly. Something—or *someone*—was in the garden.

She found him on the gnarled bench built around the base of a tree.

"Haret!"

She threw her arms around him as the dwarf rose to his feet. He swayed at her embrace—Haret, who had always stood as solid as stone. "Are you hurt? What's wrong? Where's Hoysta?"

"In the tunnels . . ." He sank onto the bench, and Abisina noticed his bandaged hands. He tucked them out of sight. "Where are the others?" he asked.

"Findlay's asleep." She sat next to him.

"That's all?"

"Kyron, Elodie, and Erna are going through the Cleft."

"Why?"

"We found Frayda."

Haret's black eyes widened.

"She—she's gone mad, I think. We decided to bring her here where she can find peace."

"Peace," he echoed bitterly.

"Haret, what happened?"

"I wish I could lie to you," he said with a sigh. "When Grandmother was captured by the überwolves, I went after her. Thank the Earth they prefer live prey. There were three. I shot one, then I was throttled from behind by one that I hadn't seen. I woke up slung over a wolf's back. Grandmother was unconscious on another wolf, and I knew she was almost gone. So, I fought them."

"Three überwolves at once?"

Haret nodded. "They'd taken my arrows, but I had my knife. I killed the first easily. Got the second in the belly. The last tossed Grandmother aside, ready to fight. I threw my knife."

Abisina gasped. "If you'd missed . . ." It was one of the rules on patrol: Don't throw your last weapon; if you miss, you can't outrun an überwolf.

Haret wiped a hand over his face. "But I didn't. Thank the Earth."

"Why didn't you come back to us? You couldn't have been that far."

"I couldn't leave Grandmother. She had so many wounds,

but the worst was a gash across her wrist. I tried to stop the bleeding—tried everything. Then, I tied off her hand."

Abisina gasped again.

"It worked, but—in the end, I had to get my knife from the body of the überwolf. She woke up when I started to cut, and I . . . knocked her out again. It saved her life but not her hand."

Haret's head sank to his chest, and tears fell onto his beard.

"Haret," Abisina said, touching his shoulder. "You had to. She's *alive*."

He raised his head. "No. Don't stop me until I've told you all of it."

Abisina swallowed. "Go on."

He drew a ragged breath. "By the time she could travel, I knew you'd be gone. We couldn't go to Watersmeet, so I decided to come here. For the peace." He spat the last word. "On the way, I had to pass . . . the Mines."

His bandaged hands, his anguish. It all made sense now. "Oh, Haret!"

He grimaced as if her cry had hurt him.

The dwarves called it Obriumlust: the desire for the Obrium metal that drove some of them mad. Haret's ancestors, and most of the dwarves in Watersmeet, had come from a great city built in the roots of the Obrun Mountains. The wealth of the city came from the only known lode of Obrium, and the dwarves were masters of Obrium craft. But a catastrophic earthquake destroyed the city. Impenetrable rock rose from somewhere deep in the earth and blocked all access to the city and the lode. The longing for this metal never left the dwarves. They'd get to the sealed entrance to the Mines and dig. When their tools broke, they'd dig with their hands—not eating or sleeping—until their hearts gave out. Haret lost his parents to the Obriumlust.

It had seized Haret soon after he and Abisina had arrived in Watersmeet. The other dwarves saved him, but he'd been crushed to learn that he could be so "weak." And now, it had happened again.

"How—how did you get away?" Abisina asked.

"I dug for three straight days. Grandmother tried every-thing—reasoning, threatening, cajoling. Weak as she was, she tried force. But I couldn't even *see* her. There was nothing but the pull. At last, she put herself between me and the wall. I—I—Oh, the Earth!" Haret's voice broke. "I struck her," he whispered, then sat up straighter. "No, I will say it all. I will hide nothing." He was speaking to himself now.

"I beat her. She hit her head. I cut her cheek open—"

"Haret—" Abisina wanted to spare him, but he went on.

"I knocked out her last tooth, broke ribs, her other wrist." He choked. "And then raised my hand—to do what? Would I have killed her, Abisina?" He searched her face.

"No, Haret," she said softly.

"I finally *saw* her," he said. "She lay there, staring up at me, accepting. . . . My mind cleared. I wanted to run." Tears coursed down his face. "I wanted to get out of there before it seized me again. I almost left her. But then I picked her up and carried her out." He cradled his arms as if he held her again. "I brought her here." He stopped, then lifted his face to Abisina. "Now you know what a monster I am."

She pulled him to her and let him sob. Findlay came toward them, grinning with happiness at Haret's arrival, but his face fell, and, without a word, he slipped away.

The dwarf quieted. "I thought I had conquered it," he said. "But it is part of me forever."

Abisina helped him to his feet. "You both need to rest. Let's find Hoysta."

Findlay was pacing near the cave entrance. "Hoysta's in there sleeping," he said as they approached. "She's been beaten!"

"Tell him, Abisina," Haret said wearily, and went into the tunnels.

She let herself cry as she told Haret's story to Findlay.

But she stopped before she got to Haret's final words: "It is part of me forever."

CHAPTER XVII

FRAYDA DIDN'T WAKE FOR THREE DAYS. WHEN SHE DID, her eyes were clearer, and she called Abisina by her name for the first time. She mentioned Watersmeet, but she didn't refer to Rueshlan in any way.

Haret and Hoysta also slept the days away. The pain on Haret's face faded, replaced by a sadness that Abisina feared might never leave.

Hoysta, too, carried a sadness, but it was all for Haret. She dismissed the loss of her hand, pointing out how well Haret had sewn her up. "Grandson of a healer. You can always tell." But she lowered her voice when she spoke to Abisina about the Mines, the one time Haret left her alone. "Can't forgive himself, even though I've forgiven him."

Haret didn't speak about what happened. Abisina poulticed his bruises, rebandaged his hands daily, and respected his silence.

She and Findlay needed to continue the journey; Kyron and the others should have reached the Cleft. But she couldn't leave Haret so beaten down.

They gathered to share their supper on the bench where Abisina had found Haret. Frayda hummed nearby as she strolled through the fruit trees.

Hoysta had taken up a handful of dirt, as she did before every meal, to thank the Earth for its gifts. She let the dark soil trail through her fingers and announced: "You folk need to get going. Frayda should not be left alone. She might get lost in the tunnels and never get out. I like these tunnels and caves, even though they're *up* in the mountains. I'll stay here, tend to Frayda, enjoy the smell of earth again."

"But Grandmother," Haret said, "our folk are rebuilding Stonedun. We . . . we planned to see it together."

Hoysta sighed. "I'm tired, Grandson. And old—I've lost track of how many winters I have. My home destroyed, the journey to Watersmeet, the battle—it's taken a toll."

"Then I'll stay with you," Haret said, pleading.

"Haret," said Hoysta gently, "you have work to do. So do I. Frayda needs healing, and I'm a healer."

"Plenty in Vranlyn will need healing."

"And you have Abisina for that." She touched his bandaged hands. "Please, Haret, let me rest."

Haret bowed his head.

"Thank you, dearie," she said, her voice husky.

Haret strode off toward the tunnels.

"We always return to the Earth when we're troubled," Hoysta said. "A dwarf's strength."

"We'll miss you, Hoysta," Findlay said. "We just got you back!"

Hoysta chuckled. "I'll miss you, too, dearies. But it's better this way. Haret needs time without me as a constant reminder. You'll look after him, won't you?" She lifted her craggy face to them, her cheeks wet with tears.

Abisina hugged Hoysta to her. "We'll look after him as if we were you."

They left the next morning. Abisina didn't know if Frayda understood what was happening, but she hugged Abisina and Findlay tightly.

With a dwarf's instinct, Haret found a tunnel that would lead them out. Abisina and Findlay went a few steps down it, leaving Hoysta and Haret to say good-bye.

"We're saying good-bye to the north," Findlay said. "At least for now."

Abisina nodded. "Once we cross these mountains, something else begins, doesn't it?" She felt a flutter in her stomach. "I wish I were sure that we're making the right choice." She remembered her hopes as she arrived at the garden. "Maybe you can never be sure. About anything."

"I'm sure about one thing," Findlay said, pulling her to him.

Haret strode down the tunnel, Hoysta's axe tucked in his belt. "Let's go," he muttered as he brushed past them.

They emerged into the bright light of a narrow plateau. To their right, the Obruns marched to the Mountains Eternal. In the near distance, a double rainbow created by the mist rising from the waterfall marked the arrival of the River Deliverance—or the Great River, as it was known in the south—through the mountains.

Though it was sunny along the Obruns, clouds shrouded the Mountains Eternal. Abisina had never seen their peaks. The jagged slopes created a wall of stone, a barrier to the west that was uncrossable.

Except for Vran and Vigar. It wasn't the first time Abisina had been struck by the strange coincidence that both Vran and Vigar had crossed these peaks from the west: Vigar founding Watersmeet; Vran founding Vranham, the first of the Vranian villages. What kind of world lay beyond that mountain range to give rise to such different leaders? What had enabled two humans to cross mountains of such dizzying heights?

My father did it, too. Rueshlan had never described his early life—where he came from, what he did before arriving at Watersmeet, how he had crossed the mountains. *Something else I'll never get the chance to ask.*

Halfway up the mountains a deep fissure stood out against the lighter stone. Abisina might not have noticed it—there were crevasses, ravines, and rifts all over the mountains— but this one had a different quality. It was much larger, and the blackness was not just darkness; it was more of a void. And something—lots of somethings—moved around it as if thousands of tiny ants swarmed a dropped piece of honey cake. She had once seen a dragon fly to the Mountains Eternal. But dragons were known for being solitary. What could this be?

"We have to climb down that?" Findlay asked as he peered over the edge of the cliff, calling Abisina back to their immediate problem. She knew the cliff could be scaled. She and Haret had come up it once. But no matter how long Abisina and Findlay paced back and forth, they couldn't find a foothold for the first step. Haret tried to help, but the height made him so dizzy, he had to step away to settle his stomach.

By noon, they all sat dejectedly on the ground. Somewhere inside the stone fortress behind them, Hoysta and Frayda wandered in the lush garden, but here it was dry and cold. Findlay flung pebbles over the ledge. Haret had his eyes closed, but his jaw was tensed. Abisina fixed her gaze on the cliff's edge.

"I could find the path if I had the necklace!" she exploded.

"You said the same thing on the other side," Findlay pointed out. "But you found a way in."

"How did you do it?" Haret growled.

"Frayda. We held onto her when she was let in," Abisina said.

Haret squinted at her. "Well, we don't have Frayda now."

"I know," Abisina snapped.

"So—any other ideas?" Findlay asked.

They went through the possibilities again. Finally, they decided to lower Abisina a few lengths down the cliff face with a bit of rope. Perhaps a new view would help her find the path. Findlay was tying one end of the rope, and Abisina had just cinched the other around her waist when a bird about as big as her hand swooped in and hovered around her head, calling frantically. Abisina ducked.

"Hey!" Findlay waved his hands around Abisina's head.

The bird kept diving between them, flapping its wings and plucking at Abisina's hair. Once it was sure it had their attention, the bird alit on a rock and fixed them with bright, black eyes. It was a kestrel.

It fluttered to the lip of the cliff, wagged its head at them, and hopped forward, as if it were about to fly off. Instead, it hopped over the edge, landing on an unseen perch, its head peeping over the top. The bird chittered and hopped again until only its crown was visible. Then, it bounded back toward them, its head and body reappearing.

"It—it found the path," Abisina breathed.

"How?" Findlay asked. They crept closer and watched the bird hop down an almost invisible shelf of rock. The striations on the cliff face and the sun glittering off bits of mica made it hard to see. And if she had, Abisina would've dismissed it as too narrow to stand on.

"Do you think . . ."

"Oh, no," Findlay groaned.

Haret joined them at the cliff's edge. He took one look and said, "I will never go down that."

"But that's what the bird is telling us!" Abisina said.

"The *bird* is telling us?" Haret barked. "Since when have birds told us anything?"

Another groan from Findlay. "Since the kestrel outside Watersmeet," he said.

"Exactly! It's Neriah helping us," said Abisina.

"How do we know it's Neriah's bird? It could be one of Reava's." Findlay glanced at the ledge and shivered.

"Reava seems to use falcons, and we haven't seen any since we got to the garden," Abisina said.

"I don't care if the Fairy Mother herself is offering to carry me down," Haret declared. "I will not set foot on that ledge."

"You've done it before, Haret," Abisina reminded him.

Their deliberations were too slow for the kestrel. With a shrill *klee*, it took flight and dove at their heads again.

"All right, all right," Abisina told the bird. "I'll show them." She scooted to the edge and rested her feet in the place the bird had perched.

"I've got you, Abby," Findlay said, grabbing onto the rope still tied around her waist.

By turning sideways, two-thirds of each foot was on rock. She slid her feet forward until her thighs rested on the cliff. If she went any farther she would have to stand. Below her a field of sharp boulders waited.

The bird landed at her feet and looked at her brightly. It hopped a little farther, and Abisina took a deep breath and stood. Behind her, Haret moaned. She moved her feet farther along, the kestrel hopping ahead, and the ledge widened.

"I don't know why we couldn't see it. It gets wider almost right away." She guessed it was some trick of the light and the colors of the rock. "All you have to do is watch the kestrel," she called up. The bird stayed in front of her, checking every few steps to see if she was coming.

"Abisina!" Findlay peered down at her. "I think I can do it, if I look at you—not down," he said. "But what about Haret?"

Abisina slid back up the pathway. At a cry from the bird, she said, "I need to get my friends." The kestrel followed her.

Haret was unpacking his bag, ready to give his gear to them and return to the garden. It took Abisina almost an hour to convince him that they needed him in the south. "We have to reach out to the dwarves at Stonedun!" she told him. "Who else can do that? And you know the terrain in the south much better than I do."

In the end, it wasn't her persuasion, but her muttering that she'd never known a dwarf so willing to run away from a challenge that got him to throw on his satchel and stamp his way to the edge. She'd been afraid to push him after what he'd been through, but now she wondered if her coddling over the last few days had made him doubt himself more.

They started down: Abisina first, led by the bird; then Haret, holding onto her waist; and then Findlay, with his hands on Haret's shoulders. Abisina was so focused on helping Haret that she didn't have time to think of herself.

They reached the bottom. At Abisina's first step onto the

rocky ground, the kestrel took to the air, and with a last *klee*, sped off to the northeast, the setting sun gilding its wings with fire. Above them, the same light stained the cliffs reddish-orange and erased the path they had just come down.

Haret sank to the ground, not looking like he'd be getting up anytime soon. Abisina and Findlay joined him, pulled out their water skins and some of the garden's fruit, and watched the sunset. They could see nothing of the country they were heading into, only the acres of boulders in front of them.

Findlay nudged her. Haret was asleep, with his brow creased. Abisina hoped he wasn't dreaming of the Mines.

"Do you know where we're going from here?" Findlay whispered.

"Vranlyn was the second of the Vranian villages. The first, Vranham, is on the banks of the Great River. Vranlyn will be east of it."

"Well, the river's west, so we should head southwest?"

"No," Abisina said emphatically. "Giant's Cairn is due south, and I don't want to go anywhere near it. We'll go west first." Giant's Cairn was an enormous pile of rocks that served as a hideout for the centaur Icksyon and his herd; it was the last place that she'd had all ten of her toes. Ever since she had considered going south, Icksyon had been in the back of her thoughts, slipping in and out of the shadows.

Findlay knew the story and said nothing.

"I'm worried about getting Haret down the rest of this mountain," Abisina went on. "After these boulders, we'll come to the Mines' southern entrance. Haret could feel the Obriumlust again."

"Can we avoid the Mines?"

"I don't know another way down. We'll need to keep a close watch on Haret. If he so much as twitches in that direction, we'll have to drag him away."

Findlay looked doubtful—the Obriumlust often brought an uncanny strength—but again held his tongue.

Abisina yawned. They each wrapped themselves in their cloaks and snuggled in together, their body heat welcome in the cool mountain air. Abisina fell asleep with her head on Findlay's shoulder.

When Haret woke in the morning, he said little, ate nothing, and his face was pinched. Abisina and Findlay hurried through their breakfast, as eager as Haret to put the Mines behind them.

By midafternoon they had crossed the expanse of boulders and began to climb down a slope of loose gravel. Haret stopped. The Mines were close. He squatted down to dig in the gravel at his feet. Abisina panicked. *He's trying to dig to the Obrium!*

But before she could say anything, Haret scraped up a handful of dirt and held it to his nose. He inhaled deeply. "The Earth," he whispered. He stood up and said, "I'm ready."

He went down the slope, hand clutched to his lips as if tasting the dirt. Abisina and Findlay followed him past the

Mines' entrance, a yawning hole in the side of the mountain. As soon as Haret's feet touched the cracked paving stones of the ancient dwarf road leading to the Mines, he started to run away from the mountains. Though his legs were short, he was quickly out of sight. Abisina and Findlay chased after him.

"He'll stay on the road," Abisina said, slowing. Her centaur-self had stirred as she picked up speed. "He just needs to get away. We don't have to keep up."

Findlay slowed, too. "We made it," he panted. "Maybe that will be our biggest challenge between here and Vranlyn."

But they both knew better.

Haret was waiting for them at the end of the road. The paving stones became more and more broken until they petered out all together, ending in an alpine meadow, the last open land before a dense forest. The green grass and wild flowers contrasted with the gloom of tall trees.

Haret's face was drawn, and he had circles around his eyes, but he smiled at them and held up two squirrels he had shot. "I'm waiting for the pot," he said, reaching for Abisina's bag. "We're going to have a real supper tonight."

Abisina did her best to join in Haret's celebration, but they were in Icksyon's country now, and she kept straining her ears for the drum of hooves.

"I saw plenty of evidence of überwolves," Haret said. "We should post a watch and build the fire higher."

"Abisina and I will get the firewood," Findlay offered.

"Abisina should not be hauling firewood with that wrist," Haret grumbled.

"It's a lot better." Abisina demonstrated how easily she could move it. "The garden must have hurried its healing."

"Hmph," Haret snorted, as Findlay took Abisina's hand. "Keep your eyes out for wood—not each other," he said, but Abisina caught a quick grin beneath his beard.

The meadow was bathed in gold. They wandered along the forest's edge, staying in the open where the late-day sun took the chill out of the air.

"There's what we need." Findlay pointed to a large fallen branch. Picking up a limb, he pulled it farther into the meadow and began to cut it into usable lengths with Haret's axe.

A faint light glimmered amidst the trees. Abisina listened. It was a peaceful afternoon. She called to Findlay, "I think I see a Seldar grove. I won't go far." He waved back as he wiped the sweat on his face.

She wove among the trees: firs, beech, oak, and maple. Glancing behind her, she could see the meadow, could hear the dull thud of Findlay's axe. Was the light she saw a grove or just a break in the trees? *A bit farther*, she told herself.

Snap! A branch cracked to her right, startling her. *Probably an animal. If I could find a deer—or any hoofed animal—I might be able to ask about überwolves or centaurs around here.* Ahead of her, the light was gone. *Must have been a sunbeam.*

She headed back to Findlay. His axe! She couldn't hear it! She broke into a run. *Maybe he's resting.* She had gone farther into the wood than she thought, and now trees and branches and roots blocked her way out.

"Findlay!" she yelled.

She heard hoofbeats.

Reaching the meadow, she raced into the open. A huge black centaur barreled down on her, lips twisted in a malicious grin—and Findlay, limp, slung over his shoulder. The centaur had a broadsword in his hand, but Findlay's body blocked him from slashing at Abisina as he galloped past.

She nocked an arrow, shot, and hit his haunch. His steps faltered, but he kept going, swerving closer to the trees.

Her next shot was more difficult. In her worry that she might hit Findlay, she missed.

He's getting away! The wall between her human and centaur shapes slipped. She fought it—*Findlay will know*—but truth conquered fear. *Findlay will die.*

Power surged from her rear legs as she galloped after Findlay. When she was in range, she drew back her arrow, focusing on keeping her shoulders even, her hands steady, regretting how little practice she'd had shooting as a centaur. The arrow sailed over the black centaur's head.

I'll get one more chance, she thought as she drew another arrow. Her strength was waning.

With a burst of speed, she pulled closer to the black centaur, her arrow in his haunch slowing him down. Findlay stirred, tried to struggle. *Not now,* she begged. She was going to shoot for the centaur's torso, but with Findlay moving, it was too dangerous. She was forced to take a less deadly shot at the centaur's haunches. She let fly—and hit him, again on the right leg. This time the arrow went deeper.

The centaur kept on moving, but Findlay used his captor's broken rhythm to twist away, and he tumbled to the ground. Abisina raced past him, ready to stop and shoot again if the centaur turned.

But he'd had enough. He galloped on, blood glistening on his rear leg, his pace uneven, his whole body shuddering each time his injured leg hit the dirt.

Abisina reeled back to where Findlay lay on the grass.

Is he—

Findlay lifted his head and shook it before raising his eyes to her.

"Get away!" he screamed.

Chapter XVIII

In an instant, Abisina transformed. Findlay dropped his head to the ground again. She should go to him, check his wounds—but those words, *Get away,* stopped her. She was back in Vranille: the taunts of the other children, the loneliness, the self-hatred. For all her resolutions and Kyron's reassurances, deep down she had never wanted anyone to know. Especially not Findlay.

Haret ran up. The confusion on his face told her that he had seen her as a centaur. "How—" Haret began, but he didn't go on. He knelt next to Findlay and carefully prodded his skull and neck. Findlay winced at one spot. "It's his head."

"I'll get my medicines," Abisina said mechanically.

"Build up the fire," Haret called after her. "I'll bring him back."

Abisina ached all over as she ran, and she let the pain drown out the memory of Findlay's cry. She stopped at the fallen tree and gathered the cut wood and Haret's axe.

The fire was roaring by the time Findlay wobbled into the campsite, supported by Haret. Without a word, she handed Haret some salve and her cloak. The dwarf wrapped Findlay in her cloak and his own and lay him down near the fire. Abisina had brewed yarrow tea, and Haret spooned some into Findlay's mouth, only to have him vomit it up.

"Keep trying," Abisina said as she picked up Haret's axe and headed to the fallen tree. She chopped and lugged wood until nightfall, bringing far more than they could burn.

Forced back to the fire by darkness and her aching wrist, Abisina sat as far from Findlay as she could. He had slept fitfully through the early evening, waking as the moon rose. He managed to keep down a few mouthfuls of tea and could sit for a short time without support, but he didn't speak. He was settling down to sleep again, when he picked up Abisina's cloak and studied it. He said slowly, "You need this."

"No," she said. "It's important you stay warm." He lay down and fell asleep. He had spoken to her at last, but he hadn't looked at her.

Haret and Abisina sat up late, Haret checking Findlay regularly, Abisina stoking the fire. The night was half gone when Haret laid a hand on her arm. "You should sleep, human," he said.

"Don't call me that. You saw what I am."

Haret sat down next to her. "How long has this been happening?"

"On the journey back from the Motherland, Kyron got stuck in the Fens. He almost drowned, and when I tried to pull him out, it happened."

"And you've been keeping it secret?"

"I had to." Her words barely escaped her tightening throat. "His face! He was *afraid* of me, Haret. I knew this would happen if he—if anyone found out."

"Human," Haret said, "he had been captured by a centaur. He didn't recognize you. He thought you were one of them."

"I *am* one of them!"

"Is that what this is about? You think that your physical shape changes who you are?"

"Doesn't it? Do you know what I was thinking the whole way to the Motherland—every day, maybe every hour? I was thinking it had actually happened to me. Somebody *loved* me. Haret, I never thought that was possible. Now, that's gone."

Haret sighed and rubbed his beard.

"Say it," she demanded.

"You're not going to like this," he said, "but you need to hear it. You are more Vranian than you realize. And you're a hypocrite."

"What?"

"You left Watersmeet because it was not the place your father helped build. You were right. So right, that all of us followed you. But *you* don't believe in Watersmeet yourself." Abisina stared at him. "Hiding what you are from Findlay.

From me. Sometimes you act like Rueshlan's daughter—when you stood between the armies and stopped the battle—"

"That was the necklace," Abisina protested. "The necklace worked *through* me."

"Like it's working through Glynholly?"

"What do you mean? It's done nothing for Glynholly."

"Exactly. The necklace belongs to you. Vigar, Rueshlan, your mother—*that* is your heritage. Start acting like it!"

Haret stalked away from her into the darkness. She wanted to be mad at him—*that stupid, opinionated, grouchy dwarf!*—but what if he were right?

She dreamt of the necklace all the time—as if it were calling to her. Was that her heritage?

What if I can't live up to it? What if I'm not strong enough?

Findlay rested the next day. Abisina was desperate to wander off by herself and think, but Haret had other ideas. "You're the healer. You look after Findlay." He set off with his bow.

By midafternoon, Findlay was on his feet—although wobbly—and had kept down a whole bowl of gruel.

Haret came back, and threw two rabbits on the ground. "They were hard to get. The überwolves know we're here. The area is crawling with them now. No one should go off alone. Had to do your trick of climbing trees, human." He shuddered. "No new centaur tracks," he added.

"How many centaurs were there?" Findlay asked. "I can't

remember much of what happened. There was the one who got me, but was there another one? I thought—it's all confused."

Haret cut his eyes at Abisina, waiting.

He doesn't remember. Findlay would never have to know. How easy it would be to say there was one centaur! She could keep her secret.

And continue to be a hypocrite.

"There were two centaurs," Abisina said dully. "The one who captured you . . . and me."

"What?"

"I—I'm a shape-shifter, Findlay. Like my father."

Findlay gaped. "You're like Rueshlan?"

Abisina nodded.

"You've known for—how long?"

"Since Midsummer."

"And you haven't told anyone?"

"Kyron was there the first time it happened. And Erna knows. I transformed when the überwolves took her."

"Why didn't you tell . . . anyone else?"

"I was afraid. I thought it would make folk see me differently."

"Of course it will make us see you differently, Abisina! It's a big change. For you. For all of us. But I think we—I think *I* deserved your trust." Two spots of color flamed on Findlay's cheeks.

"I'm sorry," Abisina said softly. "Growing up in Vranille . . . It stays with me."

"I understand that. I really do. But by coming on this journey, I've put my trust in you. Left my family. The least you could do is trust me as much."

Abisina nodded, unable to speak.

"I—I need to lie down again," Findlay said, and he stumbled. Abisina reached out to catch him, but he stepped back. He lowered himself to the ground, wrapped himself up in his cloak, and shut his eyes.

They had to spend another day in the meadow before Findlay could travel. The tension was thick for all of them. Twice they had to defend themselves against überwolves. This kept them all close to the campsite—and each other.

They broke camp on a cool, overcast morning. The temperature would make Findlay's first day back on the trail easier. Abisina and Haret had shared out Findlay's gear so he would have nothing to carry. They went west along the edge of the forest where the walking was easier, until the meadow met the forest, and they had to plunge in.

The strain between Abisina and Findlay eased a little once they were on the trail. They made a point of speaking to each other; Abisina checked the lump on Findlay's head, and Findlay carefully left his boots next to where she slept every other day. But they no longer walked side by side, shared a secret smile when they touched by mistake, or sought each other out to share a particularly beautiful mountain overlook.

Haret was more garrulous at meals to cover the uncomfortable silences. He told jokes that Abisina had heard several times, and he laughed too loudly if either she or Findlay forced themselves to offer a joke in return. It was almost a relief when they crossed the tracks of überwolves, centaurs, or minotaurs because they could focus on something outside of their group. Though Abisina no longer needed to hide, she transformed away from the other two, and more and more often she offered to go ahead and scout. If she hoped that Findlay would come with her, she told herself that it was better he didn't.

Abisina's only comfort was that she now felt completely in control of her shape-shifting.

As they went first west and then south, they found little game, and they had numerous skirmishes with überwolf packs. They took to sleeping in the trees, which Haret hated, and often woke to silver shapes prowling around their roosts. They retrieved their arrows from killed überwolves when possible, but they lost or broke enough that they had to stop for an entire day to make more.

Abisina worried about Icksyon, especially when they found hoofprints, but Haret assured her that from what he knew, Icksyon's herd never came this far south. "He stays near the Cairn."

Abisina hoped he was right. She had recognized the centaur that attacked Findlay. She had seen him when Icksyon held her captive in Giant's Cairn.

In the piedmont below the Obruns, they tramped through forests, into valleys, over small mountains, and across green meadows that made Abisina long to gallop. After spending days in a dark forest alive with überwolves, they stepped into the open space at the lip of a gorge, a river running far below.

What a relief to be in the light! But the gorge was too wide and deep to cross. Haret knew of the place—the dwarves called the river Couldin—but he had never seen it himself and wasn't sure where they could cross.

"To the east, it's not much of a river, and there's no gorge," he said. "But Vranlyn should be west of here. Let's head that way; we'll find a place to cross."

They set off. They were two weeks from the autumnal equinox and there was a touch of fall in the air. As if to prove that fall was on its way, a misty rain set in with a chilling wind that chafed their wet hands and faces.

By midafternoon, the rain had stopped, and the sun was trying to break through the clouds. The gorge had widened, the river so far below, it was a distant murmur. Abisina peered over the edge and smelled damp and decay. The walls were rutted with stone outcroppings, recesses, and entrances to caves.

"It's so deep," she said.

Haret stood away from the edge. "Soft rock here," he muttered. "A lot of it. The river eats through it like an axe on a rotted tree."

"Listen," Findlay whispered.

Something was coming toward them from the brush on their right.

To their left was the precipice. The cliff top provided no

cover. Where could they go? Whatever was coming, it sounded big.

Haret threw himself down and pressed his ear to the ground. "Centaurs," he hissed. "Eight or ten."

The cliff below offered ledges and caves. *Our best option,* Abisina thought. Seeing nothing at first, she jogged along the edge a few paces. She spotted a ledge with room for all three of them. Findlay was tall enough that he might be able to get to it.

She beckoned to him, and he understood immediately when she pointed at the ledge. He lay on his belly, swung his legs over the side, and slid backward until he supported himself on his elbows. "Not quite there," he whispered. Abisina got on her belly and clutched his hands. Findlay inched down, hanging from Abisina's hands. She slipped on the wet stone and scrabbled for a toehold. If she couldn't stop herself, she and Findlay would both slide over the cliff. She gritted her teeth, pulling against Findlay's weight. But now Findlay's hands were sliding out of hers! She had no idea how close he was to the ledge. If she lost him . . . Hands clamped around her ankles—*Haret!*—but then Findlay slipped from her grasp. Abisina stifled a scream.

She scrambled to the edge and looked over.

Findlay stood on the ledge, his face white.

The crashing in the brush got closer. Haret still crouched behind her, frozen with fear. "Not now, dwarf," she growled, and her words woke him from his trance. Haret lay on his belly and inched backward, his hands in Abisina's. With Findlay below to guide him, it should have been easier, but as Haret's waist reached the cliff's edge, he panicked. His fingers dug into Abisina's wrists, and he uttered a strangled cry as his chest scraped down the cliff. Haret became dead weight, pulling her forward.

Findlay commanded, "Let go!" Haret clung to her a moment longer, then dropped.

Abisina couldn't stop to find out if he'd made it. She had seconds to get herself onto the ledge. She lay on the cliff, legs over the side, but she had nothing to grab, nothing to keep her from falling past the ledge, past her friends, into the abyss.

"Keep coming," Findlay whispered urgently from below, but Abisina couldn't move.

The first of the centaurs broke through the trees.

Icksyon!

The giant, white centaur. Grimy, knotted beard; sacks of fat hanging off his chest and belly. Red-rimmed, insane eyes. As he stepped into the light of the cliff, he squinted and held up a hand as big as a paddle to shade his gaze.

Abisina saw the necklace of human toes before she let herself fall.

CHAPTER XIX

THERE WAS NOTHINGNESS. THEN HER FEET SMACKED against rock as Findlay grabbed the front of her tunic. Her toes gripped the ledge. A desperate but silent battle ensued as Findlay fought to pull her in without losing his own balance. Haret clutched Findlay around the waist, trying to anchor him. Abisina's satchel swung out behind her, and as Findlay jerked her in, one of the mugs shook loose, arcing out into the chasm. All three waited for the pottery to shatter on the rocks, but the clatter of hooves on the cliff above them drowned out any other noise.

Abisina clung to Findlay as she stared up. The jut of the cliff, which had made reaching it so difficult, now provided some cover from anyone who looked down. Behind the ledge, a small space was hollowed out, and Abisina and Findlay pressed into it. Haret huddled next to them.

"Well?" came the rumble of Icksyon's voice—a sound

Abisina would never forget. "You said they were walking the cliff, Madra. Where are they?"

"Along here . . . somewhere, Lord Icksyon," a nervous voice answered. "I tracked them to this gorge, and they've been heading west, making for the Great River."

"Does anyone see them?" Icksyon's light tone belied the threat underneath.

"Nothing up ahead!" a centaur called.

"Or behind!" cried another.

"And tracks, Madra? What do you see?" Icksyon continued.

"They're hard to read on stone. And with the rain . . ." She trailed off, and Abisina could imagine Icksyon's wild eyes boring into her.

"Madra . . ." Icksyon paused, and the tension grew. "A *centaur* wounded Murklern. But you found tracks from humans and a mud-man."

"A centaur follows them, or shadows them—at times." Madra's nervousness had increased.

"At times?" Icksyon asked, cold and mocking.

Madra didn't answer.

"Why did you bring us out here, Madra? We fought our way through the woods—and for what?"

"You told me to track them," Madra whined. "It wasn't easy. They were in the forest. There are other tracks, uneven ground, tree roots, and—"

"No more excuses." Goose pimples rose on Abisina's arms.

"You said you could deliver us the quarry, but you're not even sure what creatures we're chasing."

The shuffling as the centaurs shifted their weight was replaced by more deliberate hoof-falls. Then it grew still, as if the centaurs were poised, waiting.

"I swear, Lord Icksyon." Madra was panicked. "Two humans and a mud-man. I'm sure of it. But there are also hoofprints. They come and go, but—"

Madra broke off with a cry, and a rain of gravel fell past their hiding place.

Oh, the Earth! Abisina thought. *They've got her at the edge.*

"Please, Lord Icksyon," Madra begged. "I'll start at the road again. I'll—"

"I'm afraid it's too late," Icksyon said. "I was forced to kill Murklern. I didn't want to. He was strong and useful, but he returned to us—useless. And I cannot allow any centaurs to get away with an attack on one of mine. You had your chance to find this traitor, Madra, but it's time to say good-bye."

Abisina heard the centaurs move, there was scrabbling at the edge, and a large shape dropped past. A scream echoed off the chasm's wall. Then stopped.

Abisina and her friends pressed harder against the cliff.

"Edom, you take your group to the east. I'll continue with the others to the west," Icksyon said, as if nothing had happened. "The humans and mud-man may know something about this centaur. At the very least, the humans' toes will add to my collection."

Hoofbeats receded in either direction. When Abisina allowed herself to breathe again, she noticed that her cheeks were wet. Findlay broke their huddle. But their legs remained touching as they sat on the ledge—the strain between them gone. Abisina knew things couldn't return to how they were, but she was grateful to have Findlay next to her.

They considered how they might get back to the cliff top. Haret's contribution was a loud "No!" when Findlay suggested that Haret stand on his shoulders. Once one of them got to the top, the rope would help the other two, but how could they get the first one up?

As the gulf grew darker below them, Findlay reexamined a series of hand- and footholds to the right of the ledge—cracks and juts they had rejected earlier.

"I think I better try," Findlay said, and Abisina winced. "Try" implied that falling was a possibility. But there seemed no other choice, and Findlay's height gave him the best chance of success. Abisina wanted him to tie the rope around his waist so that she could catch him if he fell, but he refused: "I would pull you down with me."

Findlay did well at first. He had to spread his legs and arms apart to reach the best holds, but he inched upward steadily, like a spider, until the cliff began to angle out above him. Abisina knew this moment would come—Findlay would cling to the rock while the weight of his own body pulled him off it—and she fought the urge to turn away. His legs and hands shook with the effort. As he neared the top, he groped blindly on the cliff. His right foot slipped off a tiny outcropping, just as he found a hold, and Abisina cried out before she realized that he was pulling himself up. When his legs disappeared over the lip, she leaned against the cliff, weak with relief.

He poked his head back over. "I made it," he said, voice trembling, "but I need to rest. My hands are cramped, and my legs won't hold my weight. As soon as I can stand, I'll anchor the rope."

Abisina sat down to wait. Haret looked catatonic.

Findlay wasn't ready until the sun went down. Before he had scaled the cliff, they'd decided to get Haret up next, worried that he'd be too distracted by the height to tie himself into the rope alone. Haret was supposed to help Findlay by climbing where he could and using his arms to pull himself up, but he hung on the line like a dead weight. Findlay lowered him down. "I can't do it after that climb," he called to Abisina. "I'll get some vine. Then you'll have to tie him in and I'll help you climb. Once you get up, we can lift him together."

Abisina climbed up the cliff as the moon rose. Her progress was slow in the tricky light, but it helped that she couldn't see the depth of the abyss below her. She convinced herself that she was close to the ground. Her injured wrist ached, but with the vine, Findlay's help, and careful balance, she made it. Getting Haret up was quicker, but the dwarf was completely done for when he landed at the top, reeled in like a fat fish. "No more heights!" he wheezed.

They all needed to sleep and headed for the trees. Findlay offered to take first watch, but his climb had taken far more energy than Abisina's, so she said she'd do it. There was no talk of Haret taking a watch. After two hours, Abisina would wake Findlay and snatch two hours of sleep herself. They wanted to travel at night when Icksyon's band would gather around their fire to drink mead. The überwolf risk was higher, but by carrying torches, they hoped they could keep them at bay.

Abisina's turn sleeping felt like an instant. Findlay woke her, and she stumbled to her feet, then walked in a daze hardly distinguishable from sleep. Through the night, they got nearer to the river, the rushing water growing louder. The gorge had narrowed and its sides sloped more gently.

"Should we try to cross here?" Abisina asked Findlay.

"It's still steep."

Abisina let out a mammoth yawn.

"I agree," Findlay said as he, too, yawned widely. "Let's find a place to sleep. We can cross at sunset."

"The sooner the better," Abisina put in. "We need to keep going south."

"How much farther, do you think?" Findlay asked.

They both turned to Haret.

The dwarf shrugged. "I'm not really sure. Two weeks? Maybe a little more."

They climbed into a tree and wrapped themselves in their cloaks. Haret was too tired to complain.

Tired as she was, Abisina couldn't sleep. *In two weeks I*

could be among the Vranians again. The thought so unsettled her that once the others were asleep, she climbed down. She needed a gallop.

In a leap she was on her way, racing between trees, jumping rocks and small streams, swerving around boulders. The sun was not yet up, and the woods were dusky. She focused on the uneven ground, thinking only of the next hoof-fall, and how she might go faster.

She stopped at the bank of a stream that would lead her back to the others. She waded into the cold water and let it soothe her tired hooves. The sun had risen, and light dappled the water. A fish swam by her ankles, and she regretted that she didn't have a hook. Fish for breakfast would be a nice break from dried rabbit meat.

Staying in the stream, she made her way back. The flush of exercise faded, leaving the exhaustion of the last few days. *And the weeks before that.* It was unlikely that things would get easier in Vranlyn.

Will there be any other outcasts from Vranille? Names surfaced from her memory: Paleth, Jorno, Urya, Garm. . . . A few had been friends. Most outcasts considered Abisina even lower than they were; her coloring demanded that she be left outside the walls as an infant. Only her mother's role as healer had saved her.

She smiled ruefully and swished her tail. *What if they could see me now?* But her smile faded. She hadn't let Findlay see her as a centaur since the day he was attacked.

He said I could trust him. I need to.

She was afraid. She couldn't deny it. At times, like during a gallop, she could almost embrace her new self, but more often it felt like a curse.

Abisina saw Findlay crouched by the stream, lifting a handful of water to his mouth. She hadn't realized she was so near their camp. Before she could speak, he drew his sword. But as he raised it, he faltered.

"Abisina?" A crimson blush crept up his cheeks.

"I'm sorry. I—I didn't mean to scare you," she stammered.

"No, I'm sorry," he said as he sheathed his sword. "I woke up, and you were gone."

"I couldn't sleep." Abisina was excruciatingly aware of her centaur body, but couldn't make herself transform in front of Findlay. "Could you—could you turn around, Fin?"

"Oh, yes. Of course," he said. "I didn't think anything had happened to you really," he went on, as if talking would cover their embarrassment. "There were no other footprints, and—"

"Wait," Abisina interrupted. "I—I don't need you to turn around. I mean, you said I could trust you. So, it's okay."

"Are you sure?" Findlay asked, still turned away.

"Scared—but sure."

He faced her. Abisina knew she looked as nervous as he did. She tried to smile, and he did, too. "Well, here goes," she said.

The wall between her two selves dissolved. There was no division. There was just *her.*

Then the wall was back, her centaur-self behind it, her human-self stepping forward. She was a human girl, standing up to her bare shins in the cold water.

"Here," Findlay said. He held out a hand, and she took it and climbed out of the stream. He wrapped his arms around her as she shivered, and he rubbed her back. It felt good.

"Better?" He pulled away from her a little awkwardly.

She nodded. "Thanks."

They walked toward the tree, where Haret was snoring.

"Abisina?" Findlay stopped. "You know, that day when the centaur had me, I—I didn't recognize you. I mean, I wasn't expecting you to be a centaur."

"I know." She dropped her eyes. It was the first time they'd talked of that day.

Findlay sighed. "Haret told me that I said 'Get away!' You know I would never say that to you—no matter what. I have to get used to this . . . part of you . . . but it doesn't change how I feel about you."

Abisina took his hand.

"It does scare me," Findlay said, "but not in the way you think. Your shape-shifting proves that you're special. Like your father. I love you, Abisina. It's a little frightening to love someone who is marked for a special destiny."

"I don't know if I have a 'special destiny.' My father was a shape-shifter. So am I. Isn't it that simple?" She wondered if Findlay heard her pleading with him: *Tell me it's that simple.*

"Maybe," Findlay said. He moved closer to her. "But it

may also be a lot more complicated." He pulled her to him and rested his cheek against her hair. The sounds of the forest seemed to grow around them: the stream, a squirrel chittering in the trees, the wind in the leaves.

"I love you, too, Findlay," Abisina whispered.

CHAPTER XX

IT WAS SUNRISE A FEW DAYS BEFORE THE EQUINOX WHEN they came upon a heavy path of überwolf tracks. Since they'd crossed into the south, they'd seen an alarming number of tracks—überwolf, minotaur, centaur, and even troll. But the size of this trail shook them. It looked like a pack of forty or fifty.

They climbed into the trees to sleep, but Findlay couldn't get comfortable. "I can't wait to reach Vranlyn—just to sleep in a bed!" he muttered. His cheek was imprinted with the beech tree's bark. Abisina had similar ridges on her cheek.

"A cave is what I need," Haret grumbled. "But I'll take a bed on the ground over this lunacy."

Abisina lost herself in a strange dream. She stood in a bright, green place filled with a blinding light; the necklace glittered on her chest. She caught sight of fruit on branches— and tasted sweetness on her tongue. *The garden,* she thought—

and it *was* the garden, though in the way of dreams, it looked nothing like it. By squinting, Abisina could make out a single Seldar, standing in a ring of dazzling white stones. With an arm across her eyes, she stepped over the stones, reaching for the tree. But before she could brush her fingers against the bark, the ground beneath her trembled. A crack appeared at her feet, and the earth buckled. She was pitched toward the Seldar, but it was gone. She struggled to maintain her balance as a chasm opened beneath her, and—

"Abisina!"

Findlay?

"Abisina! Watch out!"

Her eyes snapped open as she slipped from her perch, just catching a tree branch with an elbow. Her feet dangled dangerously close to the head of a troll.

This was no dream.

Around the troll's feet, twenty or more überwolves circled like dogs waiting for scraps from the master's table. The troll's head was down, its shoulder bent to the trunk as it tried to uproot the beech. Its hide, rough and scarred, was an earthy gray color with splashes of lighter gray and green—like living rock covered with lichens. In the clamor of barks and howls, the troll didn't hear Findlay's shouts, or notice how close Abisina was to its grasp.

Abisina swung her feet sideways and hooked them over another branch. She climbed toward Findlay, who shot several arrows at the troll, only to have them glance off its tough hide.

Haret was in another beech, climbing, panting, and trying not to look down.

With each ram of the troll's shoulder, the trunk shivered beneath Abisina's hands, and then—*crack!* Some of the beech's roots had snapped. It was not going to last much longer.

"Fin," Abisina said, as she reached him, "we've got to get off! We can move to that tree." She pointed to another beech.

Findlay nodded. "Go. I'll shoot überwolves until you've crossed."

From his own tree, Haret also readied an arrow.

Abisina climbed out on a limb as thick as her thigh, but it grew thinner as she neared the second tree. Shivers from the trunk rippled out until she felt like she was riding the rapids below Watersmeet.

Yips and whines from the wounded überwolves filled the air; some wolves were now circling Haret's tree. Abisina moved fast, but her branch was so thin that she expected it to snap. How would it hold Findlay?

She'd gone as far as she could, but the next tree was still far away. Her beech gave another shudder, and the ground shook as the massive root system started to lift from the earth. Findlay had stopped shooting, following her out on the branch. *It can't hold both of us!* She had to jump.

"Last arrow!" Haret called.

Abisina threw herself at the next tree. She missed the branch she was aiming for but caught a lower one. Much lower. As she hung there, she heard a snarl, and something snatched at her foot.

Luckily it was her turn with Findlay's boots, and the überwolf came away with a mouthful of dirty leather. Abisina swung into the new tree and took aim at the remaining wolves.

CRRAACK!

The first tree—with Findlay on it—crashed to the ground, burying most of the überwolves in a tangle of branches, leaves, and roots.

The troll started ripping the tree's limbs off one by one, shaking each as if Findlay or Abisina might tumble out.

Findlay must be hurt! If the troll doesn't get him, the wolves will! Slowly, two, then three wolves crawled out from the chaos of branches, followed by more. Abisina took aim. *Where are you, Findlay?*

The troll was working its way down the felled tree, getting closer to where Findlay must be hidden. *I have to stop it,* she thought. But her arrows were useless.

The sound of grunting and smacking and bone-crunching drove all other thoughts from Abisina's mind. She stared between the branches at the hulking troll, bits of its meal dropping with wet glops to the forest floor.

She shrieked.

The troll whipped around. The hind leg of an überwolf protruded from its mouth.

It's not Findlay!

But the troll had spotted her. She scrambled to the far side of the tree, as the troll stalked toward her, bent its shoulder to the trunk, and rocked it. Abisina held on. With the troll distracted, Findlay could get out! Few überwolves were left, and most of those were injured.

Abisina got ready to drop to the ground but saw Haret racing to the troll, axe drawn, face set with grim determination. *What's he going to do?*

Abisina dropped and transformed as the troll reared back with a thunderous roar. Now was her chance! She leapt toward the fallen tree, but a burning pain seized her shoulder. She ignored it.

Haret tore out of the troll's path as it stumbled. He had severed a tendon in its leg. The creature screamed and fell to the ground, just missing Findlay, who emerged from the downed tree—pale and shaken, but whole and alive.

"This way!" Haret yelled, and Findlay staggered after him. Abisina checked for überwolves, but those that were left, smelling blood, attacked the troll's ankle, dodging its attempts to smack them away.

Abisina caught up with Findlay, transformed into a human, and offered him her shoulder for support. She noticed then that blood stained her tunic.

"Over here! Over here!"

Abisina thought it was Haret. Instead, a blond man raced past, threw himself down, and disappeared into a narrow crack in the ground. Abisina and Findlay dropped to their bellies.

She was aware of a nagging pain in her shoulder as she crept in. Haret scurried behind them.

"Oof!" Findlay groaned in front of her.

"Keep going," the blond man said. "I've got to close it up."

Abisina moved aside as the man came by her. Her nose filled with the smell of unwashed human.

"Hey! Not *your* kind," the man shouted at Haret.

The dwarf muttered, "Try and stop me."

Suddenly the dim light went out.

Abisina groped forward in the darkness, the ground sloping downward.

"Watch out!" Findlay's voice, followed by a thud.

Then Abisina tumbled into space.

"Ouch!" She landed on top of Findlay. The fall, though small, made the pain in her shoulder worse.

Haret scrambled down next to them and helped Abisina to her feet. "I smell blood," he said.

More scrabbling from above and another thud as the man landed in the dirt near them. A flint scraped against steel, and a light spluttered to life, showing the deeply scarred face of their rescuer and the rough dirt walls of an old tunnel. Above them, claws scratched at whatever their rescuer had used to keep the überwolves out.

Abisina was shivering as the man led them down the tunnel. Her feet behaved oddly, too. The ground was smooth, but it wobbled beneath her, and she stumbled into their rescuer.

The man cried out, but after glancing at Abisina, he said, "Help her. She's hurt."

Findlay took her in his arms. The burning in her shoulder grew as she jostled against his chest. She could vaguely hear Haret hurrying after them, but pain clouded everything.

The walls expanded around her. Findlay laid her on the dirt floor of a large cave. The man left the smoking torch in a bracket on the wall and rekindled the remains of a fire.

"She's been shot," Findlay said, and he touched her shoulder. Abisina groaned. "Arrow's got to come out."

"I've got water on to boil," the stranger said. "And here's something to pull out the arrowhead. The shaft must have broken off."

She tried to recall what had happened. She remembered the heat in her shoulder. Findlay was under the tree then, and Haret was out of arrows. Who had shot her?

"Thank you," Findlay said to the man. "We all owe you our lives."

"I didn't intend to save a dwarf," the man said roughly.

"The dwarves built this hideout," Haret noted. "I guess the dwarves have done you a good turn as well."

"Hmph. I found this myself—and there were no dwarves in it."

"I'm sure they've all gone to . . . Vrandun," Haret said, and, even through her haze of pain, Abisina recognized his diplomacy. This man might not take well to Haret using the dwarf name for the village.

"Where . . . where are you from, friend?" Findlay, too, was treading carefully.

"Name's Sten. I *was* from Vranhurst. Not that it's even a place anymore. Now I'm from wherever I want. Today, here suits me."

"Are there others with you?" Findlay had his hand on his sword.

"I'm not in one of those gangs, if that's what you mean," Sten responded. "I had enough of being told what to do in Vranhurst and then on the campaign with the Worm. I'm on my own now." The others were silent. Abisina listened to the crackle of the fire. "Water's boiling," Sten said dully. "You got anything for pain?"

Haret fumbled for Abisina's herb pouch. "Water-dragon," Abisina mumbled. She had collected the plants in a marshy area a few days earlier.

She lay there, trying to ignore the pain, until Haret came to her side, lifted her head, and poured the hot water-dragon tea into her mouth. Findlay murmured to Sten in the background, and she knew they were deciding who would hold her arms and legs. The water-dragon would help only so much.

"Ready, Abby?" Findlay asked gently. He hadn't used her pet name since he'd seen her as a centaur. He managed a half smile.

"A little more time," Abisina said. "The water-dragon needs to work. . . ."

"Damn überwolves. And trolls," Sten said to no one in

particular. "They get worse all the time. They're coming from the Mountains Eternal."

"You know that?" Findlay asked.

"I haven't been there, of course, but that's what I've heard."

"We thought the Worm brought them."

"The first ones, yes. There are a lot more now. There're stories of a rift in the Mountains—the Worm must have opened it. And they're coming from there. Those minotaurs with their hags, too. Who knows what else!"

Abisina remembered standing outside Vigar's garden, looking at the mountains: the black gash. What had she seen swarming out?

Abisina felt hot breath on her face as Sten leaned over her.

"Your eyes," he gasped. "You're a healer." The Vranians believed the healing gift came with green eyes.

"My mother was," Abisina said.

"I was married to a healer once. Before Charach turned the village against her. That woman had cared for every last person—" He shook his head.

"What was her name?"

"Nonna," he whispered.

"My . . . my mother was Nonna's sister—Sina."

"I—I knew Sina," he stammered. "Not well. She left Vranhurst when I was a kid, but Nonna talked about her." Sten studied Abisina. "But you can't have grown up in Vranille. Look at your skin. You're dwarf-dirty."

Abisina clenched her teeth against this familiar insult. "My father was from Watersmeet. I look like him."

Sten accepted this more easily than Abisina anticipated. "I was in the battle," he said. "Saw all those outcasts from Watersmeet. Wait—is that where you're coming from? Watersmeet?"

Abisina nodded

"I had you figured for a Vranian," Sten said to Findlay. "But it explains him." He pointed a thumb at Haret.

"I think she's ready now," Haret said, ignoring Sten. Abisina realized she had grown calm, sleepy.

The calm was destroyed when Sten returned from the fire with a pair of iron pincers.

Findlay took hold of Abisina's arms, Haret took the pincers from Sten, and the man squatted by her legs.

"Stick," Abisina said, and Haret understood, placing a piece of kindling between her teeth.

Let this be quick.

But it wasn't. The arrow was imbedded beneath her collarbone. The searing of the hot pincers was nothing compared to the sensation of the arrow being pulled out, cutting a new path through her flesh.

Findlay cried, "You got it!" just before she passed out.

She couldn't have been out for long. When she came to, Findlay still had her arms, but he released them as she groaned. "Did he . . . get it?"

When no one answered, she looked at Sten. He was studying the bloody arrowhead.

He dropped it suddenly, pulled an arrow from his quiver, and aimed at Abisina.

"That's *my* arrow I pulled out of you. The only beasts I shot today were überwolves—and a centaur!"

CHAPTER XXI

FINDLAY AND HARET LUNGED AT STEN, KNOCKING HIM aside so that his arrow shot into the dirt.

"Let him up," Abisina said, after they had taken his quiver, the knife at his waist, and a dagger from his boot.

"What kind of magic is this?" Sten cried, his fists cocked.

"You were at the battle," Abisina said. "You saw Rueshlan."

Sten nodded, his gaze shifting between them, as if trying to decide who was most likely to attack.

"He was my father," Abisina went on. "A shape-shifter, human and centaur. I have his coloring and his ability. But I have Sina's—Nonna's—eyes."

The fists dropped a fraction.

"My father came south and met my mother. They fell in love, like you and Nonna. Sten, you're my uncle."

Sten dropped his hands farther. "I see her in you."

Findlay let out his breath.

"We need to clean the wound," Haret said.

Sten sat down on the other side of the fire, letting Haret sew Abisina's wound and put a poultice on it. As much as it hurt, the wound wasn't dangerous if they could keep out infection.

Sten spoke only to Findlay, telling him where to sleep, offering him some dried venison—which Findlay forced down, though no one in Watersmeet ate deer meat—and pointing to a whetstone to sharpen his sword. Now and then, Abisina caught Sten staring at her, but when she tried to meet his eyes, he looked away.

Finally, Abisina spoke to him. "Have you heard of a centaur called Icksyon?"

"An enormous one with a dirty-white coat?" Sten said. "He's come from the north, uniting the herds. Are you one of *his*?"

"No! He's tried to kill me—twice."

Sten said nothing more, and he didn't look at Abisina again.

In the morning, Findlay asked Sten how far they were from Vranlyn. He looked suspicious. "Why?"

As Findlay explained, Sten scowled. "You're here to help Vranians?"

Abisina answered: "Vranlyn offers another way. The Vranians hurt you, too."

"I *am* Vranian," he insisted.

"So am I," Abisina said.

Sten got to his feet. "I've done what I can for you. I'm going out now. When I return, I want you gone."

He picked up his bow, slung his quiver on his back, and headed for the tunnel, but before he got there, he turned to them. "You got lucky meeting me. I hate überwolves and trolls. Anyone who kills them is my ally. It won't be so easy in Vranlyn. If they find out about you," he thrust a finger at Abisina, "they won't be as understanding." He strode out.

Haret found a second tunnel that led them south before surfacing in a thick forest. For the final leg of their journey, they would travel during the day, sleep on the ground at night—Haret refused to return to the trees—and build fires to keep the wolves at bay. Abisina's shoulder ached, and it bled if she moved too much. They were on constant lookout for the usual dangers, but now they also worried about the gangs of Vranians. Sten had told Findlay that there were several between his hideout and Vranlyn. "They don't care who they kill: men or beasts. They think of nothing but food." And Reava's falcons were back. A pair spent the day shadowing them before disappearing to the north.

Two days after the autumnal equinox, they came upon a wide, slow-moving river running south.

"This isn't the Great River, is it?" Abisina asked Haret. The tranquil waters couldn't be the torrent they knew from the north.

"I don't think we've gone far enough west," Haret agreed.

But the river's sandy banks made for easy travel. They followed it south, hoping it would lead them to Vranlyn.

They discovered debris on the shore: under-shirts that might have floated away while being washed, a stick with wool on top that could've been a child's lost plaything, shards of pottery. A human village must be close. It was late afternoon, so they set up camp and took turns bathing in the river.

After supper, Abisina said what was on all of their minds: "We could be in Vranlyn tomorrow." Findlay stopped whittling, and Haret held the knife he'd spent the last half hour throwing into a rotting stump. "I think Findlay should go in first. And I don't think we should tell anyone that I can . . . that I'm a shape-shifter."

"What about Corlin?" Findlay asked.

Abisina shook her head. "It's not worth the risk."

The next morning, they left the riverbank for the cover of the trees and came upon a section of forest recently burned by wildfire. Black, leafless trunks stood like specters, their few remaining branches rattling in the wind. Abisina could see the river through the trees but couldn't tell how far the charred forest extended.

"Forage, firewood, game—all gone," she said. *Has Vranlyn survived?*

The fire had stopped at a swath of cleared land between the forest and fields that had once been cultivated. Now tall weeds and saplings grew in place of crops. Beyond, they could make out a high, forbidding stone wall. The wall itself was black, but it was dotted with watchtowers built of grayer stone. The wall's size suggested a settlement large enough to be called a city. Abisina had assumed Vranlyn was the same size as Vranille, but it was much older. It would be bigger, more settled.

The three of them stopped at the edge of the trees. The air was still.

"I don't like it," Haret said.

Abisina scanned the wall. Someone moved in one of the watchtowers. Her stomach tightened. "This isn't Vranlyn," she realized. "It's Vranham. Look at the wall. Perfectly sound. Corlin said Vranlyn's wall needed repairs."

"Maybe we can't see the damage," Findlay suggested.

"Those watchtowers—they're new. And think of the river. We dismissed it because it didn't look like *our* river, but it's enormous. It's got to be the Great River."

"I thought the river was farther west, but I really don't know. It could swing east," Haret said.

"I'm going closer," Abisina announced.

"What are you talking about?" Findlay cried and then dropped his voice. "If this is Vranham, we should get out of here as fast as we can. You're the last one who should go near it!"

"We need to be sure," Abisina insisted. "I'm smaller than you, Fin, less likely to be seen."

"Haret's smaller than both of us, and he knows better than to get closer," Findlay countered.

"He's a dwarf! They'll kill him on sight!"

"The same thing they'll do to you! It has to be me. If I get caught, I'll say I'm a refugee," Findlay argued.

"Corlin said that no one gets out of Vranham," Abisina shot back. "If I get chased, I can transform and outrun any pursuers."

"And I suppose you'll be safe as a centaur?"

"Fin, I have the best chance!"

In the end, it was Abisina who left Findlay and Haret in the trees. She was sure it was Vranham, but she had to see it for herself.

She crept through the tall grass, doubled over.

Thunk, thunk, thunk. The sound of hoes against hard earth.

Abisina dropped onto her belly and crawled. Through the tangle of weeds and brush, she approached the wall of the city, a watchtower rising above it. Two sentries stood at the parapets, one scanning the fields, the other watching whoever was hoeing below. She froze. Could they see her?

But no cry came from the sentries. Instead the snap of a whip and a scream interrupted the rhythm of the hoes. In the tumult of shouts, cries, and continued whipping, Abisina scooted forward until she could see into the narrow band of planted fields between the wall and the abandoned cropland.

A man stood over a huddled figure, his whip flying again and again against his victim's back. A group of guards, some clutching whips, others armed with swords, jeered and called out to their comrade.

"You show him, Iker!"

"Give him a lesson he'll never forget!"

A second group—men, women, and children holding hoes—stood to the side, faces averted. They were emaciated, dressed in rags, and barefoot. Their legs were manacled and several of them bled from beneath the irons. A few small tubers were strewn on the ground.

"Enough!" One of the guards separated himself from the others and stepped between Iker and the outcast at his feet.

The whip paused.

"You want me to go easy on him, Teg?" Iker scoffed.

" 'Course not," Teg said, with a glance toward the watchtower. "But we need them to work for us, don't we?"

A low groan came from the outcast in the dust.

"Sounds like softness to me," Iker said. A few of the guards shouted their agreement. "What do you lot think?" Iker called to the guards in the watchtower.

Another figure had appeared at the parapet. His hair was grayer, his face thinner, but his hooked nose, hard eyes, and cold smile were the same as Abisina remembered.

Theckis.

As the guards on the ground caught sight of him, they dropped to one knee and murmured in unison, "There is no Vran but Vran." At their words, the outcasts threw themselves on the dirt, hands over their heads.

"Softness to outcasts is a dangerous charge, Iker," Theckis said. "Are you sure you want to bring it against your comrade?"

As much as Abisina had loathed Iker as he was beating the outcast, she pitied him now. She heard judgment in Theckis's voice. He had already assigned guilt to Iker and Teg and the whole group of guards and outcasts. He was enjoying their fear.

"This one," Iker pointed to the outcast, "was eyeing the fields. He was taking a step toward them when I stopped him. He was trying to escape, Eldest. Anything short of death is softness." But his knuckles were white where he gripped his whip.

"We have a conflict," Theckis mused. "As Iker says, this creature was, perhaps, attempting to escape. He must die—as *all* who even think of escape must. Teg, then, must be punished for softness."

"Eldest—" Teg began, but Theckis cut him off.

"You, too, spoke truly, Teg. We do rely on outcast labor, and Iker has deprived us of this man's. If he had been vigilant, if he had been doing his job, the outcast would not have dared raise his eyes to the fields. So Iker must also pay."

"Eldest—" Iker leapt to his feet.

But Theckis's game was over. "Leave the outcast to die. Bring Iker and Teg to the smithy to be manacled as outcasts. The rest of you guards will help with the harvest today. Get hoes and shovels. Other guards will be sent to ensure that none of you think of escape."

Two guards took hold of Teg and Iker as they struggled and protested. No one spoke against the illogic of Theckis's sentence. They simply mumbled, "There is no Vran but Vran," as Theckis turned away.

Then Teg, with a defiant look at his captors, shouted at Theckis's back, "Kill them all! But we'll die right along with them! Don't you see it? We're—"

With a quick cut of his sword, a guard slit Teg's throat.

Theckis was shaking with rage. "Does anyone else dare to speak such treason?" he screamed.

In the ensuing silence, Abisina could hear the panicked breathing of the outcasts.

"Teg died too quickly, with too little pain," Theckis said. "If anyone else dares—a guard, a captain, an Elder—yes, even they will envy Teg's easy death when they see what I can do."

"There is no Vran but Vran," the guards and outcasts mumbled again. With a last look of fury, Theckis turned and disappeared from view.

The guards and outcasts marched around the side of the wall toward the gate into Vranham, leaving Teg's body and the beaten outcast behind. Abisina crawled back toward the burned wood. She longed to help the outcast, but the guards in the watchtower still stood at their post.

Haret and Findlay waited where she left them.

"It's Vranham," she said. "And it's as bad as Corlin said."

Haret picked up his satchel. "Then let's get out of here. We've got the afternoon. There's not much of a moon tonight, but we'll get as far away as we can."

It took three more days of traveling east along a small river before they reached Vranlyn at last. Another walled village surrounded by cultivated land, Vranlyn was smaller than Vranham but much larger than Abisina's village.

In the forest outside of Vranlyn, Haret found an abandoned hidey hole that had been used by dwarf scouts. It was a tight fit for Abisina, but it would give her and Haret cover if needed while Findlay was in Vranlyn. They stowed their gear and walked to the edge of the forest.

A sentry patrolled the top of the stone wall—no watchtowers here—and a hammer clanged on metal. Piles of rubble were scattered on the plain where the wall had been breached. A few figures worked near the rubble.

Haret winced at the hammering. "Humans know nothing of cutting rock. . . ." he muttered.

As in Vranham, the people had managed to plant some grain and vegetables, but it would be a poor harvest. Weeds choked most of the fields; the plants were spindly and weak. Other crops had been raided—by gangs? Icksyon's herds?—leaving bent stalks, trampled leaves, and the smell of rot. No one was at work in the fields.

"This has got to be Vranlyn, but I don't like the idea of Findlay going in alone," Abisina said.

"We've been over this. He'll be less threatening alone. And we'll be watching from here, arrows ready," Haret assured her.

Their arrows would do little at this range. With a tense smile, Findlay left the shelter of the trees.

Abisina watched him, his back straight and strong. *If something happens to him . . .*

Once the sentry spotted Findlay, three more figures joined him on the wall, watching. When Findlay got close, he stopped, and there was some talk Abisina couldn't hear. At one point, Findlay raised his hands and rotated on the spot, as if to show them that he wasn't hiding anything, and then resumed walking. A small gate opened. Findlay passed through it, and the gate came down with a clank that carried across the fields.

He was inside.

Haret and Abisina lingered, keeping watch. Nothing moved except the sentry. Haret handed Abisina a blister root—a dwarf favorite.

"Why is it taking this long?" she exploded. "Corlin *wanted* us to come."

"The river's not far," Haret said. "Remember that cress we saw?"

Abisina shot Haret a look. "I know you're trying to get rid of me, dwarf. I'll get your cress, but if you see *anything*, you better yell."

Haret was still staring at Vranlyn when Abisina returned with the watercress and their gear. "I'm not going to hide out while Findlay's in there," she replied when Haret grunted. "And don't act surprised. You weren't planning on going back, either." Haret's short bark of laughter told her she was right.

Before they could eat, the gate lifted. Three figures came out. One walked with Findlay's loping gate.

"Thank the Earth!" Abisina said. "Is that Corlin to the left of Fin?"

"Can't tell from here. Vranians all look the same to me."

As they got closer, Abisina was sure she recognized Corlin's hunched shoulders. The third man seemed familiar, too. Was he from Vranille? *It doesn't matter where he's from,* she reminded herself as her heart raced.

The setting sun was shining onto the faces of the young men. The third one lifted his hand to his eyes, stumbled slightly, and she knew him. *Jorno!* He'd been outcast in Vranille. He wasn't born there, but the summer before Abisina fled, he showed up with his foot half severed. Anyone maimed by centaurs was automatically outcast; Jorno had also appeared simpleminded. Abisina had later discovered that Jorno's behavior was a ruse. Believing him a fool, people had spoken openly in front of him, and he funneled what he learned to the tiny underground rebel movement, which included Abisina's mother.

Abisina had learned of Jorno's trick on her last day in Vranille—the day Jorno had saved her life. As Charach whipped the Vranians into a rage, Jorno had kept his head and told Abisina to run before the mob came after them, giving her the time she needed to get out. She'd assumed he was killed by the mob, but here he was, striding across the field, with the barest hint of the limp he'd once made so pronounced to fool the Elders.

Abisina ran to them.

"Human, what are you doing?" Haret whispered, but she didn't slow.

She was so relieved to see Findlay, to know that Corlin had made it home, to find Jorno alive.

"I can't believe you're here!" she said to Jorno.

Jorno's fair skin turned pink. He was Abisina's height, and his blue eyes stared right into hers. "I had my hopes about you," he said. "I didn't see your body among the others. But when I couldn't find you anywhere in the village afterward, I assumed they got you. . . ."

"Welcome to Vranlyn," Corlin said a little wryly. "Such as it is. You couldn't have come at a better time."

"Did Findlay tell you about Haret?" Abisina asked.

"That's what took so long. I had to prepare the people for a dwarf to arrive," Corlin said. "Findlay also told me about Watersmeet. I'm sorry."

Abisina tried to make her voice light. "They'll find their way. Things have changed too fast for them. We thought we might be more help down here. Others are coming. They may be hiding nearby, waiting for us. Elodie and Erna—a faun—and Kyron."

"Kyron?" Jorno said sharply.

"I told Jorno about meeting you and Kyron," Corlin explained.

"No centaurs," Jorno insisted. "You're pushing people too hard, Corlin. Did you see their faces when you said a dwarf was coming?"

His intensity startled Abisina.

"Haret's here now. We'll figure out Kyron—and Erna—when they get here," Corlin said.

As they walked to Haret, Abisina looked at Corlin closely. His arm had red scars running down it, and his hand was bandaged where two of his fingers were missing.

"It's been a hard summer," Corlin said, noticing her gaze. "We've had a troll in the area. It brought the wall down where the minotaurs had already weakened it—and took my fingers. There have been so many raids, the people have refused to work in the fields until we fix the wall. I've tried to convince them that the wall won't matter if we have nothing to eat."

"If we don't stand guard every night," Jorno added, "and sometimes even when we do, centaurs or the gangs of men take what they can get."

"You've been fighting centaurs?" Abisina asked nervously. *What if Kyron has already been killed?*

Corlin understood. "I'd recognize Kyron, Abisina. And they always attack in herds."

"How about Icksyon? A big white centaur that leads the herds? Have you seen him?" Abisina held her breath.

"Not yet," Corlin said with a frown, "but we've heard of him."

They reached the edge of the forest, and Haret came into the fields. "Corlin," he said gruffly.

Corlin shook Haret's hand. "Thank you for coming, Haret."

"This is Jorno," Abisina said. "I knew him in Vranille."

Haret nodded at Jorno, but Jorno looked past him, cheeks flushed.

"How did you escape Charach?" Abisina asked Jorno, as they headed back to Vranlyn.

"I slipped out of the village and into the trees while the mob . . . burned the bodies."

She knew he was thinking of her mother. "I was there, too."

"I wish we had found each other then," Jorno said. His intense blue eyes sought hers. "When I couldn't find you, I left. I knew I would find nothing to the east but centaurs, fauns, and—" He caught himself before saying "dwarves," but his disgust was clear. "It made the most sense to return to Vranhurst."

"You were from Vranhurst?" Abisina realized she knew almost nothing about Jorno. "Did you know my mother from there?"

"She left right after I was born, but I knew her sister, Nonna."

"We met Nonna's husband, Sten. He lives alone west of here."

"I knew him a little," Jorno said. "Nonna talked a lot about your mother. So when I got to Vranille, I asked for Sina. They would have killed me on sight. I was out of my mind after what the centaurs did to me, but I said your mother's name, and that made them pause." He glanced at Abisina. "That's when I first saw you. Your mother healed me."

At the mention of her mother, Findlay took Abisina's hand and squeezed it. Jorno's eyes flitted between them.

"What about Paleth?" Abisina asked. The only Vranian child who'd ever reached out to Abisina, Paleth had been close to death when the mob came after the outcasts.

Jorno shook his head. "I hid with her under the storehouse. She died while I was there. It was better that way. If they had found her . . . Even if she'd survived the mob, the life we all had to live after that . . ."

When they reached the wall, the sentry stared down at them. *Hostile or curious?* Abisina wondered.

"I can't promise that you won't be kept at arms' length," Corlin warned. "Or that Haret won't be deliberately shunned."

"Are you all right with that, Haret?" she asked.

He snorted. "Reminds me of when I met you."

Abisina smiled in spite of herself. "That's why we're here," she said. "I know how hard it is to change." She could almost feel the centaur-self in the back of her mind nodding in agreement.

Chapter XXII

Like all Vranian villages, Vranlyn was built in concentric circles. The outcasts had lived on the outer circle, closest to the forest where they collected wood—and closest to the first wave of attack if centaurs breached the wall. At the center were the Elders' houses—spacious and solid.

The outcasts' huts had been deserted for two years, and most were falling down in disrepair. Seeing them, Abisina remembered how small, dark, and cold these huts had been. Her mother kept theirs clean and neat, but most outcasts gave up any pretense of home.

Findlay stared. "You lived in one of these?" he whispered to Abisina, and when she nodded, he squeezed her hand again.

As they walked, Abisina caught glimpses of people—all blond, blue eyed, and fair. *And all dirty, skinny, and worn out.* They hurriedly looked away if Abisina looked in their direction. Haret kept his eyes on the road. One man spit, and a few others' jaws dropped. *How could I have let Haret come here? I knew what it was going to be like.*

Corlin was calling out to everyone, greeting them by name. "They're from Watersmeet!" he announced. "They've come to help us." Jorno also greeted people, but Corlin was the leader here.

A small pack of children followed them. Children had always been cruel to Abisina—throwing stones, kicking her, stealing any food rations she managed to get. She risked a glance at them. Their faces were only curious. One little boy yelled, "Did you know Rueshlan?"

"They know my father?" she asked Corlin.

"They've heard the story of how he killed Charach," he said. "They understand that the one who rid them of the Worm was a friend, though they don't understand how he could be man and centaur. But very few of these people were at the battle, and most that were, fought for the Worm."

"What?" Findlay stopped.

"They were enslaved," Corlin reminded him. "They had to fight to survive."

"You managed to get away," Findlay said.

"I got away early. I was never a good Vranian." Corlin smiled. "Both of my parents would've been outcast if the Elders had any idea how they were raising me. I could see what Charach, the man, was doing before he showed himself as the Worm."

"I didn't realize I'd meet folk here who I fought against," Findlay said. "I figured they'd all be in Vranham."

"Those who *chose* to fight for the Worm are there," Corlin agreed. "The folk here want to live a new way."

Toward the center of the village, there were more people in the streets, but no one approached them. Abisina had grown used to the wide variety of folk in Watersmeet. For the first time in almost two years, she was very aware of her dark skin and black hair.

Corlin led them to one of the Elders' houses—easily six times larger than the huts behind it. Abisina hung back. She'd never been in an Elder's house. She imagined spacious rooms, thick animal skins on beds and chairs, pots of preserved food lining the shelves, vast fireplaces fueled by wood that she and other outcasts had risked their lives to gather.

"We use this house for meetings," Corlin said. "No one lives in the Elders' houses anymore. We're trying to get away from Elders and classes and divisions. In fact, we've pulled down some of their houses across the common." Corlin pointed to two rubble-filled gaps. "More will follow. People use the logs to fix their own homes, and we're taking the stones to the wall."

"I slept in one for a night," Jorno told Abisina. "I had to know what it was like." His tone was light, but she heard an eagerness that unsettled her.

As Corlin led them inside, Abisina couldn't escape the feeling that someone was watching her. Looking up, she expected Elder Theckis or Kayn or Waldrin to be staring down at her from the beams high above her head. There was a big fireplace, though only a small fire burned in it now. The chairs pulled to the hearth were rough. The people had probably helped themselves to the Elders' more refined furniture.

Abisina stopped. Tails hung over the fireplace—white, black, and brown, row upon row.

Her stomach heaved, and she raced for the door, making it outside before she vomited. The children who had followed them were milling about, but Abisina ignored their stares.

Findlay came to her. "What is it?" he asked.

"Did you see the chimney—the 'trophies' on display?" He shook his head. "Centaur tails, Fin!"

In Vranille, they had tacked centaur tails to the outer walls of the village—a warning to the other centaurs that might attack. She hadn't thought twice about the practice then. Centaurs were demons that needed to be driven from the land. Now she knew that this display was as barbaric as Icksyon's necklace of toes.

"I will not walk back into that room," she told Findlay.

Haret came out the door. "I explained why the tails upset us," he said. "We're going to Corlin's house instead." He frowned. "This is not going to be easy."

Corlin had invited all of Vranlyn to meet them, though Abisina suspected that "insisted" was more accurate. It was a tribute to Corlin that so many came. A few men and women who'd been at the battle greeted Abisina. No one called her names. No one tried to hurt her. But most didn't look at her. No one touched, spoke to, or looked at Haret.

Findlay was the only one who people talked to comfortably, thanking him for coming, asking questions about Watersmeet, and wondering if he had met Rueshlan. Abisina's father seemed to be a revered figure and Watersmeet an almost mystical place.

There were a few people from Vranille. Two were former outcasts, Urya and her son, Brack. They had been outcast when Urya hid Brack from the Elders gathering men to fight off a centaur raid. They had considered Abisina beneath them after they were outcast and now seemed embarrassed by their former treatment of her. She wanted to reach out to them, put them at ease, but they looked so uncomfortable when she approached them, she said nothing.

A thick-necked bear of a man came up to Abisina and spoke in a loud whisper, all the while gauging the crowd's reaction to his words. "You had us all fooled in Vranille, eh?" he said, wagging his bushy eyebrows at her. "Daughter of an Elder, I hear. I always thought that mother of yours knew what she was up to."

The man's name came to Abisina—Dehan—but she had no idea what he was talking about. Corlin explained, "The people think of Rueshlan as an Elder."

"Your mother healed my husband," a woman put in, folding Abisina's hands in hers. "The Worm got him in the end, but I would've lost him earlier if not for Sina."

A girl of seven or eight winters rushed up to Abisina, got within half a length of her, and stopped. Like all the people of Vranlyn, she was skinny and sallow, but she had a spark in her green eyes. "My mother was a healer like yours," she said.

"I can tell by your eyes," Abisina said, and the girl grinned. She wore a tunic far too large for her that she belted at the waist with a collection of rawhide pieces.

"I'm Thaula," the girl said. "I would have been outcast like you." She thrust a knobby knee at Abisina and pointed to a large, brown birthmark. "Here, we don't have to hide. We're free. Because of your father. I want to be just like you some-day," she announced. "I want to show people what outcasts can do!"

Abisina bent to the girl's height. "You're already showing what you can do."

But I'm not. And yet, how could she transform in front of people who couldn't even accept her dark hair? Who had centaur tails on display?

It was late by the time the hut cleared out. Thaula had fol-lowed Abisina the rest of the evening until her father shooed her home. Beside Corlin and Jorno, three others stayed behind: Dehan, a young man who'd been at the battle, and the woman who'd prepared a meager supper for them. *Anything is better than trail food,* Abisina thought, biting into a piece of coarse bread. *And they don't have much to share.*

"Corlin," Abisina asked, "do the humans here understand that dwarves live in Watersmeet? And fauns and centaurs?"

"I've told them," he said.

"I don't understand. They want to build a community like Watersmeet, they're fascinated by Rueshlan, but they can't look at Haret!" Abisina said.

"Do you really think we can do what you want?" Haret said bluntly. "I came to help, and I will, but oh, the Earth! What a job."

Haret hadn't spoken since arriving in Corlin's hut, and the Vranian woman seemed surprised, as if she'd expected Haret to speak gibberish.

"We're not giving up!" Abisina said firmly. "If we leave now, these people might go to Vranham to join Theckis." She saw again the manacled feet of the outcasts and the one left to die. "We're not giving up," she repeated.

"Of course not," Findlay said. "But I don't think we understood how hard it would be, Abisina."

Haret grunted. "I thought these folk would be different from other Vranians."

"They *are* different," Corlin said earnestly. "But it will take time. I tried to set up a Council, but they couldn't do it. They think I'm an Elder, no matter how many times I tell them I'm not. They're used to being led. So I lead—but I am pushing them to take some power. They are a proud, strong people. I see them changing every day—in small ways. Please trust me. They want you here. They just need to get used to you and recognize what you can teach us."

"Then, we need to *show* them our skills," Abisina said. "How do we begin?"

Chairs scraped as everyone pulled closer to the table. Corlin listed problems Vranlyn faced as winter approached: the wall needed mending, the fields needed to be harvested, the storehouses were almost empty, and many sick and injured people couldn't work.

"Don't you have a healer?" Abisina asked.

"There's Eder, Thaula's father, who was married to a healer," Corlin said. "He can sew wounds a little. A few others know some herb lore—like Ivice here." The woman at the table smiled shyly.

"What about the healer's hut? Are there any medicines or herbs?" Abisina asked Ivice, who sat farther back than the men.

"We're not sure what we have," Ivice admitted. "Only healers and Elders could read. We have neither here, so we can't read the labels on the jars."

"Well, that's my task then," Abisina said. "If you can take me there, Ivice, I'll get to work tomorrow morning."

"Can I bring my son, Landry?" Ivice asked, pointing to the younger man. "I think he has worms."

Landry turned red. He was about Abisina's age.

Haret spoke up. "You want the folk to see how I can help? Let me at the wall."

"We could really use you. None of the masons returned," Corlin said. "We were using mud as mortar, but the stones fall out when it dries."

"Mud?" Haret groaned. "Stones *want* to fit together. They'll tell you how if you listen to them."

"I don't know who will consent to work for the dwarf," Jorno said.

"Well, I know one who *won't*," Dehan, the bear-necked man, put in with a chuckle.

Landry nodded. "Heben."

"There are plenty of others," Corlin agreed. "Jorno can take a group to the armory. Our weapons need attention: spears and swords are dull, bowstrings are brittle, arrows need new feathers. We'll also need a group to fill the storehouses. Findlay can lead them. We'll assign those jobs before we ask people to help Haret."

"I saw lots of forage outside the walls," Findlay said.

"Forage?" Ivice frowned.

"We're not used to foraging," Landry explained. "That's seen as . . . well, the beasts' way of feeding themselves."

"The people of Vranille foraged," Abisina said. "Right, Dehan? Every Founding Day the Elders told the story of that first winter, when people found food in the woods."

"We've heard that the newer settlements were forced to extremes in order to survive," Landry said, "but in Vranham and Vranlyn, it's been generations since we've had to act like beasts."

"Well, we have to now," Corlin said simply.

"What will we find—out there?" Ivice asked doubtfully.

"It's nut season," Findlay answered. "There's nothing like good hazelnut flour. The pond we passed had cattails and reeds—very good eating. My mother is the captain of a foraging team in Watersmeet," he added.

"So it's women's work," Landry concluded.

"There are more men than women on my mother's team," Findlay told him.

"And your mother is *captain*?" Ivice asked.

"She's a drill captain for archers, too." Findlay clearly enjoyed seeing the amazed faces around the table.

The meeting ended past midnight. Corlin and the other villagers went hut to hut with the news that all were to meet on the common ground at sunrise. Ivice walked Abisina, Haret, and Findlay to a vacant hut she'd prepared for them. Animal pelts lay on the sleeping platforms, and yarrow tea and a small loaf of bread were set out for their breakfast. Findlay climbed into the loft, after offering it with a laugh to Haret; Abisina fell into the bed right below. After such a long day, Haret's buzzy snore from the floor soon lulled her to sleep.

Abisina arrived on the common as the sun rose. At one end, the huge stone slab that had served as an altar had been tipped over. She wished it had been removed altogether.

"I look at that altar every time I walk on this common." Abisina hadn't heard Jorno's approach. "I can still see him—Charach—standing on it," he said. "You noticed it right away, didn't you? The Worm inside the man?"

"Almost right away." At first, she'd been taken in by Charach's beauty and power. His head of gold curls, his broad shoulders. She thought he was Vran, though Vran had been dead for generations. But in the depth of his black eyes, she'd found the Worm. "Did you see it?" she asked.

"I didn't *see* the Worm until he actually shed his human form, but I felt it. They were all screaming for him—even the outcasts. I hear them sometimes . . . when I sleep."

Abisina noticed the shadows under Jorno's eyes. *It's been harder for him. I've been in Watersmeet. What has his life here been like?*

He took her hand. "You have your mother's hands, you know," he said, smoothing her palm. "She always said you had more of the healing gift than she did."

"I'll need whatever gift I have today." Abisina drew her hand away. Findlay and Corlin were coming toward them.

"I have bad news," Corlin said. "One family and several men left for Vranham this morning."

Abisina bit her lip. "I'm sorry, Corlin."

"It was bound to happen. And a few of them were going to make our work today much harder. It's just as well."

Abisina wasn't sure she believed him, but Corlin seemed confident as he began the meeting, standing against the common's fence, not near the altar as an Elder would have. The people gathered around. Abisina estimated there were two hundred, maybe a few less.

Corlin first called for a group to go with Jorno to the armory. Abisina paid particular attention when Heben—a big man with a hard face—volunteered. Corlin next asked for people to work in the fields. He didn't mention that some would be foraging until the volunteers were ready to leave, and many grumbled. "Our people have foraged before," Corlin reminded them. "There's no shame in it."

Findlay quieted some of the protests by telling the men that he would need them as guards. "In Watersmeet, we send out patrols to defend the foragers," he said. Abisina had to smile. Findlay didn't mention that two girls and a faun had made up one of the best patrols. "I'll get those men foraging yet," he whispered to her as he left.

Those were the easy assignments. Following Findlay wasn't such a stretch. Abisina came next.

"Some of you know Abisina," Corlin said. "She's a healer, and she's going to the healer's house now to help any of you who need it. Everyone must be well. Our success depends on our work."

Standing in front of a sea of Vranians, Abisina couldn't help thinking, *They could turn into a mob so easily.* She hid her shaking hands behind her. "I could use several people," she said. "Folk who know herbs, and someone to tend the fire while I make teas. If anyone has beeswax for salves . . ."

According to plan, Ivice raised her hand. No one else. Abisina waited.

"I'll do it!" A high, young voice spoke from the back.

Thaula shouldered her way through the crowd.

"My mother didn't get a chance to teach me much," she said, "but I can tend a fire."

"That will be your job, then," Abisina said, wanting to hug the girl.

An old woman near the front raised her hand. Then a second woman.

"That's four," Corlin said. "That should do it."

With a smile of relief, Abisina led her helpers and the sick and injured off the common.

An angry murmur rose behind them. They had hoped to get as many people away as possible before Corlin assigned Haret's crew. But Abisina's group turned back.

"What is it?"

"What's going on?"

"He's put the dwarf in charge of the wall!" a man on the common yelled.

"I know what you're thinking!" Abisina cried, running toward the common. She wouldn't leave Haret. "I used to think it, too," she said. "But then I *lived* with the dwarves. And do you know what they did for me? They clothed, fed, and healed me. In one winter, I received more from this dwarf and his grandmother than in my fourteen winters with the Elders. You remember standing in line for tiny portions of cheese and meat and flour. You know how the Elders lived. How fat they were. Some of you were widows, orphans, or outcasts like me. Did you ever have a full belly? Were you warm in the winter?

"Haret is offering his help, even though we've done nothing but harm him and his folk. And there is no one who knows more about stone than a dwarf. Let him teach you. When we fought the White Worm, who dug the battle trenches? The dwarves! Rueshlan, my father, would never have considered asking anyone else."

She paused, and Corlin, pressing the advantage, exclaimed, "I'm going with Haret! Who else is coming?"

Dehan's hand went up, then a few more. It wasn't an overwhelming victory, but it would do.

As Haret left, he whispered to Abisina, "You know, human, Rueshlan didn't *ask* us to build trenches. We just did it."

"I know, Haret," she said.

He cocked his head at her. "A teacher, eh?"

There'll be no living with him now! Abisina laughed to herself, and led her group to the healer's house.

Chapter XXIII

THEY HAD TWO MONTHS, IF THEY WERE LUCKY, BEFORE the snow came. And they dreaded an attack by Icksyon. They were racing to fill the storehouses and secure Vranlyn.

Abisina moved into the healer's house, getting to work as soon as she woke each morning. In the afternoons, she went out with the foragers to fill her stores with herbs, roots, and plants. She and Findlay always searched for signs that Kyron and the others had arrived. Twice, Abisina sneaked away, transformed, and searched further. She found nothing. She asked Corlin to talk to the sentries, but Jorno argued against it. "People left when the dwarf arrived. You want to tell them a centaur's coming next?"

They revere my father, Abisina thought. *If I gain their trust, I can teach them that not all centaurs are evil.* It was terrifying to imagine standing in front of Vranians as a centaur. *I couldn't even show Watersmeet!*

But I've wondered ever since if the folk would have listened to me if they'd seen my true self. I don't want to have the same regret here.

Findlay was the first to convince the villagers that these northern strangers could help them. "Taste how sweet this is!" he would insist, offering his foraging crew a bite of a may-apple. "But *never* eat it when it's green," he warned. He explained that the carrion flower smelled foul, but its young shoots were delicious "when cooked for a quarter of an hour at a roiling boil." The women giggled when Findlay talked about cooking. More than a few men, still officially "guards," picked plants when they thought no one was watching. The hollowed-eyed look of the hungry softened in Vranlyn.

It took the villagers longer with Abisina. Many who needed healing didn't want her "dwarf-dirty" hands to touch them. But as word spread that her elderberry and yarrow poultices stopped bleeding quickly, that her feverfew tea eradicated worms, and that she sewed wounds with a gentle touch, people viewed her differently—or her hands, at least.

She met a similar barrier when she began to offer archery training. Only the women came, even when she bested most of the men at target shooting. She kept teaching, and enjoyed watching the women progress. All Vranians were taught to shoot, but none of the men had been willing to teach the women more than the basics.

One morning, as Abisina left the healing house to get firewood, she discovered a new pair of leggings folded neatly at her doorstep. A pair of boots sat next to them. She'd been wearing boots and clothes that she'd found in an abandoned hut. The boots were huge and the leggings had ripped knees. She no longer worried about transforming unexpectedly, but she hadn't taken the time to make herself new clothes. Someone had noticed.

The leggings were supple and soft, the boots snug and warm. They fit perfectly. She asked Thaula to find out who'd done this for her—the little girl seemed to know everything that went on in Vranlyn—but Abisina never discovered the giver.

As the weeks passed, the villagers treated Abisina with a grudging respect, but she had few real friends.

Except Thaula. The little girl shadowed Abisina's every move. The Worm had forced Thaula's mother to travel with his army as a healer, and she had never returned.

"My mother was related to Imara, the original healer, who came across the Mountains with Vran," Thaula told Abisina once.

"So was my mother," Abisina said. "In fact, all the healers are supposed to have descended from Imara. You know what that means, don't you?"

"What?"

"It means you and I are cousins."

The child's face lit up.

Haret couldn't understand why Abisina cared if the Vranians were cold to her. "Be glad they're not running at you with clubs."

"Doesn't it bother you that they can't get past seeing you as a—"

"Mud-dweller? Don't look so shocked, human. I *am* a mud-dweller. We had names for them, too. It's going to take generations to change."

"If Kyron arrives—" She stopped. "*When* Kyron arrives, what will happen to him?"

"We need to prepare them," Haret said pointedly.

"You mean *I* need to prepare them by showing them what I am. And I will. When they're ready. I just convinced a couple of men to take down the centaur tails." Abisina had refused to enter the meeting house until the tails were taken down, but they had simply been moved to the outside walls. "They thought I was overreacting."

Haret looked at her skeptically.

"Haret, I *will*. When the time is right."

"Hmph."

It was early evening, and Abisina was working on a poultice for a boy who'd been burned by a gang's flaming arrows. The sharp, sweet odor of stoneroot flavored the air. Thaula was out delivering another poultice. Abisina expected Findlay, but it was Jorno who came through the door, bringing a cool draft.

"Evening," he said, without glancing at Haret.

Haret got up. "I'm off to bed for a few hours before I start my journey." The wall building was going slowly, and Haret was leaving that night for Stonedun to persuade the dwarves to help.

"I wish you'd take someone with you, Haret," Abisina said.

"We've been through this, human. You and Findlay can't be spared. This is a delicate matter. I could only take someone who knows dwarves. I'll be fine."

Abisina walked him to the door. "Look for Kyron and the others." She put her hands on his shoulders. "And be careful, dwarf."

"I'll see you soon, human," he said and left.

"Do you think he'll succeed?" Jorno asked, taking a seat by the fire. He picked up the spoon and stirred Abisina's poultice.

"He has to." Abisina checked the pot. "Stop stirring, Jorno. It needs to sit."

"I've been thinking about you, Abisina," he said. "Well, when am I *not* thinking about you?" Abisina studied her poultice. Jorno had begun to hint that he had feelings for her—strong feelings. She was sure he knew about Findlay, but that didn't stop him.

Jorno continued: "I've been thinking about what it must've been like for you to meet your father. It must've been horrible when you realized he was a centaur. I mean, you know what they're capable of."

"If you knew my father or Kyron . . . Jorno, it's the most important lesson I learned living in Watersmeet. A centaur, a dwarf, a faun—like you and me—can *choose* to be good or evil."

"Some creatures always choose evil," he said. "Not just centaurs," he added, as Abisina frowned. "Trolls. Überwolves. They're all the same really."

"I don't think we understand those creatures. Überwolves are hunters—and we're food. And trolls seem . . . dimwitted."

"Well, I don't 'understand' centaurs."

They lapsed into silence. Abisina didn't understand Jorno, either. As an outcast, and one who'd worked in the underground movement, he should've been easy to convince.

There was a knock on the door, and Findlay strolled in.

"Hey, Abby," he said. "Oh—hello, Jorno."

"Hey, Fin," Abisina said. "Here." She offered her stool to him, pulling up the smaller stool Haret had been sitting on.

"Take mine, Abisina," Jorno offered. "I have to go talk to Corlin."

"I just left him at the meeting house," Findlay said.

Jorno headed to the door. Findlay, walking to the hearth, had to step aside to keep from colliding with him. "Sorry," Jorno said tersely.

Findlay sat down and picked up the spoon. After a glance in the pot, he put it down again.

"Goodnight, Abisina," Jorno said from the door. His gaze lingered on her. "I enjoyed our conversation."

Haret returned two weeks later, bringing only three dwarves with him: towheaded brothers, Dolan and Werlif, and a darker blonde female, their cousin Prane. Abisina wondered if Haret had chosen them for their lighter coloring, but he said he'd taken who would come. "They're as suspicious of the Vranians as the Vranians are of us. Only the youngest ones were interested. And I don't want to think what Breide will say when she finds out I brought a female!"

Werlif was so young that he didn't have a beard yet. Dolan's beard was patchy, and Abisina learned that it had fallen out in places where he'd come into contact with the Worm's poison, which soaked the ground around Stonedun. All three of the dwarves had burns on their hands and faces from working in the noxious soil.

The poison had destroyed so many plants and trees that the Stonedun dwarves had little to eat. They lost days of labor on their new home, transporting food over many leagues. Gangs of men, hungry enough to eat dwarf roots, raided their caravans.

"They've talked of leaving Stonedun," Haret said, "but they have dreamed of returning to it for so long. And they'd have challenges anywhere in the south. For now, they're staying."

"Any news of Kyron and the others?" Abisina asked.

Haret shook his head. "Any sign of the fairy spies?"

"No. Maybe they've given up, now that we're this far south."

With the arrival of the new dwarves, several more people left for Vranham.

Findlay took the loss personally. One of the men who left had become an avid forager. "He was truly curious about the folk who live in Watersmeet. I guess curiosity isn't enough."

Corlin remained stoic. "Several men have come to me to say that I'm pushing them too hard. They don't want another Vran, but they don't want 'demons,' either." Corlin rubbed his eyes. "We're going to lose some. But that doesn't mean we stop."

In one day of work, the dwarves almost doubled what the villagers had done on the wall. That afternoon, the entire crew of men—and a few women and children—gathered around to watch the progress, hypnotized by the dwarves' skill and precision.

Abisina suspected that Haret was showing off a little. As he selected rocks, he sniffed them, rubbed his cheek against them, and sometimes touched them with his tongue or held them to his ear.

The other dwarves placed the rocks Haret chose and then twisted, adjusted, and readjusted, as they found their grooves and contours. Once, Prane returned a rock to Haret, her face red to the tips of her ears.

"I'm sure it's me, chief," she said, "but I can't fit this one."

Haret took the rock and ran his hand over it. He cocked his head and slowly walked over to the place it belonged.

"Chisel?" Prane asked, and Haret rolled his eyes.

Dolan and Werlif stopped their work to watch. The crowd held its breath.

Haret licked his pinkie, pressed it down in the center of the rock, and lifted it to his face to examine something so small Abisina couldn't see it. The onlookers shrugged.

Deliberately, he flicked the offending speck away. Prane reached for the rock. Before Haret relinquished it, he warned, "Let it dry."

"Dry, chief?" Prane asked in a small voice.

"My finger was wet!" He held up his pinkie. Prane smiled sheepishly. She blew on the rock and tried again. When the rock fell into place, a loud cheer went up from the crowd.

The next morning, when Haret stopped by, Abisina learned that the dwarves had staged the entire drama.

"What?" she cried.

"Human, you're not going to tell me you believed that. The rocks fit very, very closely—closer than a human could ever sense—but a bit of spit?"

"Prane . . . the other dwarves . . . they were all in on it?"

"Of course. We have to show these Vranians that we have unique skills. And we do. We just made it a little more obvious for them."

Abisina had to smile, though she wasn't quite sure she agreed with Haret's trick.

"Last night," Haret went on, "some men stayed at our fire for blister roots. They learned some of our songs and we learned some of theirs. I've never heard sterner music! They make those centaur songs sound almost jolly."

As Haret started to leave, Abisina couldn't resist asking one more time. "But really, Haret—the whole stone thing was a joke?"

"Dwarves never joke about stone. The joke was about the

humans. A bit of wet." He chuckled. "Now a full grain of sand, on the other hand . . ."

When Haret was in Stonedun, more people had begun to spend their evenings around Abisina's hearth in the healer's house. Even when he returned, the dwarves worked late on the wall, and the people continued to come. Ivice often drank a cup of tea before heading home, joined by Dehan. They'd been married recently—both had lost their spouses to the Worm. Ivice's son, Landry, would stop in. Brack, the outcast boy from Vranille, sometimes slipped in and brought his friends. Although it made Abisina angry that they came only when Haret was gone, she was heartened to think they were making any progress. It felt good to be a hostess. *A party of Vranians in my house*, she marveled.

There was a growing sense of well-being in Vranlyn. The storehouses were filling, Haret's crew made improvements on the wall, and the gleaming weapons in the armory added to their feeling of security.

Minotaurs and überwolves harried the foragers regularly, but the centaur attacks had slowed. Abisina wondered if finally convincing the villagers to remove the centaur tails from the outer walls had helped. She was thankful for the reprieve, whatever its cause.

Seeing a kestrel in the forest as she gathered herbs also raised Abisina's spirits. She knew that Neriah was following their progress.

But Kyron, Elodie, and Erna had not come.

A group gathered at Abisina's hearth one cold evening when the fire was particularly welcome. Haret was with the other dwarves. Findlay and Jorno sat on either side of the room; Abisina was near the middle with Corlin, Ivice, and Dehan. Thaula played at Abisina's feet with her friend, Hilagar. Brack and two of his friends rounded out the group.

"What do the Vranians do for celebrations?" Findlay asked.

"Celebrations?" Brack looked at him in surprise.

"We didn't have celebrations," Corlin said. "Just rituals. Like the Day of Penance."

Abisina met Jorno's gaze. It was on the Day of Penance that the mob had killed Vranille's outcasts. Brack shifted uncomfortably, too.

"Do you still observe the Day of Penance?" Findlay asked.

"We don't observe any of the Vranian rituals," Corlin said. "I've often thought we need to replace them, but there's been no time to figure out how."

"The rituals were horrible," said Abisina. "Chants that reminded the people how undeserving they were, how Vran had given them so much and they'd achieved so little. I was amazed when I arrived in Watersmeet at Midsummer. Feasting and dancing, songs and stories . . . There was nothing like that in Vranille."

"At Vran's Birthfest we got a little more to eat than usual," Dehan noted.

"And the Elders took most of it," Ivice said bitterly, then clapped a hand over her mouth.

Despite the changes in Vranlyn, women rarely disagreed with their husbands—especially in public.

Dehan looked from his wife to Corlin, unsure how to respond.

"When was Vran's Birthfest?" Findlay asked, breaking the tension.

"The summer solstice," Corlin said.

"What about now? What did the Vranians celebrate at this time of year?"

"The Day of Penance," Abisina answered. "What are you thinking, Fin?"

"Celebrations aren't just joyous," he said. "They bring folk together. We need to celebrate what we've done here, show them that this new life is different. Better."

"You're right, Findlay," Corlin said. "We need a celebration of some kind. It's been too long."

Thaula let out a huge yawn, which prompted Ivice to do the same. Ivice got to her feet and announced, "It's bedtime."

The others began saying good-bye and heading toward the door.

"Fin," Abisina said, "can you stay? I have something I want to ask you about." They had made this plan earlier in the day. The night before, Jorno had stayed to talk after everyone had left, despite Abisina's hints that she wanted him to leave. She didn't want that to happen again—and neither did Findlay.

Corlin was the last to leave. "It serves another purpose, celebration," he said. "We're trying to pull down the memory of Vran, but we've provided nothing in place of him."

"What do you mean?" Findlay asked.

"Well, Watersmeet has Vigar, right? Isn't she someone you look to for guidance, to provide some . . . model for how to live?"

"Yes," Abisina said. "But she didn't become a deity to the folk of Watersmeet the way Vran did for the Vranians."

"She's a hero," Findlay said. "Her founding idea for Watersmeet is what drove us to leave and come south."

"Maybe we need a 'hero.'" Corlin paused, a half smile on his lips. Then his smile turned into a grin. "We're really doing it, aren't we? We're building something here—something new."

He sauntered out of the hut, whistling as he walked through the dark village.

CHAPTER XXIV

ABISINA WENT ABOUT HER HEALING THE NEXT MORNING in a light mood. *If only Elodie, Kyron, and Erna would get here . . .*

A woman on the foraging team came in with a sick child in her arms. "I need help," Trima said. "Espen's been sick for days. His cough . . . He can barely catch a breath!"

Abisina reached for the little boy, limp in his mother's arms, but Trima pulled away. "Do you have to touch him?"

It had been weeks since anyone had balked at her touch. "I don't have to," Abisina said gently. "But it will help me find out what's wrong." The boy's breath rattled in his chest. Heat radiated off him. "Please, Trima," she said. "He's very sick."

At another gasping breath and a spasm of coughing, the mother relented and gave her child to Abisina. "He's all I have left of his father," she whispered.

"I'll do everything I can."

A hand to the boy's chest confirmed what Abisina already knew. She needed to clear his lungs—fast. Abisina pinched the flesh on the top of his hand; instead of springing back, the little ridge of flesh remained. He needed to begin drinking immediately.

"Get as much of this between his lips as you can, while I brew a sun-dew tea," Abisina instructed, handing Trima a cup of fish broth set aside for her own mid-meal.

Poor Espen had no energy to resist as his mother poured broth between his lips.

Abisina waited for the water to boil and wracked her brain for any other remedies. Then it came to her. "Snakeroot! The dwarves make a tea that has worked in some of the worst cases. I'll—"

"You will not give my son anything from a dwarf!" Trima shook with rage, holding Espen tightly against her.

"Trima, the sun-dew will help, but I don't know if it's enough."

"No demon medicine!" Trima stormed out, with her son in her arms.

Abisina called after her, "I'll send the tea over with Thaula as soon as it's ready. Keep giving him broth and water."

Her good mood had evaporated. *She can say what she wants to me, but to put her child's life at risk . . .* The water was boiling. With a sigh, Abisina took the sun-dew leaves and dropped them in the pot. *I'll brew the snakeroot anyway. If she changes her mind, I'll be ready.*

There was a Seldar grove a short walk from Vranlyn, and Abisina liked to go there early in the morning. The next day she woke up anxious to stroll through the trees. Thaula had delivered the sun-dew tea, and Trima hadn't brought Espen to Abisina in the night—a good sign.

Both Findlay and Jorno had warned her about leaving the safety of the village by herself—it was one of the few things they agreed on—but the quiet of the morning, the brisk fall air, and the time alone with her thoughts tempted her.

As she approached, the grove seemed to rise like an island of light from the pearly mist of morning.

A dark figure moved among the Seldars.

Abisina raced to the grove, caution forgotten, throwing her arms around a very surprised Elodie.

"Abisina!" Elodie cried and hugged her back.

"I've been so worried."

"I'm so glad to see you."

"You're thinner," they both said at once and laughed.

"Are you all here? Erna and Kyron?" Abisina asked.

"They're hidden nearby. With Darvus."

"Darvus!" Abisina exclaimed.

"We stayed with Erna's folk for a while—to recover. Few are left, but they took care of us, welcoming me, and even Kyron, when Erna explained who we were. I knew you'd be worried, but we had no choice."

"Can you take me to them, Elodie?"

"Of course. It was all I could do to keep Kyron from storming Vranlyn last night."

"Vigar's braid! We've made progress," Abisina said, "but they're not ready for that."

Elodie nodded. "It's the same with the fauns. We heard Icksyon's name everywhere. We had to convince them that Kyron wasn't spying for him."

The girls hurried away from the grove, but before they'd gone far, they heard Findlay call, "Abisina?"

She motioned Elodie behind the trees. "Over here, Fin. Are you alone?"

"Yes. I really wish you wouldn't come out—" He stopped as he caught sight of the other girl. He broke into a wide grin. "Elodie!" They hugged each other. "How are you? Where are the others?"

"I'm taking Abisina to them now. Findlay, I think you're actually taller!"

The others were hidden about half a league away. A large pine had fallen and taken a few other trees down with it. The jumble of trunks and branches made several leaf-caves that kept all of them—even Kyron, if he lay down—out of sight.

"Look who I found!" Elodie called. "You were right, Kyron. She came to the grove!" The others emerged from their bowers. Everyone but Darvus was exhausted and thin. Kyron bore several new scars on his chest and flank and a fresh cut on his forearm. Abisina unslung her medicine pouch and examined his wounds.

Though Findlay wanted to stay and hear about their journey, he offered to get Corlin. "And I'll bring some food," he added, exchanging a worried look with Abisina.

"I can see that you've had a hard time," Abisina said after Findlay left. "What happened?"

Except for a few überwolf skirmishes, their trek to the Cleft had gone smoothly. But at the mouth of the Cleft, they stumbled into a large group of refugees fighting a pack of überwolves.

"Kyron and I took out more than half the wolves," Elodie said. "But the refugees barely spoke to us afterward."

"They barely spoke to *you*," Kyron put in. "They completely refused to speak to *me*. Now that we're in the south, we understand." He shook his head. "The centaurs here! Abisina, I knew what they did to you . . . but I hadn't seen them for myself."

Erna whimpered at the mention of centaurs. Darvus put his arm around her and cooed in her ear.

"We were congratulating ourselves that we made it to the Cleft," Elodie went on. "Little did we know what waited on the other side."

"Icksyon?" Abisina asked.

"Almost as bad—one of his herds."

Darvus explained, "All the centaurs in our area have joined together under Icksyon's leadership. With food getting scarcer, they're after the deer, stag, and wild donkeys near our home."

"It's the same down here," Abisina said, "though Icksyon's herd hasn't attacked Vranlyn yet. If anything, we've seen fewer centaurs lately."

"The centaurs we met at the Cleft didn't know what to make of me," Kyron said. "At first, they thought Elodie and Erna were prisoners and assumed that I was taking them to Icksyon."

Erna shook as Darvus held her closer, rocking her.

"Apparently 'tribute' is common," Kyron growled. "Barbarians! But I was ready to talk—to offer them the centaur greeting. Then the leader cut me in the side, and that spurred the rest into action. We'd used so many arrows against the überwolves, I didn't dare face them. But with Elodie and Erna on my back, I didn't have much hope of outrunning them."

"So your fairy helped us," Elodie said.

"Neriah? You saw her?" Abisina asked.

"No, but we saw her birds. A whole flock of kestrels swooping in on the centaurs, pecking at eyes, causing mayhem. It must have been her."

"Did you see any of Reava's birds?"

"Not after we left you," Elodie said. "But after the fight at the Cleft, we traveled at night, so we might have missed them. It slowed us down, but we couldn't risk another fight with centaurs."

"Then we got to *my* community." Erna spoke up for the first time.

"Yes." Elodie smiled at the faun. "We were worn out, hungry—even sick." Elodie glanced at Kyron.

"I was getting weaker and weaker," he said. "I'd gotten several wounds in the fight with Icksyon's crew. They festered . . ."

"Kyron looked so frail, our folk didn't run from him," Darvus explained.

"It's been hard for our folk," Erna said, her lip quivering. "We lost so many to the Worm. The centaurs have killed more."

"That's why I never made it to Watersmeet," Darvus said. "There was too much to do, and few fauns left to do it. And then there was Erna's mother." He took Erna's hand in his, and she sniffed.

"Is she . . . did she . . ." Abisina stopped, afraid to upset Erna more.

But Erna answered, "Yes . . . She did. It was a lovely ceremony." She sniffed again.

"I am sorry, Erna," Abisina said.

"I know I shouldn't be sad," Erna said. "He'll be good to her."

"He?"

"Her new mate," Erna said woefully.

"Your mother got remated?" Abisina exclaimed. "Why Erna, that's wonderful! I thought she had died."

Erna stared at Abisina and burst into tears. Darvus led her away from the group, giving Abisina a reproachful look.

"What just happened?" Abisina asked.

"Well, you said that it was 'wonderful' that her mother remated," Elodie said with a little smile.

"How can that be worse than dying?"

"She thinks her mother remated too soon. It's been only fifteen winters since her father died."

"Fifteen winters—Elodie!"

Now Elodie grinned. "You know Erna," she said.

"Darvus actually makes it worse," Kyron noted with a glance over his shoulder to where the two fauns huddled together. "She was getting quite . . . Well, I won't say strong. Maybe a little less helpless. Now, she's worse than she was in Watersmeet."

"She was shocked that so many fauns had died," Elodie said.

When it was Abisina's turn to describe her trek south, she hesitated and then said, "I have something to tell you first, Elodie. I should have told you before."

Elodie's face turned serious.

"I've learned that I'm . . . I'm a shape-shifter. Like my father."

Abisina held her breath, waiting for Elodie's reaction.

"A shape-shifter? You can become a centaur?"

Abisina nodded.

"That's fantastic!" she cried. She hugged Abisina to her.

Abisina felt a surge of strength. She was done lying to her friends.

Elodie released her and said, "I *knew* it!"

"You did?"

"You've become more like your father. Going to the Motherland, the way you handled Glynholly, the decision to go south. You've *felt* more like Rueshlan's daughter. You carry yourself differently—with more confidence."

"You're right, Elodie." Kyron beamed.

When Erna and Darvus returned, Abisina took Erna's hand and said, "You don't have to lie for me anymore, Erna. Elodie knows I'm a shape-shifter."

"Really?" she whispered. "You were so . . . scared."

"I was," Abisina agreed. "But you were right. My friends love me."

Erna's face shone. "You mean, I helped you?"

"You did," Abisina assured her.

"Do the humans in Vranlyn know?" Kyron asked.

"Not yet," Abisina admitted. "They're not ready. Corlin perhaps."

Abisina was explaining what life was like in Vranlyn when Corlin and Findlay arrived, bringing several loaves of bread and salted fish.

Corlin didn't hesitate as he greeted Kyron and the fauns. When he met Elodie, however, he paled. He took her offered hand, and long after Elodie had released his, he held it at his side, fingers curled as if holding something he didn't want anyone else to see.

Elodie seemed shaken, too. Abisina glanced at Findlay, and he winked at her.

"I wish I could be sure my people would welcome you

as much as I do," Corlin apologized. "Especially after what Watersmeet has done for them. But I think we need to go slowly. If I showed up with all of you . . ."

"We have to convince the villagers that we can be useful," Abisina said. "You've never seen a forager like Erna. Maybe we should start with the fauns."

Erna blushed at Abisina's praise.

"I think Elodie should be first," Corlin said. "As a human, she's easier for the people to accept."

"I'm ready," Elodie said with a smile at Corlin. He grinned, too.

"Are you coming back now, Abisina?" Findlay asked.

"I need to check on Espen, but I'm worried about leaving the others here."

"Don't worry about us," Darvus said quickly. "Fauns can melt into the woods like tree spirits. We'll look after Kyron for you."

"Look after me?" Kyron grumbled, his mouth full of bread. "I'm the one everyone fears!"

"I'll come back this afternoon—if Findlay will let me off foraging duty," Abisina said.

Findlay pretended to think it over. "I'll let myself off, too," he concluded.

When Abisina clasped Kyron's forearm in farewell, the big roan leaned in to her and whispered, "That was a brave thing you did, Abisina, telling Elodie."

"I should have done it sooner."

"You've done it now." He squeezed her arm. "I'll see you after noon," he called.

Corlin and Elodie fell into step, absorbed in conversation. Findlay chuckled.

"What?" Abisina said.

"Corlin looks like I did when I met you," Findlay answered.

Abisina took Findlay's hand. She thought Elodie was beautiful with her smooth, ebony skin, bright eyes, and cascading hair, but she had never imagined that a Vranian could appreciate this beauty. Even a Vranian like Corlin.

Maybe he is ready to see me as a centaur. . . .

CHAPTER XXV

COMING THROUGH VRANLYN'S GATE, THEY ENCOUNTERED A group of people delivering baskets to the storehouse. Corlin called out: "We have a new visitor from Watersmeet!"

Abisina knew he was counting on the strength and mystery of "Watersmeet" to temper their reaction, but one woman stared at Elodie in shock, huddling closer to her husband. An older man threw his basket down and stomped back to the village. A woman Abisina knew from the healer's house welcomed Elodie curtly without taking her offered hand. As the group retreated to the storehouse, Corlin said under his breath, "Not as bad as it might've been."

Elodie looked dazed.

The next group they met—the men working with the dwarves on the wall—didn't go any better. Haret came over and embraced Elodie while the men glared. Elodie answered them with a friendly smile, which forced some to gaze at their feet.

"Corlin, a word," Heben said. Abisina knew that Heben had threatened to leave several times, and she braced herself. He pulled Corlin aside and spoke intensely, punching his fist for emphasis. Corlin nodded, the flush of anger creeping up his cheeks. He returned to Findlay and the girls and offered Elodie a tight smile, but said nothing.

When they reached the center of the village, the common ground should have been alive with activity. The fires were stoked, and the smell of smoked meat hung in the air, but the work had ceased. Across the common, Abisina saw stony faces. Only the children fidgeted, glancing from one group to the other in confusion.

Jorno stood among the villagers, arms crossed, frowning. Corlin and Abisina had agreed that they would not tell Jorno that Kyron, too, had arrived. When Abisina suggested this, Corlin had questioned whether it was necessary, but Jorno's face reassured Abisina that they had made the right decision.

"I'm taking Elodie into the meeting house," Abisina said quietly. "Findlay, I think you should stay."

"Why should we hide Elodie away?" Corlin argued. "If we don't force them to accept her—"

"We are forcing them to accept Elodie," Abisina cut him off. "She's here. But they're scared and angry. We *can* push them too far, Corlin."

"But—"

"Please. Trust me."

"Corlin," Findlay said, touching his arm. "You need to talk to them. Now."

Corlin faced the crowd.

Abisina and Elodie ducked into the house. Abisina thanked the Elders for building such sound houses; once the door was closed, voices droned from the common, but they couldn't hear the words.

Elodie sank into a chair, head in her hands. "I knew it would be difficult. But that—"

Abisina paced. *It could have been worse. They could have come after her.*

Elodie raised her head. "To think that you used to live like this," she said softly, and Abisina realized her eyes were full of tears.

"Of course you are kind enough to think of *me* right now," Abisina said as she knelt in front of her friend and put her arms around her.

"I'll just have to get used to it," Elodie said. "Now that I know what I'm dealing with . . . Why did you leave the common?"

Abisina grimaced as she got to her feet again. "I can think like a Vranian," she said. "Findlay is a man and he looks like them; they can respect him. He also represents Watersmeet, which is a powerful symbol. Watersmeet killed the Worm."

"Your father killed the Worm. Wouldn't *you* be a more powerful reminder?"

"Most of them weren't at the battle. Rueshlan's a legend to them. In reality, they would see him as a demon. How can you owe your freedom to a demon?"

"I can see why you haven't told the folk here that you're a shape-shifter," Elodie said, "but you don't even seem angry."

"I'm angry sometimes. But I can't force them to change. I can only show them how. It's going to be slow—and painful."

Findlay came in and took a chair next to Elodie with a sigh.

"What's going on out there?" Abisina asked.

"Several men are leaving. There might be more." Findlay leaned forward, elbows on his knees. "When Corlin began talking, most of the women faded back, letting the men carry on the discussion. I thought that was changing, but when there's a threat, those habits return. One of the men leaving is on my team. He had told me he'd *never* go to Vranham. He had two children with dark hair left to die outside the walls. But now he says he'll be gone within the hour."

"What did Corlin do?" Elodie asked.

"Stood his ground. He feels terrible about what you've had to go through. He'll be here soon to tell you himself."

Abisina wondered if they would've had more luck bringing Erna. Though Abisina knew Elodie was kind and funny, she appeared strong and intimidating at first. Or maybe her friends shouldn't have come at all. *To be treated as monsters . . .*

"I know what you're thinking," Findlay said, "so stop it. We *want* to be here."

Abisina couldn't help but smile.

"Abisina?" Thaula poked her head in the doorway. "Are

you coming to the healer's house? There's a line of people waiting for you."

Abisina got up. "I'll be right there, Thaula. I think I'll stay in the village this afternoon," she said to Findlay. She didn't want to leave Elodie. "Will you go see Kyron?"

"I'll tell him that you'll come tomorrow," Findlay said.

Abisina appreciated the distraction of the busy healer's house, losing herself in her tasks until she heard a groan at the doorway.

Trima was there, Espen clutched in her arms. His breathing was worse, his frail chest struggling to rise, his lips blue. Trima had been giving him broth—he was no longer pinched with thirst—but this was little comfort.

"Do what you have to do," she said hoarsely. "Just save my boy."

Abisina returned to the meeting house after noon. The snake-root had already started to work and Espen was sleeping more peacefully. When Abisina arrived, Findlay had just left to visit Kyron. Corlin said good-bye to Elodie reluctantly, off to try one more time to convince the families to stay.

"I have to get out of here," Elodie said once Corlin was gone. At the look on Abisina's face, she laughed. "Not out of Vranlyn. Out of this house. It's oppressive."

"The Elders' spirits have seeped into the walls." Abisina shuddered. "But are you ready to face the people out there?"

"That's why I'm here, isn't it?"

"Elodie, I will never stop admiring you," Abisina said, as she opened the door.

Most people were already at their afternoon tasks and the streets were quiet. Two older men frowned at Elodie's approach, but Elodie smiled at them. After the girls had passed, one of the men called to Abisina, "I need some more of that wintergreen salve, healer. If you have some."

Once inside the healer's house, Abisina released a big sigh, echoed by Elodie. Both laughed. "I don't know what it is about you, Elodie," Abisina exclaimed. "You make me laugh even at the most serious times."

"My mother calls it my 'giddiness'—a quality she does not approve of. She says you make me 'steadier.'"

"She should see you on patrol. You're as serious as Lohring when you're facing überwolves."

"Lohring? Really?" Elodie said.

"Yes, the Fairy Mother herself!" Abisina frowned. "I wonder how her plan is going. Do you think they've closed the Cleft?"

"They've had enough time to get a crew there from Watersmeet. But they'll have to spend all their energy defending themselves against überwolves and centaurs rather than building their wall."

Elodie wandered around the hut while Abisina made tea. "Did you make *all* of these?" she asked, examining the array of medicines.

"Most," said Abisina proudly. "We'll need them all to get through the winter."

"I'll miss Watersmeet at the solstice," Elodie said wistfully, then smiled. "So much for being giddy."

Abisina told Elodie about the planned celebration. Corlin had already formed a committee to work on it. "A first step toward a Council," he'd told Abisina excitedly.

Thaula came dashing into the hut, saw Elodie, and screamed.

"Thaula!" Abisina cried.

The little girl clapped her hands over her mouth. "I'm sorry," she mumbled. Or at least that's what Abisina thought she said.

Thaula put her hands down and tried again. "I'm sorry," she repeated earnestly. "You—you startled me."

"You saw her this morning at the meeting house," Abisina pointed out.

Thaula shook her head emphatically.

"I had my back to the door," Elodie said. "Is this the helper you told me about?"

Thaula took a tentative step forward and nodded.

"This is Thaula, and as you can see, she needs to work on her manners."

Thaula inched closer. "Can I . . . can I touch you?" she whispered.

"Thaula!" Abisina cried again.

"It's all right," Elodie said, laughing. "She's never seen anyone as dark as I am."

"I wanted to touch the dwarves, but I was afraid to ask," Thaula admitted.

"A good thing. I don't know what Haret would've said," Abisina replied.

"You may touch me, Thaula," Elodie said.

Thaula reached a finger toward Elodie's hand. She touched it lightly and then grinned at Elodie. "You're real."

"I hope so," said Elodie.

Abisina poured Thaula some tea. "You didn't ask to touch me."

"I *did* touch you—the first night you were here. You didn't realize it because we were all crowded into Corlin's house."

By the time Jorno arrived, Thaula was on Elodie's lap, chattering away.

Jorno greeted Elodie politely, but stole furtive glances at her. While Thaula showed Elodie the letters she'd learned, writing in charcoal on the hearth, he said to Abisina, "Is it true that all the people—folk—in Watersmeet can read?"

"Yes. There's a large library there. My father helped collect stories from fauns, centaurs, dwarves—even the fairies."

Jorno sat back in his chair. "Hmm. So they can learn."

Elodie and Thaula fell silent at Jorno's words.

"I'm sorry, Abisina. Really—I don't know how it works with them."

"*They* are as smart as we are, Jorno. In fact, they know plenty of things that humans don't. All the folk have gifts. The fauns can communicate with trees and tree spirits. The centaurs understand hoofed animals."

"They can talk to other beasts?" Jorno asked, and Abisina's brow creased.

"Hoofed animals," she repeated.

"Come see." Thaula tugged on Elodie's hand. "It's just outside."

"What's outside?" Abisina asked.

"The stool I'm building," Thaula said.

Abisina began to follow them, but Jorno grabbed her hand. "About what I said. I know it upset you."

Abisina tried to put her anger aside. "I forget sometimes that I felt the same way once. Of course it's going to take everyone awhile to get used to us."

"It's not you I have to get used to," Jorno said quickly. "I know Elodie had a rough welcome, but humans are easier for us."

Abisina remembered how she was comforted by the fairy homes in the Motherland, watching the fairies visit one another. It made them seem more like her. Wasn't that what Jorno was saying?

"Abisina, you have to know how I feel about you," Jorno blurted out. "Since we first met in your mother's hut. I said nothing then. You were young, and your mother insisted I keep my full recovery from you. But when you arrived here—I knew it was meant to be."

"Jorno—" Abisina tried to break in.

"Findlay doesn't know you like I do," he continued in a rush. "He's not Vranian. He wasn't outcast. He wasn't taken by centaurs. Abisina"—he clutched her hand—"I didn't mean to say this all now, but it couldn't wait."

Abisina pulled her hand away. "Please, Jorno."

"Just think about what I said."

Elodie and Thaula returned. Jorno met them at the door. "I have to check in at the armory," he said.

As Abisina sat down at the fire, Jorno's words lingered in her mind. She and Jorno did have a lot in common. It had been extremely hard for her to put the past behind her. But she loved Findlay. And trusted him.

And what if Jorno knew about my shape-shifting? What would he think then?

He was wrong—he didn't know her at all. They may have shared something once, but not now.

For the next two days, Elodie caught up on sleep—and food—helping Abisina in the healer's house between naps. Corlin visited frequently. On Elodie's third day, she woke and announced: "Enough sleeping. I'm here to show the Vranians that I'm not a demon. What can I do?"

Abisina suggested she come with her on the afternoon foraging trip. "The group is small, and we could use your patrolling skills. And if they're at all like Corlin, they won't be able to resist you!"

Elodie looked sharply at Abisina, then giggled. "There does seem to be a certain . . . connection between us."

They stopped in at the meeting house where Corlin,

Jorno, and Findlay argued over the coming celebration. Haret was there, too, on a rare break from work on the wall. When Abisina walked in, he was insisting that the dwarves plan the music. "Vranian dirges are not celebratory!"

Jorno scowled.

Corlin explained that the planning committee wanted to observe a penance.

Jorno turned to Abisina. "I'm sure you'll agree with me. A penance is too much like the old ways."

"A penance doesn't have to be painful," she said. "We can have a short ritual and follow it with celebration. They need something familiar."

"That's what the committee wants to do," Corlin agreed.

Jorno's scowl deepened.

He assumed I'd agree with him, thought Abisina.

"I have another idea," she said. She hadn't intended to share it so soon, but Jorno's anger startled her and the words came tumbling out. "I was thinking that the village needs a new name."

At first there was silence. Then Corlin smiled. "Of course," he said. "We're no longer *Vran*lyn."

"So what should it be called? Or have you thought of that, too, Abisina?" Findlay said.

"Well, actually, I have. Watersmeet is named for a natural feature. I thought of the Seldars, but that didn't lead anywhere. Corlin said the people need a hero, so I considered *Cor*lyn." She laughed as Corlin blushed. "Then it came to me: *New*lyn."

"Newlyn," Corlin echoed. "I like it."

There were nods around the group.

"Let's do it!" Corlin said, then caught himself. "We should take it to the people."

"Findlay?" One of the foragers stood in the door. "We're ready to go."

"Right. Are you coming, Abby?"

"And Elodie," she said.

Abisina could feel Jorno's gaze following her as they left the meeting house, but she refused to meet his eyes.

When they showed up with Elodie to meet the foragers, there were dark looks, but no one left. Brack, the outcast from Vranille, even said hello to Elodie, though his face was red with embarrassment.

Findlay led the group to the patch of wild leeks they planned to harvest. The women carried bows, the men spears and swords. Elodie and Abisina kept arrows on their strings, and Findlay kept his sword unsheathed as the rest of the group pulled the leeks.

"I think we've got enough," Findlay called, just as Elodie yelled, "Guard!"

Abisina and Findlay responded immediately, taking positions on the outside of the group.

"Get into the middle. Spears out, bows ready," Findlay commanded the villagers in an undertone. Abisina, Elodie, and Findlay slowly backed up, tightening the circle. All eyes scanned the trees and brush.

Abisina heard the twang of a bow, a short cry, and the thud of a body. "One down!" Elodie called.

Abisina saw something move in the shadow of an elm. She shot, but her arrow shivered into a tree beyond.

A villager behind Abisina took an arrow in the shoulder. "Ahh!" Taber bellowed but held his ground, blood running down his arm.

The arrow had come from above. A shaggy man perched in the elm, ready to loose another arrow. "Trees!" Taber cried.

At his yell, arrows flew. Disheveled men emerged from the trees and dropped from above, swords, arrows, and spears ready. It was one of the gangs that had been pillaging Vranlyn's fields. The wood filled with shouts and the clang of weapons.

Abisina felled two of the attackers. A man held the point of his sword dangerously close to Findlay's neck. Before Abisina could shoot, Brack brought the man down with a spear. Without pause, Abisina aimed and shot at a man leaning out from the shelter of a tree.

One of the village spearmen fell, and a woman doubled over, an arrow in her gut. Abisina spun to her left and shot twice—hitting a man in the throat, another in the side. Findlay felled another with his sword. Elodie was spraying arrows into the trees. Bodies littered the ground.

A grunt nearby caught Abisina's attention. Brack was rolling on the ground, fighting an attacker. He landed several punches on the man's face, but the man gave as good as he got, and Brack's nose bled. More blood dripped from a cut on his forehead. The attacker managed to draw a dagger. Abisina couldn't get a clean shot in the tangle of arms and legs. Taber yelled, "Come to me!" Brack rolled his adversary closer to Taber, who brought his spear down on the man's back.

The gang was finished. With a shout, the grizzled men disappeared into the trees, many of them leaving tracks of blood behind. The men carried off two bags of leeks.

Abisina hurried to check the injured. One spearman was dead, his throat cut. The woman with the arrow in her belly writhed in pain, but the arrow had missed her vital organs. Taber's shoulder bled copiously.

An attacker lay near the trees, unable to flee but alive. Abisina approached him.

"You," he said weakly.

It was Sten—the uncle she hardly knew, who had saved them from the troll.

He could expose me as a shape-shifter . . .

"We need three litters," she called to Findlay.

"I can walk," Taber insisted.

"I know. One's for him." She pointed to Sten.

"What are you going to do to me?" Sten demanded.

"Save you, if you let me."

"*We* won't let you," Taber interjected.

Abisina faced him. "I fight when I have to, but I'm a healer. I will not leave him out here to bleed to death or worse."

She turned to Sten and reached into her pouch for something to slow the bleeding.

"Why?" It was another forager, Chana. She didn't stare at Abisina but at Elodie. "Why did you protect me? That man—he had me, and you shot him."

Elodie shrugged. "You would have done the same for me."

Chana pursed her lips, and Abisina knew she wasn't so sure.

Findlay and Taber each took a litter, while Abisina dragged Sten's. Slowly, they made their way back to the village.

The sentry on the parapet spotted them as they left the trees, and a crowd came out to meet them. As the story about Elodie's expert shooting spread, the tension around her eased a little.

"Will you help Abisina teach us to shoot?" one woman asked timidly.

Fauns next, Abisina thought. *I hope Darvus and Erna are ready.*

That night Abisina had hoped to slip out of Vranlyn—*Newlyn,* she reminded herself. She couldn't use the name until it was official, but she loved the way it sounded. She wanted to see Kyron and the fauns, but the next few hours were critical for Sten. She couldn't leave him.

Sten didn't wake until the sun was high. "Nonna?" he rasped.

"No, it's me—Abisina."

He fought to rise, but couldn't lift his head off the pillow.

"Shh. Lie still, Sten. You're hurt."

He groaned. "I should never have taken up with that gang."

"Why did you?" Abisina asked.

"I thought I'd do better if I weren't on my own," Sten said weakly. "Icksyon's moving this way."

She had known this news would come, but hearing it, she felt sick. "Are you sure?"

"There's been a war. Icksyon killed a local herd leader, and brought the rival herd into his own."

"That's why we've had so few attacks," Abisina murmured. "They've been fighting each other."

Sten nodded, but the talk was wearing him out. "Go back to sleep," Abisina said. "You need your rest."

"Why are you doing this?" he asked. "I could tell them— about you."

"I know. But you're the only family I have left."

Abisina waited for Sten to fall asleep again, and then went to the meeting house to find the others. If Icksyon was coming, they had a lot of work to do.

CHAPTER XXVI

CORLIN DECIDED TO CALL A MEETING FOR THE WHOLE community.

"You can't tell them about Icksyon!" Jorno protested. "They'll be petrified!"

"They have a right to know," Corlin insisted. "We have to trust them—something the Elders never did."

Abisina felt a pang of guilt. She still hadn't trusted any of them—not even Corlin—with the secret of her shape-shifting.

She left them arguing, whispering to Findlay that she was going to warn Kyron about Icksyon. But first, she had to check on Espen. She gathered medicine at the healer's house, made sure Sten was comfortable, and went to Trima's hut. Espen's breathing was easier, and his cheeks had regained some color. Trima pressed Abisina's hand to her chest, and smiled through her tears.

Abisina was at Vranlyn's gate when Jorno stopped her.

"Where're you going?" he asked.

Abisina held up her healer's pouch. "I need some spike-nard. This string of coughs depleted my supplies."

"Do you think that's important now?"

"It's especially important now. I may not get another chance."

"You're going alone?"

"Findlay offered to come, but I'm really not going far." She hated lying, but she couldn't let Jorno come with her.

"You of all people know the dangers out there," Jorno said. "If I were Findlay, I wouldn't let you—"

"*Let* me?" Abisina said. "Findlay *offered* to come with me."

"Well, then I'm *offering* as well."

"I grew up in the woods, Jorno, and have been trained as a Watersmeet patroller."

"I worry about you, Abisina. Can't you understand that?" He took a step closer to her. "It's not like it was then. You're not an expendable outcast." Jorno spoke quietly, but his anger burned against her skin.

She forced a laugh. "I'd have a full sack of spikenard by now if I hadn't run into you. Spikenard must be picked when the sun is high." Another lie. "It's getting late. It won't take me long once I get out there." She walked through the gate and didn't look back.

Abisina transformed as soon as she was hidden in the trees. After her conversation with Jorno, it felt liberating to gallop.

Kyron was waiting near the tree-fall. "I almost gave up," he said as she trotted toward him. "But I thought you'd come today. The fauns and I have been on the move. Seems safer. I've been here since noon."

"I meant to get here sooner, Kyron. I'm sorry."

"Well, you're here now. Are you ready for a run?"

"I wish I could . . ." Abisina told Kyron about Icksyon.

"Do you know when an attack might come?"

"No. We're trying to get ready. I don't like you being out here. We might be able to get the fauns in, but you're tougher."

"I can take care of myself, Abisina," Kyron said. "It's you I'm worried about. I can't protect you when I'm out here."

"I'll be as safe as anyone inside Vranlyn," Abisina said. "My father would agree."

Kyron frowned, but didn't argue.

"Maybe all three of you should get away from here," Abisina went on. "We have food, weapons—things Icksyon wants. You'd be safer to the east."

"And leave you?"

Abisina recognized the set of Kyron's jaw. He was staying.

"I'll ask Haret to come tomorrow—find you a cave. He's been working so hard on that wall, he barely sleeps," she said.

Abisina agreed to a short gallop. Kyron seemed lonely; Erna and Darvus, newly reunited, would be poor company. She said good-bye as the sun began to set. Findlay—and Jorno—would be worried.

She couldn't see the village yet when she heard the *klee-klee-klee* of a kestrel overhead. She glanced up, and—"Oh!"

Neriah herself stood astride a branch, a black shadow against the red sky. "Sorry," the fairy said as she leapt to the ground. "I thought a kestrel call would be less startling than if I just appeared." She didn't show any surprise to see Abisina as a centaur.

Of course—her birds have been watching me.

Neriah wore the familiar loose black tunic and pants, and a long coat that seemed to be spun of night. The silver band of leaves was just visible through her hair.

Abisina noticed again that she was comfortable with Neriah in a way she wasn't with any other fairy.

"Are you alone?" Abisina asked.

"No one else even knows that I'm here," she said.

"I have to thank you, Neriah. I'm not sure I—or any of my friends—would have made it here without your help."

"You were brave to come, Abisina. I wanted to do what I could."

"What's happening in the north? In Watersmeet?"

"The Mother's plan is going forward," Neriah said. "Glynholly has sent dwarves to the Cleft, but she didn't send enough folk to guard them. They often have to stop their work to defend themselves against centaurs, überwolves, and refugees. The dwarves asked for more support, but Glynholly refused."

"Why?"

"I don't know. The Mother's been . . . vague. My birds have shown me skirmishes between Glynholly's soldiers and the refugees. I think she's afraid to leave Watersmeet defenseless."

"Glynholly is *fighting* the refugees?"

"Watersmeet is like a fortress now. Very few leave—and no one goes in."

"What about Neiall and the others that Glynholly captured? Do you know what's happened to them?"

"They were captured?" Neriah looked surprised.

"They met me when I returned from the Motherland. When I was called a traitor, they—"

"You—a traitor?"

"Because I went to the Motherland. Reava said that I had asked the Fairy Mother to help me overthrow Glynholly."

"But that's not true!"

"They exiled me anyway. Either Glynholly lied or Reava did."

Neriah stared at Abisina.

"I thought you knew all this," Abisina said. "You sent the kestrel to warn me."

"I sent a kestrel to keep me informed. It never returned."

"I saw peregrine falcons kill it. The kestrel carried a Seldar leaf. I assumed that the leaf was to tell me you had sent it."

"The leaf was to tell Reava and her falcons that the kestrel was mine. I knew something had gotten him, but not that it was my own sister. Reava wants the crown," Neriah said grimly.

"But you're the eldest daughter, aren't you? Isn't the crown yours?"

"Not necessarily. I have to prove myself. If Reava can show that she has more ability than I do, she could become Mother. Lohring herself wasn't the eldest daughter, but her older sister was seen as unstable."

Abisina considered how Neriah seemed somehow less constrained—more "human"—than the other fairies. *Is she considered "unstable"?*

"This has to be Reava's work," Neriah continued. "The Mother is willing to go to great lengths to protect the Motherland, but she wouldn't have stooped to this."

"Will you tell the Mother?"

Neriah considered. "Reava is my rival. Anything I say will be seen in that light. Reava will certainly deny it. And the Mother has gotten what she wanted. The dwarves are walling up the Cleft. She doesn't *want* to know how that result was purchased, as much as she would disapprove. In the end, Reava thinks the Mother will thank her by giving her the crown."

"Doesn't helping us hurt your chances to be the heir?"

"Perhaps, but closing off the south is wrong. And it will not work. The threat has grown too large. There are more überwolves, minotaurs, and trolls than ever before."

Abisina nodded. "They're said to be coming from the Mountains Eternal." She described what she'd seen from the cliff: the black gash crawling with bodies and the rift Sten had talked about.

"I've seen it, too," Neriah said. "I was at Vigar's garden. In fact, that's why I came. . . ." She reached into her long coat and withdrew a metal box. "Here." She laid the box in Abisina's hand.

The box was solid Obrium. The intricate designs etched into the metal reflected the light in dizzying patterns. "Where did you get this?" she asked.

"Vigar took this box to her grave. After several weeks in the garden, Hoysta must have felt its presence. She fought, but eventually she started to dig with her one good hand."

"In Vigar's grave?" The peace of the garden, the stillness of the grave, torn apart by Hoysta, mad with Obriumlust. "Is Hoysta all right?"

"She's weak and ashamed, but Frayda's helping her. It's good for Frayda, actually. She needed to help someone else."

"How did you know to go there?"

"Birds can report what they *see*, but they do not understand our speech. I wasn't sure why you left Hoysta in the garden, so I kept an eye on her. When my birds showed me images of Vigar's destroyed grave, I had to go."

Abisina ached, thinking of the pain this box had caused Hoysta. "What's in it?" she asked.

"I couldn't open it," Neriah said. "*You* must open it. You are Vigar's heir."

Abisina tried to hand the box back to the fairy. "I don't know what you mean. Glynholly's the Keeper. She's Vigar's heir."

"On Reava's last visit to the Motherland, she mentioned

that the Keeper's necklace is tarnished; it appears 'powerless,' according to her. As I understand it, Vigar gave the necklace to your father, and he gave it to your mother, even though it was the Keeper's necklace. Is that right?" At a nod from Abisina, Neriah asked, "Has that ever seemed strange to you?"

"I think he gave it to her because he loved her."

"Of course, that's part of it. But did the necklace continue to *shine* with Sina?"

"Yes."

"Why would it shine for a Vranian woman and not for Glynholly?"

"It shone for me, too. On the journey to Watersmeet and after I got there. Well—except when I ran away from my father. It died then."

"But then you stopped the battle with it," Neriah said, "and it was 'alive' again?"

"I just wore it, held it, followed where it led me," Abisina insisted.

"It did not lead you here, but I suspect it would respond to you even now. Your whole history is surprising, Abisina. From what I know of the Vranians, it is unusual that they allowed you to live. And yet you did," the fairy noted.

Abisina looked down at her hooves.

"Your shape-shifting is another sign of your unique destiny," Neriah said.

"Findlay said that once: that I have a special destiny." She stared at the box in her hand.

"If you are not meant to open it, it will stay closed. As it did for me."

The box was shut by a clasp of twisted Obrium threads looped over a tiny knob.

Abisina moved her finger to the loop, and the light around the box intensified. She remembered the dream she had before she'd arrived in Vranlyn: a powerful light came from Vigar's grave. Could Neriah be right—this box was meant for her? In one quick motion, she touched the loop, and the box sprang open with a flash.

A folded piece of vellum sat in the middle of the box and under the vellum, Abisina saw the imprint of the Keeper's necklace in the dark cloth that lined the bottom.

"The necklace came from this box!" She picked up the vellum, brittle with age, and unfolded it carefully.

"What does it say?" Neriah asked.

Abisina scanned the words, written in a hasty scrawl. She gasped, and the box nearly fell from her hands.

"What is it?" Neriah said.

Abisina read aloud:

> Vigar,
>   I cannot stay. I will find you in the valley.
>   Still your loving brother,
>   Vran

CHAPTER XXVII

"Vran and Vigar . . ." Abisina couldn't go on. She tried again. "How can the founders of Watersmeet and Vrania be sister and brother?"

Neriah said nothing.

"'*Still* your loving brother'—what happened between them?" Abisina stared at the box and the letter clutched in her hands. Vigar had touched this! Vran, too! Vran, who had brought so much pain and hatred to the world, had *loved* Vigar—the woman who had fought and died to bring folk together.

Understanding crept over her: she had been given a gift. "This changes everything," she said slowly. "Knowing these two were related could bring folk from Watersmeet and the Vranian villages together . . . as my father wanted. I have to tell my friends. Can I show them the box?"

"It's yours, Abisina."

"I can't keep it with me. If it did that to Hoysta, what would it do to Haret? Come with me now. We'll talk to my friends. Then you can take the box."

Neriah glanced at the moon. "I should get back . . . tell the Mother."

"Please, Neriah," Abisina said. "I want to show it to them, but I can't keep it."

"I will come briefly."

Neriah leapt to the trees and Abisina stayed in her centaur form. Once they reached the fields surrounding the village, Abisina transformed and Neriah joined her on the ground. The fairy was hard to see. Only her circlet of leaves flashed in the moonlight.

Abisina put the box in her satchel, keeping a hand on it as she walked. It was warm through the cloth, and she checked several times to see if the satchel glowed at her side; it didn't seem possible that the cloth's rough weave could contain all that brilliance. *Will Haret sense it right away?*

As they entered the village, Neriah took to the roofs, leaping from hut to hut. Abisina headed to the healer's house. Her friends would be gathered there, wondering where she was.

On the common ground, a large group was assembled. Abisina stopped.

". . . going after spikenard. Be ready to face anything."

Jorno. They're organizing a search! "Wait!" Abisina called, running across the common. "I'm here."

The group turned to her.

"Vigar's braid!" Findlay's voice, filled with relief.

"The Earth, human! What were you thinking?" And Haret's.

"I—I found some feverwort," Abisina said. "There's not much around here, so I stayed out to collect some. I'm sorry that I made you worry."

"At least you're safe," Corlin said. "Return to your suppers, everyone. Tell any others on their way that she's turned up. And thank you."

The crowd shuffled away, but Abisina's friends besieged her. Thaula almost knocked her down with a fierce hug.

"Where have you been, human?" Haret asked suspiciously. "You've harvested every bit of feverwort within leagues of here. What's really in the bag?" He reached out and touched her satchel, then snatched his hand away as if he'd been burned. "Wh—What have you got?"

"We need to go inside. Not the meeting house," Abisina said, speaking low. "We have a visitor."

"Kyron?" Findlay asked.

"The centaur?" Jorno broke in.

"Neriah—a fairy." Abisina avoided Jorno's stare.

"To the healer's house?" Corlin suggested.

"Sten's there."

"To mine then," Findlay said.

"Thaula," Abisina bent down to the little girl, "I need you to stay with Sten. I'll come home as soon as I can."

"Can't I see the fairy?" Thaula pleaded.

"Not this time, dear heart. And I need you to be *very* careful that you tell no one about her. Do you understand?"

"I can keep a secret." Thaula put both hands over her mouth, squeezed her eyes shut, and nodded three times to confirm her promise. Then off she went, a tiny shadow racing across the moonlit common.

When they reached Findlay's hut, Abisina called out to Neriah, and the fairy leapt from a roof. Corlin almost stumbled. Jorno went white, and even Elodie looked nervous.

"Let's get inside." Findlay was the first to recover.

Once in the hut, Neriah was ill at ease. The mundane items—a table, stools, and sleeping platforms—seemed to emphasize her wildness. *She looks caged*, Abisina thought. *But we need privacy for this.* For now, the news of Vran and Vigar had to stay among the folk she trusted.

Do I trust Jorno? He wasn't one of the folk she had planned to tell. He'd been there since she'd arrived in Vranlyn, part of the organizing, the work, the leadership of the village. Why wouldn't she include him? But that anger, those intense eyes, and flattering words . . . *It's too late now. I can't dismiss him the way I did Thaula.*

Haret also worried her. He was sweating, though the night was cold. He was short of breath, and he kept glancing at Abisina. She tried to sit as far from him as possible as they pulled stools and chairs to the fire. Neriah remained standing. An anxious silence fell over the gathering.

Abisina told of the latest events in Watersmeet and the

status of the wall at the Cleft. She confirmed Reava's treachery and that the creatures that plagued the south—and now the north in increasing numbers—came from the Mountains Eternal.

"I didn't want to believe the rumors," Corlin said.

"That's why Neriah helped us come south," Abisina said. "We must come together, the north and the south, if we hope to protect ourselves."

Haret jumped to his feet. "There's more!" he cried. "I can feel it in this room." He pointed a shaking finger at Abisina. "You're hiding something!" He lunged toward her.

Before Abisina could respond, Neriah leapt forward and stood between them. She towered over the dwarf, and her voice filled the room. "Dwarf! Will your madness hurt someone else you love?"

Haret cowered before the fairy, then fled.

Around the circle, faces were stunned.

"It's this." Abisina drew the box from her satchel. The room turned as bright as day.

Jorno raised a hand to shield his eyes. "What is that?"

"Where did you get it?" Findlay asked.

"It was Vigar's." Abisina explained how Hoysta found it. "The box used to contain the Keeper's necklace." She opened it. "Look at the imprint in the cloth. Vigar and my father wore the necklace. Glynholly wears it now. But the light in the metal has gone out. Neriah thinks I need to wear it . . . that it's meant for me."

Findlay nodded at her.

"There's something else," Abisina said. "This letter here—it says that Vigar had a brother. A brother named Vran."

Gasps met her words.

"What can it mean?" Elodie asked.

"Don't you see?" Abisina said. "This could be the key to getting north and south united. With the threat coming from the Mountains Eternal, it is even more important to come together. This letter gives us a means to do that."

"What are you thinking?" Corlin asked.

"We need to reach out—to *everyone*. Dwarves, fauns—they're the easy ones. Theckis and Vranham will be much harder. And then there's Icksyon."

"Icksyon?" Corlin exclaimed.

"Believe me," Abisina said, "the thought of talking to—of working with Icksyon—terrifies me—"

"No!" Jorno's cry echoed around the room.

"Jorno, we have to," Abisina said. "None of us is strong enough to survive alone. We need to work with the centaurs—and all of the folk."

Jorno started to argue, but Neriah cut in, "We have to think beyond our own communities. We're not very good at that—especially the fairies—but we will not survive unless we do."

"What about Watersmeet?" Elodie asked. "The folk there need to be part of this."

"Of course," Abisina said. "We have to bring this news to Glynholly. She'll see now that Watersmeet's destiny is linked with the south."

"You can't go, Abisina," Elodie pointed out. "You're too much of a threat."

"I'll go," Findlay said. His eyes met Abisina's.

"I should go, too," Elodie said softly. "You'll need my bow."

"Will Haret agree to go to Stonedun?" Neriah asked.

"I think so," Abisina said. "And Erna and Darvus can go to the fauns."

"That leaves Theckis and Vranham to me," Corlin said. "All this time, I've tried to keep people here, and now I'm going to Vranham myself. . . ."

"And the centaurs?" Neriah asked.

"Think what you're saying!" Jorno protested. "An alliance with *centaurs!*"

"It makes all of us uneasy," Corlin began, "but—"

"Uneasy? The rest of you—even you, Abisina—have forgotten what it's like to live in fear of them. Out there, in the village, *they* have not forgotten. *I* have not forgotten!"

"It's true," Corlin said, "that some of the folk here questioned Charach when he brought the centaurs into his army. It was a betrayal. But Abisina is also right. We have to work with the centaurs now."

Abisina would ask Kyron to go to Icksyon. She was sure Corlin knew this. It wasn't necessary to say it here, in front of Jorno.

"Wait!" Abisina said. "What should I do?"

"They'll need you in the village," Corlin said. "To keep the work going."

Abisina didn't like the idea of staying. Jorno would be there, and once Findlay was gone, there would be little to stop him from pressuring her again with how much he loved her. *But the people here trust me. I'll show them who I am, teach them not to hate centaurs.* Fear welled in her chest, but she ignored it. *We need the centaurs.*

As she looked around the room, it came to her.

"Seldara," she whispered. She said it louder: "Seldara. That's what we can call this land when all the folk have come together."

"Seldara," Findlay repeated, and across the room, folk smiled. Except Jorno.

Neriah would leave now; the others would leave in a week's time—after the celebration. Corlin would gather the people to explain the need to reach out to other communities. For now, he would not mention that this included centaurs and fairies. "That will come in time," he said.

"Please," Abisina said, pressing Vigar's box into the fairy's hand as Neriah started to go. "Take this."

"Are you sure?" Neriah asked.

Abisina nodded. She wanted the box. And the note inside—the proof that bringing north and south together was right. They made her feel strong. But Haret was more important. *And it's time to do this on my own.*

Chapter XXVIII

THE DAY OF THE CELEBRATION DAWNED BRIGHT AND clear. In the healer's house, Thaula slept on a pallet near Abisina's bed, having begged to spend the night. Sten, getting stronger every day, had moved into a vacant hut the day before. For now, he planned to remain in Vranlyn.

Abisina bustled around the house putting together packets of the most useful herbs and salves for her friends' journeys. The past days had gone fast. Darvus had agreed to return to his home community. "It's gotten so bad around us, they'll understand that drastic action is necessary."

Erna surprised everyone—including herself—by refusing to go. "I came here to show the humans that fauns can help them. Abisina needs me."

"But Erna, *I'm* going home," Darvus insisted.

Erna squeaked. "Abisina needs you to talk to the fauns. M-My work is h-here." Her lip quivered as she spoke, but she didn't change her mind, even when it came time to say good-bye to Darvus.

Darvus left, casting long looks back at Erna as if expecting her to run after him, but she gripped both Abisina's and Elodie's hands, wept profusely, and stayed put.

Introducing Erna to the village didn't cause the stir Abisina feared. Maybe the people were getting used to the folk from Watersmeet. Maybe Erna was so timid, no one could see her as a menace. Or maybe, thoughts of the celebration preoccupied the village. Only Heben threatened to leave, and that was halfhearted.

Findlay and Elodie would return to Watersmeet via Vigar's garden; Kyron would go with them as far as Giant's Cairn. Neriah had promised to send a kestrel to help them up the cliff and to alert Hoysta and Frayda that they would need their help to get in.

When Abisina told Haret about Hoysta, he almost set out for the garden himself. But he relented when Findlay and Elodie swore to send a message through Neriah's birds if she was not mending speedily.

Corlin, who had a short journey ahead, spent all of his time helping Elodie, while Abisina helped Findlay. Both couples were hardly apart. Neither had anticipated a separation so soon.

Jorno stopped by the healer's house a few times but said little. Abisina knew he was upset with her, and she feared the anger smoldering below his surface.

Thaula was mumbling in her sleep. "It's time to get up, sleepyhead," Abisina said as she shook the girl's shoulder.

Thaula was up in an instant. "I'm going to meet Hilagar and Ora before the penance. Right near the goat pen. We can sit wherever we want. When I was little," she said, standing up straighter as she braided her hair, "we had to stand far from the altar. Oh—I forgot. There is no altar!" Her last words were muffled as she pulled her tunic over her head.

Abisina laughed. "I've been worried about being lonely when my Watersmeet friends leave. How can anyone be lonely with you around?"

The penance would be short, and there would be no public humiliation or punishments. After that, the committee had planned a day of feasting, with archery and spear-throwing contests. The dwarves would lead the singing, for which Abisina was extremely grateful. Findlay had tried to convince the people to try dancing, but his descriptions made no sense to them. "Abby and I will show you," he had promised.

There's good reason to feast and sing and—if we can manage it—dance. Both storehouses were full. The wall was mostly sound, and the other dwarves had agreed to stay and shore up the weaker places after Haret left. Abisina had stocked the healer's house with medicines.

Findlay arrived right after Thaula ran off to meet her friends. Abisina threw her arms around him. "I'm going to miss you so much, Fin." She pulled him to her and tried to say with her kiss all that was in her heart.

They walked to the common ground, hand in hand. The bright sun and Findlay's jaunty stride made Abisina smile. *Enjoy today*, she reminded herself.

At the Vranian Day of Penance, the Elders had permitted no talk and patrolled the common brandishing long poles topped with iron bars that they brought down on the heads of anyone behaving "in a manner insulting to Vran." The people stood ranked around the altar: men, boys, women, girls, widows, and outcasts. Faces were grim, knowing that a day of hunger, cold, and grueling ritual was ahead. By nightfall, many would collapse. The Elders would outcast more people, based on their confessions. And someone would be driven from the village for crimes so "heinous" they could not be cleansed.

In Vranlyn, the changes they'd made were powerfully displayed. Folk smiled, greeted one another, and shared gossip and advice. Delicious smells rose from the food laid on tables at one end of the common. There were no ranks. Haret and the dwarves were among the crowd. Erna stood next to Elodie, holding her hand. Corlin beamed. For the first time in days, Jorno met Abisina's eyes.

Corlin had refused to lead the penance like an Elder. Instead, a group of men and women led it. Confessions took place in silence, in each person's heart, and the leaders asked people to consider their strengths as well and how they might use them in the coming year.

When the penance ended, Corlin addressed the crowd: "You have ensured your own future by facing challenges with

courage. Many folk took on a new task in learning to forage."
Cheers for the foragers. "Jorno, a former outcast, has led our
work in the armory." Cheers for Jorno. "You have learned new
techniques for working with stone." Whoops for the men and
dwarves who worked on the wall. "Some of you have tried new
medicines." Amid the shouts, Abisina saw Trima touch Espen's
cheek; he was past danger now. "Eder carried more wood than
anyone else, though he would've seen the task as beneath him
before." A roar for Eder. "And Yera can identify any edible
plant within a league." Laughs and whoops for Yera. "You have
worked hard. I have never been more proud than I am today, to
be part of this community, to be able to call you—all of you—
my friends."

"Hip! Hip! Huzzah for Corlin!" Brack cried. Soon everyone picked up the cheer.

Corlin blushed and bowed several times before calling for
quiet. "I—well, several of us—have a proposal for you to consider. We are building a new life here. We have kept the tradi-
tions that made us strong and rejected what weakened us. We
are a *new* community." Deafening cheers drowned him out.
"So here's our proposal," Corlin called when the shouts died
down. "We do not disrespect Vran," he said carefully. "But we
are no longer simply a *Vranian* village. We need a new name!
A name that reflects who we are: Newlyn!"

The cheers gave Corlin his answer. When he held up
his hands again, his tone shifted. "As you know, a few of
us will undertake a journey tomorrow. We still face many

challenges. Icksyon. Minotaurs. Trolls. Wolves. Gangs. Perhaps other creatures from the Mountains Eternal." The cheering had faded into silence. "We will survive this winter through our partnerships with Watersmeet, Stonedun, and each other. Haret will go to Stonedun again. Erna's mate, Darvus, is on his way to the fauns. Sten has agreed to talk to the gangs. Findlay and Elodie will return to Watersmeet to carry the news of our success. And to tell the refugees who have gone north that they can make a home in the south again."

Cries of happiness erupted. Many had friends or relatives who had gone north.

"I will go to Vranham to talk to Theckis, tell him what we've done. Perhaps he, or his people, will want to take this journey with us. I have asked several folk to work together to provide leadership while I'm gone," he continued. "I hope this is a model we can use in the future. Jorno, Dehan, Heben, Ivice, and Abisina will serve as a Council to address problems as they arise."

Abisina worried about having Heben on the Council, but when she brought this up to Corlin, he insisted. "We need men like Heben to see that they have a place in this community. If they don't, we'll lose them to Vranham."

"For now," Corlin concluded, "we celebrate!" A final cheer went up from the crowd.

The folk approached the laden tables and heaped their plates with food: loaves of bread made with hazelnut and acorn flour, goat cheese, and roasted blister roots. The dwarf Dolan played a lively tune on his pipe. The children chased each other in a game of tag, almost knocking over one of the tables.

"Even Jorno looks cheerful," Findlay whispered to Abisina.

Thud, thud, thud.

Abisina heard the sound over the din of music, laughter, and chatter. It came from the western part of the village.

"What's that?" Findlay asked.

"Let's go find out!" Abisina said.

But before they had gone more than a few steps, they saw a sentry running toward them, yelling.

"Battering ram! Centaurs attacking!"

The cry spread, and everyone began to run to the western wall, knocking over the tables, and trampling the food. Abisina reached for her bow, but she had no weapon. The arms contests were to be held outside the walls; none of them had brought weapons to the celebration.

"The armory!" Jorno screamed. He was right next to her. A similar scene flashed into Abisina's mind: fleeing the common ground in Vranille, Jorno beside her, the mob of murderous Vranians on their heels. *But this time we're all together*, Abisina reminded herself.

The armory was on the north side of the village, and the crowd veered as one toward it. Jorno and Abisina reached it first, and they flung the doors wide. "Bows to the left!" he shouted. Abisina ran in that direction while Jorno raced to the spears glittering row upon row. He ripped them from the wall and tossed them at whoever entered the armory.

The women ran to Abisina, but Ivice pushed her aside. "You go. My shot is nothing to yours." Abisina grabbed a bow and quiver and raced to the door.

As she neared the wall, the blows of the battering ram grew louder. The whiz of arrows, shouts of command, cries of pain, and a staccato beat like a hundred pickaxes added to the cacophony.

The assault targeted an expanse of wall most in need of repair. At each ram stroke, clods of mortar fell away. Some people had ripped a beam from a nearby hut and were trying to brace the wall, but it was futile. The wall would crumble soon.

"Get back! Get back!" Abisina screamed. The wall would crush them! Corlin and Findlay arrived with spears and swords and echoed her command.

"Fall back and set spears!" Findlay shouted.

The men knew hand-to-hand combat; the women did not. *But they know archery,* Abisina thought. *Elodie and I have seen to that!* The ram would break a section of wall; on either side of the breach, the wall would still stand. "Women! To the sentry ladders!" Abisina cried. "Kill as many as you can *outside!*" A few women followed Abisina, and then more caught on.

Two ladders propped against the wall came toppling down. Abisina dodged them, grabbed the next one—*please, let the wall hold here!*—and started to climb. Each thud of the ram reverberated through the rungs. More women joined Abisina on the ladders. Reaching the parapet, Abisina risked a peek over the wall to take in the size of the attack: about twenty centaurs worked the battering ram—each wearing leather chest plates and armed with swords. Next to them, a line of minotaurs were driving their horns into the wall. Behind that, a sea of centaurs and minotaurs pawed the ground. The hags clustered farther off.

In the middle of the centaurs—huge, and menacing, and out of arrow range—stood Icksyon, bellowing orders. He looked up toward the wall as Abisina's eyes fell on him. A look of mild surprise registered on his face, then a malicious smile as he touched his necklace of toes.

Abisina ducked behind the wall as Elodie clambered up.

"Bad?" Elodie asked, and as if in answer, a volley of arrows flew over their heads.

When did southern centaurs learn to shoot? Abisina thought, but the missiles forced her to ignore her fear of Icksyon. "The centaurs with the battering ram first! Then the minotaurs," Abisina shouted to the other women.

As the women on the wall felled the centaurs, Icksyon called replacements from the large herd, but the bodies of the dead made it difficult to swing the ram. Abisina got into a rhythm of shooting, then ducking the next volley of arrows, but another woman caught an arrow in the neck and fell to the ground.

As Abisina nocked her next arrow, the rock beneath her feet swayed, then lurched as a section of wall crumbled. Elodie yanked her back, and Abisina fought to get onto solid stone, breathing in mouthfuls of mortar dust.

The men on the ground impaled the first wave of centaurs on their spears, but not enough had arrived from the armory to handle the next wave. The centaurs struck the men down with their hooves and charged deeper into the village. As spearmen arrived, Findlay and Corlin tried to reestablish the line of defense.

The women shot as many as they could from above, but as the wall swayed again, they began to climb down. "Elodie! Follow me!" Abisina yelled, putting one foot on the ladder. Elodie did the same. Just before the wall collapsed beneath her, Abisina pushed off the parapet. She and Elodie rode the ladder as it fell, landing on the low roof of an old hut. The roof withstood the impact, and they scurried up the thatch, and shot arrow after arrow into the advancing centaurs.

Abisina had lost sight of Findlay, but she spotted Haret swinging his axe at the centaurs' vulnerable shins. More spearmen and archers arrived.

"I'm going to need more arrows!" Elodie shouted.

"To the common ground!" came a cry from below. *Findlay.*

"Fall back!" This cry came from a different direction.

"Let's go," Abisina said, and she slid down the thatch to the ground. Elodie landed next to her. A dead woman lay near them, her quiver almost full. Abisina was pulling the arrows free when something slammed into her side, tossing her up in the air. She crashed against the wall of another hut.

"Are you okay?" Elodie ran to her and helped Abisina up. Nearby lay a minotaur, Elodie's arrow in its chest.

Abisina's side ached as they ran down a lane toward the common. The minotaur's horn had slashed her tunic but missed her flesh.

"Why are we retreating?" Abisina panted. "More spears were coming!"

They got to the common and understood. The storehouse was crawling with minotaurs. They must have broken through the gate while the village defended the wall. The creatures were grabbing bags of flour, baskets of roots, jars of honey.

The humans, led by Findlay and Corlin, charged across the common. Centaurs from the breach pursued them. Some turned to face the stampede. Abisina and Elodie took shots at the minotaurs in the storehouse.

Suddenly Jorno was there. "The other storehouse!" he yelled. "Come on!"

Abisina and Elodie followed him down a small lane, headed toward the main gate and the second storehouse. They reached a dilapidated outcast's hut and crouched in its shadow.

Four or five minotaurs clustered at the door of the second storehouse. The Elders had built an elaborate locking system of pulleys, springs, and hidden doors to protect the storehouse close to the gate from attack. Corlin had left the system in place.

The main gate stood open. Stacks of food bags and baskets were piled outside, but Abisina couldn't see who guarded them. Behind her, the battle raged on the common, but here it was strangely quiet.

The minotaurs gave up trying to work the lock and raced at the door with horns lowered. It would give eventually.

"Storehouse first," Abisina whispered, "then the food." She took aim.

The minotaurs fell before they knew where the arrows were coming from. As the last one dropped, Abisina dashed to the cover of the sentries' guardhouse by the gate. Elodie and Jorno followed.

Outside the gate, hags were loading the stolen food on litters. Were these frail women going to lug it away themselves? Then two minotaurs lumbered up with empty litters. Two hags left the stack of baskets, brandishing their staffs.

One hag pointed into the village and whacked a minotaur with her staff. It hurtled forward, and the second minotaur followed, a wary eye on the other hag.

Two centaurs approached next, their litters also empty. One growled, "Where are they going? Lord Icksyon ordered us to get the food to the forest."

The hag pointed again.

"We have to get this to the forest," the centaur argued. "You'll get your share there."

The hag raised her staff menacingly.

"That thing won't work on me, witch," the centaur spat,

but he didn't get any closer, and he and his partner galloped through the gate in the direction the hag pointed.

"Let's go," Jorno whispered.

They ran through the gate, arrows ready.

"Abisina!" The shout came from across the plain.

Kyron!

"Get the centaur!" Jorno yelled.

"NO!" Abisina screamed.

Jorno didn't seem to hear her. Abisina threw herself at him. His arrow brushed her cheek right before she crashed into him. Then the hags were on top of them, pummeling with their staffs and tight, hard fists. Abisina's bow got wrenched away. She had to get out! She had to get to Kyron—tell him to run.

She transformed, throwing off the hags. They scrambled back, stunned.

Elodie and Jorno had lost their bows, too, but Jorno pulled a knife from his belt and faced Abisina.

"Jorno—it's me!" she cried.

He drew his knife back to throw, but hesitated.

"It's *Abisina*," she said desperately.

"Demon!" he roared.

"I am not a demon!" Abisina pleaded. "My mother saved you. And you saved me." To her right, Elodie picked up a bow. The hags watched from a safe distance. "You *know* me."

"I've never known you!" Jorno shouted.

"My father was a shape-shifter. He killed the Worm." She

held out her open hands to him. "He chose good, Jorno. Like Kyron and the centaurs at Watersmeet. And me. We all chose good."

He threw his dagger.

Abisina dodged the knife as she heard the twang of Elodie's bow. Abisina didn't wait for the arrow to find its mark. She thundered across the plain, hags scattering before her.

Where is Kyron?

She didn't see him, but her hooves must have known because they carried her to the centaur's crumpled form, Jorno's arrow imbedded in his chest.

"Kyron!" She transformed again and knelt beside him.

"Abisina." He struggled to speak. His eyes sought her face.

"I'm here, Kyron, dear, dear friend."

"Your father would be so proud of you. I'm so proud of you." He winced, then smiled, his breathing ragged.

He reached for her arm, and she grasped his in the centaur manner.

"You can . . . protect yourself now." He closed his eyes again and his hand slipped to the ground.

Abisina didn't have even a moment to understand her loss. As she knelt by Kyron, her hand on his cheek, a hiss echoed overhead: the whistle of swords dealing blows; the whisper of chains rubbing torn flesh; the wind over barren lands; the dying breath of multitudes. A shadow fell over her. It was like night without stars, without hope of day. She looked up.

Three creatures. Many times larger than centaurs. They

flew on black wings. Their heads were naked with ridges of blistered skin. Cruelly hooked beaks jutted from between yellow eyes. Their thick legs ended in huge gnarled feet, each toe tipped with a barbed talon.

Reava? But no. These were not fairies' birds. *They're from the rift in the Mountains.* Abisina was sure of it.

Two of the monsters descended on the village. The third banked its flight and came to her.

She had no weapon.

She drew Kyron's heavy sword from its sheath.

The creature carried the reek of raw meat and blood. It landed within paces of her—its beak open to reveal a hard black tongue. Its head shot forward. It drove its beak into the ground, missing her by a breath. The earth shook, and when the bird raised its head for the next blow, it left a crater where its beak had landed.

Abisina swung the sword, but it glanced off steely feathers. The creature's head drove down again, and she sprang under its neck, dragging the sword with her. Hidden under its bulk, she searched for any vulnerable spot amid the folds of leathery skin. The creature brought its beak down on Kyron's chest.

"No!" Abisina yelled, and with all her strength, she thrust Kyron's sword deep into the creature's breast.

The monster recoiled, ripping the sword from her hands. It lashed out with its talons, slicing a deep cut in her arm, the sword still protruding from its chest.

Abisina fell back. With nothing left to defend herself, she

grabbed a handful of dirt and threw it into one of the creature's eyes. It reared and swung its head. Abisina threw herself at the hilt of the sword, transforming as she grasped the metal. Her added weight pushed the sword up, cutting through the monster's breast and into its neck.

Abisina stumbled clear as the bird fell sideways, crashing to the earth. Dead.

She took a step and her front legs buckled. She was on her knees, clutching her bleeding arm. And then she was surrounded by centaurs. She waited for the blows, but they rushed on. She fought her way to her hooves, just as Icksyon galloped past. Their eyes met, his burning with madness and fear.

Then he was gone, racing on with his herd, as the two other monsters rose from the village, bodies clutched in their talons. With a hiss, the birds wheeled in the air and flew after the centaurs. Abisina transformed and threw herself on the ground as the birds flew overhead.

From where she lay, Abisina could see the village, quiet again. The sun shone brightly. Had she dreamed the horrors of the last hours? Were the dwarves singing, the humans feasting, dancing?

She lost consciousness as a last hiss echoed across the plain.

CHAPTER XXIX

ABISINA WOKE IN THE HEALER'S HOUSE, THE WORRIED faces of Haret, Findlay, and Elodie crowded above her. Seeing her awake, Findlay wiped his eyes.

Elodie disappeared and returned with a cup of tea, which she held to Abisina's lips.

They wouldn't tell her much then, but over the next day, as she gained in strength, she heard the story.

The leviathan-birds, as the folk called them, had landed on the common ground in the thick of the battle. The hags had fled, leaving the minotaurs in disarray. The centaurs had also tried to flee, but the birds snatched them with their steely talons, shaking them till their necks broke. The humans and dwarves, so much smaller, did better at dodging the birds. The birds caught some as they seized centaurs, and crushed others with their beaks and feet. But the centaurs suffered most.

The birds didn't rise from the common until they had

killed all they could reach. Then they gathered the bodies they could carry in their claws and pursued the terrified centaurs to the forest.

The villagers burned the bodies of the centaurs and mino-taurs, building huge fires where each had fallen, afraid the leviathan-birds would return to get the bodies.

"Kyron?" Abisina asked weakly.

"We had to, Abby," Findlay said. "I have his sword for you. I found it in the third bird. He must have died protecting you."

Abisina nodded. She would explain later.

The storehouse near the common lay in a splintered pile, the food destroyed. But the second storehouse was intact, and some of the food taken from the first was still stacked outside the gate.

"So many were killed, there's probably enough food to get Newlyn through the winter," Findlay said sadly.

The losses were terrible: Sten, who had fought bravely, ignoring his fresh injuries; Heben, who had stayed despite his suspicions about outcasts and dwarves; Brack, who had survived the mob in Vranille; Dehan, newly married; Yera, who had learned so much of Findlay's forage skill; Werlif, the dwarf who had never grown a beard.

Thaula and the other children—led by Erna—had sur-vived by hiding in a hut near the common.

Findlay didn't mention Jorno until Abisina asked.

"We don't know what happened to him. Elodie thought she had hit him with her arrow, but we found no body."

"He saw me transform, Fin," Abisina said. "I think he's . . . gone."

"To Theckis?" Findlay asked.

"Or one of the gangs. Or maybe to become like Sten—out there, on his own."

In a few days, Abisina was strong enough to return to her healing work, but she first wanted to speak to Corlin. Findlay didn't think anyone had seen her transform—there were no rumors in the village—but Abisina knew that it was time.

When she told him, Corlin said, "We've all known there's something special about you, Abisina. And when Findlay said you killed a leviathan-bird by yourself—well, I knew there had to be more to the story."

"I should have told you sooner," Abisina said. She remembered Findlay's words when he had found out: *"I think I deserved your trust."*

"I understand, Abisina. You know too well how Vranians were taught to hate. I don't know how I would have responded even a few weeks ago. But now that we've seen what we're facing . . ." He trailed off.

Most of the people of Newlyn seemed to agree with Corlin. As the news of Abisina's shape-shifting and defeat of the leviathan-bird spread through the village, a few people avoided her, or refused to meet her eyes. But many still gathered at her hearth in the evening, though the mood had changed. At first, Abisina thought it was anger. Or fear. But then she realized it was awe.

They think I'm my father. They want me to help them as he did.

But she was careful not to shape-shift in the village. The people needed time to get used to the *idea* of her before facing her as a centaur.

"The snow will fall soon," Haret said one evening, glancing around the folk in the healer's house. "Someone needs to take the news of Werlif's death to Stonedun. I was going to go anyway."

"That's the question, isn't it?" Corlin asked. "*Are* you going? Are any of us going?"

Abisina had been dreading this question. It was more important than ever to reach out to the other communities—the leviathan-birds had proved that. But she wasn't ready to say good-bye to her friends, to Findlay.

Elodie must have shared her feelings. "You can't go now, Corlin," she said. "Newlyn needs you."

"I'm strong enough to travel," Findlay said, "but I don't want to leave Newlyn, either." He didn't look at Abisina, but she knew he was thinking of her.

"Maybe after the snow. . . ." Corlin said.

Abisina's eyes met Haret's. She nodded. "No," she said. "Of course, we want to stay together, comfort each other. We're scared—and we should be. The leviathan-birds are the newest horror from the rift in the Mountains. More will come. Our journeys can't wait."

———•◦•◦•———

Elodie and Findlay left on a cold, clear night two days later. The moon rose over the trees as they passed through the gate. Abisina and Corlin walked with them as far as the Seldar grove. Haret was already on his way to Stonedun.

Elodie turned to say good-bye to Corlin, tears glistening on her cheeks.

Findlay walked Abisina to the edge of the grove, and they embraced but said nothing. They had made their good-byes the night before, in the warmth of the healer's house. Neither could bear the moment of parting. Abisina stayed in the Seldars as Findlay walked away.

The trees had always comforted her. She wandered among them now. Snow dusted the ground. For the first time since her father's death, Abisina wasn't waiting for him to speak to her. She would love to hear his voice, would love to tell him all that had happened, ask his advice, his blessing. But she didn't *need* it.

She knew what lay ahead: she had to take Kyron's place. When Corlin returned from Vranham, she would go to Icksyon. There could be no peace, no Seldara, without the centaurs. *It's what my father would do.*

Klee-klee-klee.

"Neriah?" But instead of the fairy, a kestrel landed in a branch above her. It cocked its head at Abisina, then flapped awkwardly to her outstretched arm.

"Are you hurt?" Abisina asked as it alit, its sharp talons biting into her skin. A black chain was wrapped around its right leg. She reached for it, and the bird complied, letting her loosen its binds. The chain was attached to a pendant clutched in the bird's talons. Heart racing, she reached for the pendant, but the bird took to the air. It flew to the top of the Seldars and let the pendant drop.

Just before it landed in Abisina's hand, the light of the Seldars touched it, changing the dull iron to the brilliance of—

Obrium.

Threads of the precious metal wove into a single strand.

The Keeper's necklace.

The kestrel flew off with another cry.

Neriah sent it. Had Glynholly given it up? Was she hurt? Killed? Was Abisina the Keeper now?

Abisina had no answers, but she lifted the chain over her head and the glowing pendant fell over her heart. She sighed deeply and tucked the chain into her tunic.

Corlin waited for Abisina outside the grove. He would leave for Vranham in the morning.

"Ready to go back?" he asked.

Abisina started to go, then stopped. "Wait."

She transformed.

"I'm ready."

LOOK FOR

WATERSMEET

the prequel to THE CENTAUR'S DAUGHTER

available now:

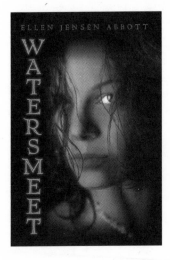

- **International Reading Association Young Adult Award Notable Book**
- **YALSA Teens' Top Ten Nominee**

"The story of an outcast on the road with a rather cranky dwarf, looking for her lost past and a better future. This fast-paced journey to the self is gorgeously written, set in a violent and diverse fantasy world, and filled with prejudice and hope."

—Cynthia Leitich Smith, *New York Times* best-selling author

From her birth, Abisina has been an outcast—for the color of her eyes and skin, and for her lack of a father. Only her mother's status as the village healer has kept her safe. But when a mythic leader arrives, Abisina's life is ripped apart. She escapes alone to try to find the father and the home she has never known. In a world of extremes, from the deepest prejudice to the greatest bonds of duty and loyalty, Abisina must find her own way and decide where her true hope lies.